*Offered by the king as the prize at a tournament,
Lady Eloise Gerrard was far from gaining the freedom
she so ardently desired. Shocked to discover the king
had every intention of winning the prize for himself,
Eloise turned in desperation to the challenger,
Sir Owain of Whitecliffe, the man who had once
awoken all her youthful passions…only to desert her.
Could she now wish to see him the victor—
the conqueror laying claim to his prize?*

"You will win tomorrow, won't you?"

Owain tipped her into the crook of his arm and studied
her face. "I shall win. Don't doubt it."

"Shall you wear my favor?" Releasing herself from
his arms, Eloise tied the cloth around his upper arm.
"There," she said, trying to smile. "If I have to accept
someone, it had best be you."

His kiss was intended to be gentle, but Eloise had
only memories to feed on for days and, despite her
reservations, her need of him was wild and undisciplined.
There, in a quiet haven in the center of Westminster's
thronging palace, his lips and hands reminded her of
their night together, and predicted those to come….

* * *

The Knight's Conquest
Harlequin Historical #673—September 2003

Harlequin Historicals is delighted to present author Juliet Landon and her magnetic medieval novel

THE KNIGHT'S CONQUEST

THE KNIGHT'S CONQUEST

JULIET LANDON

HARLEQUIN®

TORONTO • NEW YORK • LONDON
AMSTERDAM • PARIS • SYDNEY • HAMBURG
STOCKHOLM • ATHENS • TOKYO • MILAN • MADRID
PRAGUE • WARSAW • BUDAPEST • AUCKLAND

ISBN 0-373-29273-2

THE KNIGHT'S CONQUEST

First North American Publication 2003

Copyright © 2002 Juliet Landon

This edition published by arrangement with Harlequin Books S.A.

Visit us at www.eHarlequin.com

Printed in U.S.A.

Please address questions and book requests to:
Harlequin Reader Service
U.S.: 3010 Walden Ave., P.O. Box 1325, Buffalo, NY 14269
Canadian: P.O. Box 609, Fort Erie, Ont. L2A 5X3

Chapter One

The announcement of intent to marry, though softly spoken, provoked more or less the reaction expected by the lovely young woman from her elegant white-haired father, Sir Crispin de Molyns, Deputy Keeper of the King's Wardrobe.

'Well,' he said, pinching the bridge of his nose, 'I've heard of killing two birds with one stone, Eloise, but this is ridiculous. A lady of your standing doesn't marry her steward, for heaven's sake. You don't have to marry the man to retain him for another period of office, you know. I've never had to marry mine so far.'

His attempt at flippancy went unnoticed by Lady Eloise Gerrard whose defences had been rehearsed almost constantly during the two-day journey from her manor in Staffordshire to her father's home in Derbyshire. Even so, her retort was not as well chosen as it might have been. 'I don't *have* to marry anyone, Father.'

Predictably, Sir Crispin recognised the blunder and

studied her from beneath snowy eyebrows. 'You *do*, Eloise. You must know that,' he said, gently.

'Well…all right…I do.' Eloise began to pace the large sunlit solar of Handes Castle as if to recall her lines, a phrase for each step. 'I've been widowed for a year…and the king has sent for me…we all know what for…and I mean to tell him…that I've decided on a husband…thank you very much.'

Her father was unimpressed, knowing the king as well as he did. 'Well, if you think he'll allow you to marry your steward, my lass, widowed or not, you'd better think again. He won't. You're a tenant-in-chief, Eloise, and he doesn't allow wealthy widows in *his* gift to give themselves away to nobodies. There's many a knight who'll pay him handsomely for the privilege of marrying a de Molyns woman who's just inherited Gerrard's property, too. He'll not allow all that to be passed on to the progeny of a mere steward, however well born he may be.'

'There won't *be* any progeny, Father.' That was something else she had rehearsed, but somehow it had emerged too soon in the scene.

'Oh, lass! Now you *are* talking nonsense! You're far too young to be embarking on a marriage of convenience, if that's what you have in mind.' He could have said 'too beautiful' also. As the elder of his two daughters, Eloise had a regal loveliness that made men fall silent and follow her with their eyes, weaving her into their daydreams. He had seen them.

At almost twenty-three years old, she had reached a tall willowiness that had bypassed the clumsy phases of adolescence and filled out into the ripeness of womanhood with a natural grace that set her apart. Her abundant deep auburn hair was plaited loosely into a thick rope that hung well down past her waist, the last two days of uncomfortable travel having given her little opportunity to do more than keep it out of the way. But even the casual adoption of a maiden's hairstyle, which had earned a frown of disapproval from her waspish sister-in-law, could not disguise the fact that here was a woman who knew her own mind and was not afraid to fly in the face of convention.

Her eyes, some said, were her best feature, being a changeable hazel, green in some lights, brown in others, but rimmed with thick dark lashes that made each blink an enchantment. Some insisted that her mouth excelled, wide and gently curving over white pearly teeth. Others said it was her skin, honey-toned and flawless. She herself said that whatever good points she had had so far done little for her, with a string of disasters to her credit and a widowhood after only three months of marriage. The cynicism that had accumulated over the past few years could sometimes be seen as a fleeting expression by those who loved her, and they at least were in agreement that it was hardly surprising, after all she'd been through.

Eloise had hoped that, of all her family, her father would have understood her reasons for choosing to marry her steward rather than accept a man of the king's choosing. 'Other widows have done it, Father,' she said, knowing that he would not allow that to pass unchallenged.

'Yes, old dowagers well past breeding age,' he retorted. 'Of course they have, in the past, but not in the king's reign. Edward the Third doesn't release his property without expecting a good return on it, and you *are* his property, like it or not.'

Eloise disliked the label. As a tenant-in-chief, her estate belonged to the king, obliging her to keep it in good and profitable order and to supply him with a specified number of men to fight in his army each year. She would not be allowed to remain unmarried for long while heirs were required, or while men queued for the honour of adding everything she held, and was likely to inherit, to their own estates. For this, they would be expected to pay the king generously. For permission to remain unmarried, Eloise would have to pay the king a heavy fine which would undoubtedly be so great that she would find it impossible to survive. Either way, the king would gain and she would lose. The alternative was to remove herself entirely from the degrading marriage-market and return to the sisters at Fairwell Priory who had done their best to educate her.

The notion of marrying her own loyal steward had seemed like a good one only a week ago, but now she felt an uncomfortable shift of the ground beneath her feet at her father's lack of understanding. 'If I'd known I was going to be left in this position quite so soon, Father, I'd not have...'

Sir Crispin studied her, watching her flounder.

'You were in plenty of hurry to marry Sir Piers, lass,' he said. 'Regretting it now, are you?'

She was silent, affirming what he already suspected.

'Aye,' he said. 'I know. It was the other one you'd have had if pride had not got in your way. And now you're set to do the same again, even before you have to meet each other once more.'

'I don't have to meet him, Father. And you're mistaken: I care nothing for the man. I'm marrying Stephen atte Welle because we both need the security of marriage and because we have what each other needs.'

'Except the need for bairns.'

'I don't need bairns.'

'Don't expect me to believe that, lass. And you *do* have to meet him.'

'Who?' Eloise turned to her father in alarm.

The hand that she laid on the plum-coloured velvet sleeve of her father's gown was taken and clasped warmly, comfortingly, then she was drawn towards the great curtained bed at the far end of the chamber where they sat side by side on the low step of the surrounding platform as they had so often done before in rare moments of privacy.

'Sir Owain of Whitecliffe is staying here during your sister's betrothal celebrations, Eloise.'

'Here? Now? In the castle? You cannot mean it, Father.' Eloise stared in astonishment at the elegant white-haired man whose calm announcement sent dual shocks of anger and excitement through her which not even she could tell apart.

'I do mean it.'

'And you gave me no warning because you and Mother knew I'd not have come if I'd known. Is that it?'

'We did hope, dear,' replied Sir Crispin, patiently, 'that you'd have put old resentments behind you by now. After all, Jolita doesn't celebrate a betrothal every day, does she?' He could have bitten his tongue at the gaffe.

'Nor every few months, Father. Indeed no.'

'Eloise—' he took her hand again and sandwiched it upon his knee '—this new cynicism doesn't become you, you know. Nor does it do to bear grudges as long as that.'

She left her hand where it was, but on the subject of grudges she was less at ease. 'That was no small slight, Father. How can you expect me to be civil to a man who offered marriage and then disappeared from the scene, and who then had a hand in my husband's death? I was not cynical until then, but no woman could be expected to ignore those facts, surely?'

Sir Crispin was not inclined to agree, having hoped to sing Sir Owain's praises to her once more. 'He's my neighbour, my dear, a man of substance and wealth, property and—'

'And notoriety.'

'Well, yes. Some notoriety, but all jousters are

tagged with that, whether it's deserved or not. It goes with the profession.'

'I know. I was married to one.'

He held back a sigh of disappointment which he knew would not be appreciated. Her three-month marriage to Sir Piers Gerrard had shown all the signs of early neglect, and perhaps this was not the best time to revive old antagonisms with mention of his distinguished neighbour. He would speak of matters closer to his daughter's interest.

But he was mistaken. His neighbour, Sir Owain of Whitecliffe, was closer to her interest than he had thought.

'It will give me great pleasure,' Eloise said, 'to find every reason to avoid him, Father. It's going to be difficult enough having to be sociable on the anniversary of Sir Piers's death without coming face to face with the one responsible for it.'

'How can you say that, Eloise? Sir Owain was *not* responsible; it was Sir Phillip Cotterell who accidentally struck the fatal blow. You knew that.'

'They're friends, Sir Phillip and your fainthearted neighbour.'

'And they enter the same tournaments, but jousting is fought in pairs, one against one, not in trios and quartets.'

'Nevertheless, he was involved, one way or the other.'

'The tragedy was investigated to the king's satisfaction, Eloise.'

'But not to mine. I was told very little of what

actually happened on that day at Windsor, only that Sir Phillip was distraught, as if he could be any more distraught than I was. Not even Sir Phillip's closest friend could bring himself to explain to me in person.'

'Perhaps he thought you'd not receive him, my dear.'

'I wouldn't!' Eloise said. 'But he might have made the effort.'

Sir Crispin had hoped that things might be a little less complicated for him, this time, being caught uncomfortably between his remarkably spirited daughter and his distinguished neighbour, Sir Owain of Whitecliffe, though he was far too honest to deny that he himself was partly to blame for this state of affairs.

It was true that the young couple's first meeting had been brief, but both he and Lady Francesca had agreed that their instant attraction was one of those rare events it was worth a life to witness. The chemistry between Eloise and Sir Owain had been enough to send shockwaves through those who stood nearby, a palpable frisson of tension that Sir Crispin himself in his younger uncouth days would have called lust but which his lady wife referred to as 'a definite warmth', bless her. It was not that the two of them had had any time together to explore this phenomenon. Quite the contrary. Little had been said on that occasion except the usual mannered interchange which was chaperoned by the rest of the family, hardly the climate in which to liberate one's deepest feelings. He saw that now. Perhaps he should have given them time to be alone to come to some more definite agreement, but time had been at a premium before his own return to Westminster, and somehow it had seemed more important for he and Lady Francesca to talk to Sir Owain, rather than for Eloise to talk to him. That was, after all, the way of things, especially in the light of her previous contracts.

At the time, he had been sure that this view was the correct one to take, for Eloise had given him the distinct impression that her liking of Sir Owain matched his own, though on reflection she had said very little on the subject. He supposed it was the look of her, her unusual preoccupation and his wife's insistence that Eloise's silence was positively charged, rather than negative. Women were supposed to know about these things.

The problem had arisen when Sir Owain had been called to attend the king on some mission or other. No warning, no time to take things further except to send Sir Crispin a hurried note making an offer for her hand and hoping that Eloise would wait for his return in due course. Except that none of them knew how long that due course was likely to be, not even Sir Owain himself and, when all was said and done, his offer was only one of several received in recent months. There was no point in replying with an acceptance, for Sir Owain had departed from Whitecliffe at the same time as his letter arrived, and he himself was bound the next day for Westminster for another spell of duty. He could not delay it any longer. He had things to do, people to see, events to organise. Moreover, Sir Owain must have known that no offer was binding, even when accepted, any more than a betrothal was until it had been fully consummated and sanctified by marriage. Indeed, prepuberty betrothals took place all the time, and often came to nothing after all that.

With hindsight, he himself should have attended to the business more assiduously, with firmer instructions to Sir Rolph, his son. Instead of that, he had believed that her heart was set at last upon a man who looked as if he could stay the course longer than the previous two, and that Eloise's matrimonial problems were all but solved. Rolph's deputising in domestic matters had been a godsend in the past, even if it meant housing his wife Griselle and their brood for several months of the year. A capable young man was Rolph, though in retrospect perhaps not experienced enough yet to handle his sister's future with the necessary shrewdness.

He, Sir Crispin, had gone to Westminster as planned, feeling no sense of alarm when Lady Francesca's letters told him of the constant visits of one of Rolph's neighbours, Sir Piers Gerrard, of the man's gifts to Eloise, of his charming attentions, of Rolph's opinion that he would be a far more suitable match for Eloise since he was there and Sir Owain was not. Since her last two betrothals, both he and her mother had found it increasingly difficult to make Eloise's mind up for her, so he had no fears that Rolph, her half-brother, would be any better at it.

How far he was wrong in that assumption he was never quite able to tell, but by the time he returned home at the end of summer, Sir Piers had become the front runner in the marriage stakes. Eloise's determination to have him had set in as firmly as her scorn for Sir Owain, and his own hopes of having Sir Owain as a son-in-law had been dashed. And by the time Sir Owain returned from his mission, Eloise's disappointment at his mysterious departure, fuelled by Sir Rolph's and Sir Piers's teasing references to the man's notorious affairs with ladies of the court, had turned to personal affront. What was he, her father, able to say in Sir Owain's defence when Sir Piers, having warmed her heart with a constant shower of love-tokens, visits and promises, seemed at last to suggest something more permanent than a hurried offer from a disappearing rake? Her question, not his.

Nor did Sir Crispin have a very satisfactory answer for Sir Owain, the best he was able to offer being, 'I have less and less control over my daughter's marriage requirements these days, I fear. She is now inclined to make her own decisions upon these matters, more's the pity.' The tone had been apologetic, somewhat shamed.

'Then it's time she was told what's best for her, sir,' Sir Owain had retorted, far from pleased. 'Her mind is made up?'

Sir Crispin had nodded. 'We can still remain friends I hope, sir? Good neighbours?'

'No doubt, Sir Crispin. We may meet in London, some time.'

To say that Sir Owain was displeased was a typically English understatement that left Sir Crispin and Lady de Molyns highly embarrassed by the developments over which Lady Francesca, in the thick of it, had been powerless to control. It was then that Sir Crispin realised he should never have allowed his son, Sir Rolph, to handle that side of affairs, however proficient his enquiries had been about his neighbour, Sir Piers Gerrard. Nor should he have assumed that the flame he had witnessed being ignited in his beloved daughter was mature enough to burn without fuel.

None of them could have predicted how things would be after only two years, one year into her widowhood, how the confidence which had already begun to erode had, since her marriage, landslipped into a deep chasm of scepticism. Even he, Sir Crispin, had noticed it on his returns from London, though her accusation of complicity in Sir Piers Gerrard's death at a tournament only three months after their marriage could not be taken seriously. He knew Sir Owain to be a proud man, but never a rash or vindictive one. He had invited Sir Owain to Jolita's betrothal celebrations in the hope that he and Eloise might conceivably rekindle that flame, if it had ever truly died, and had been gratified to discover that, if he still smarted, he had learnt to conceal it better than she. That they both had grounds for doubting each other no one could deny, Sir Owain obviously having believed that the incredible emotional connection they had made on that day, which others had felt, would be enough to make her wait for him, for ever, if need be. Which went to show, Sir Crispin mused, that no man, however experienced, could truly anticipate a woman's mind.

As for the manner of Sir Piers's death, that was something about which she was far better not knowing, though one could hardly blame her for being doubly unenthusiastic about meeting the man she believed to be in some way responsible, however little evidence she had to go on. Even the mention of the man's name was enough to send sparks flying; a pity when the two of them would be under the same roof for the next few days. 'A pity,' said Sir Crispin, reflectively. 'Such a pity when he's looking for a wife.' He stood up, pulling Eloise with him, and together they sauntered towards the largest glazed window that looked out over the small town of Handes. Below them, the sun caught the tops of the trees in a wash of pink and, in a field beyond the thatched rooftops, the striped arming-tents fluttered with colourful pennants ready for the tournament. Flashes of silver and steel caught the sun where men practised at the quintain, and the river slithered away into the distant landscape punctuated by the splashing bodies of small children and flapping ducks. The deep window-recess was like a small ante-room in the thickness of the castle wall where people could sit in private conversation.

Eloise's response to her father's nonchalant remark was, however, hardly subdued. 'Looking?' she scoffed, loudly. 'For a *wife*? Such men don't look for wives, father, they have them hurled at their heads. They're inundated with women falling under their feet night and day. I know. I wish I'd known of it before I married Sir Piers. But I'll not make the same mistake again—' she didn't hear the door open quietly on the opposite side of the chamber '—and don't let Mother imagine she can pair me off with that great overwheening clod who prances about knocking men off horses for a living.'

'Eloise!' her father warned, placing a hand on her arm.

'He may be your neighbour, Father, but he's not mine, and I'd rather have my sober steward any day than your local punch-drunk hooligan, no matter how celebrated he is.'

'Eloise...please!' Sir Crispin said in alarm.

'I'm sorry, Father, but you must not harbour any ideas in that direction. Tell Mother to say I'm too expensive, even for him.'

Sir Crispin heaved a sigh, wiping a hand around his chin and shaking his head sadly at some point beyond Eloise's shoulder. 'You may tell them both yourself, my lady. Sir Owain had best hear that from your own lips, I believe.'

Suddenly aware of her father's attention directed elsewhere, Eloise whirled round, immediately understanding the significance of his attempts to silence her outburst. Behind them, standing on the deep clean rushes only a few yards away, were three figures, her mother, her sister Jolita and their guest, Sir Owain of Whitecliffe. Her breath stayed frozen in a distant corner of her lungs, and she found that her mouth was suddenly dry. They must have heard every word, every insult.

But while her mother, Lady Francesca, was plainly embarrassed by her daughter's aggression, her sister was just as plainly eager to witness the next bout. Her pretty eyes danced with anticipation. Eloise did not look to see the effect of her words upon the tall knight in the surcoat of deep gold velvet, though she suspected some amusement, and because she could find no reason for regret, nor could she explain her unaccustomed virulence, her instincts told her to flee while there was still a chance.

With barely a glance in Sir Owain's direction, she whispered a quick, 'I beg you will excuse me, please,' and headed for the door with as much dignity as she could summon.

In two long strides, the man she had just condemned reached it before her and placed his hand upon the latch. She thought, hoped, that he was about to open it for her, but his intention was just the opposite and, for what seemed to Eloise like an eternity, their eyes were locked in a silent battle of wills.

They had met only once, two years ago after the Essex knight to whom she had been betrothed for three months died of the terrible pox in March, 1349. He had changed little since then, except for the disappearance of a beard which had once outlined his square jaw. She supposed that the white scar along his lower cheek was the reason for its removal. Now she saw anew the keen intelligence and indomitability in his expression which had first excited her, and instead of the shifty leer of so many men, his steady gaze bored deep into her mind and found the shiver of fear at the root of her anger.

She recognised again the astonishing virility, the animal vigour and strength of him, even while motionless. There was the muscled throat and the commanding backward tilt of the head, the wide mouth that she was sure was well practised at kissing, but never her. His dark silky hair had been well cut, but was now combed back off his forehead, slipping forward to touch one angled brow. His eyes, dark-rimmed and dangerously narrowed, sloped down at each corner. And now his powerful bulk made an impossible barrier that he patently had no intention of removing. A momentary flicker of his eyes towards her father was the only minute signal Sir Owain gave that she should yield, as if to remind her of unfinished business. Incredibly, and inexplicably, she lowered her angry stare and turned to meet her father's advance.

Hoping to save a situation that appeared rapidly to be slipping beyond his control, Sir Crispin drew her away from the human barrier. 'Come, lass,' he whispered. 'For Jolita's sake?' He led her back into the private solar hung cosily with bright tapestries and lit by shafts of evening sunlight. 'Our guests will be sharing the same board for a few days, and your mother and I would prefer it if they spoke to each other. Will you not greet Sir Owain? He's been looking forward to meeting you again.'

Determined not to lose the next skirmish, she lifted her chin and turned to face again the fearless man who had come to stand by her father's side. 'Then I fear our re-introduction will be a crushing anticlimax for Sir Owain, Father. Shall we hope, sir, that the victor's crown will be a fitting compensation for any other expectations you brought with you to the tournament?'

The great man met her cold appraisal impassively and, since she had declined to curtsy, gave her no return bow. 'I shall take back everything I came for and probably more, my lady,' he said. His voice was as she remembered it, richly baritone and cultured. His arrogant reply came as no surprise; these men had to be self-confident, cocksure, or they'd not be so successful.

A surge of excitement shivered unreasonably through her, and the will to continue the battle from the safety of her family's presence spurred her recklessly on. 'Ah...' she smiled '...then your short journey must once again be scarce worth the effort. For myself, I appear to be successful only in terms of three months, like the last marriage to a man you knew well. Could it be that you happen to have a spare three months between tournaments, sir?'

He had not moved a muscle throughout her self-deprecating volley but stood with his chin up, appreciating her performance, noting every nuance of sarcasm but seeing also a quiver of uncertainty behind the amazing green-brown eyes. 'Is that what it takes, lady? Three months? Well then, yes, I have a spare three months in which I could make you passive and obedient, which is more than your father and late husband have been able to manage between them, apparently.'

'And now,' she replied, icily, 'I fear I am well beyond their control. And yours too, Sir Owain.'

'Backing off already?'

'Not as fast as you, sir!' she snapped.

'Pity. I thought I heard a challenge.'

'I was stating a fact. Claim your victor's crown at the tournament and take it home.'

'And who will you sharpen your tongue on, lady, with me gone? Your next husband?'

'Yes, Sir Owain, my next husband. A remarkably loyal man. We shall be wed later this summer.'

His eyes, which until now had been laughing, cooled perceptibly as the impact of her words clearly caught him by surprise. But he would not allow her to win so easily. 'Then I hope you've made him aware of your three-monthly terms, or the remarkably loyal man will be in for a nasty shock by Christmas, lady. Is he someone I know?'

After that rudeness, Eloise had no intention of telling him, but her father felt that this was the perfect time to place a fly in the ointment, so to speak, before the king did it less gently. 'Lady Eloise intends to marry her steward, Master Stephen atte Welle, a man of—'

'Her *steward*?' Laughter and incredulity returned

together, and Eloise could happily have killed both him and her father on the spot.

Rather than wait for the next provoking remark, she turned quickly away, taking Jolita's hand as she passed. 'Come, Jollie. Pray excuse us, Mother. We have much to talk about.'

Lady Francesca de Molyns intercepted her daughter's brisk departure as only a mother can. 'Child,' she said, enclosing her as the men moved to the far end of the solar. 'Child...hush now! Sir Owain is our neighbour, you know. He and your father are bound to meet socially and exchange news. Don't allow him to anger you so.'

'Insensitive, Mother,' said Eloise, her voice low with displeasure. 'For my father to choose this particular time for Jollie's betrothal *and* to stage a tournament *and* to have that man staying here at the castle. Insensitive!'

'Unavoidable, my love,' her mother cooed, lifting a strand of the glossy copper-beech hair to one side. Her fingers were soft and gentle, her own hair streaked with threads of silver through deep red coils. She was still a beautiful woman. 'It was not *our* choice of dates. It had to fit in with your father's duties at Westminster, and with Lord and Lady Pace. And think how the men would be without a tournament. They'd not know what to do with themselves except hunt. At least this way we get to be with them. And as for Sir Owain not being invited—well, it would have been unmannerly to leave him out, wouldn't it?'

'Obnoxious creature!'

'You didn't have to pick a fight, my child. Not with such a man.'

Three pairs of eyes strayed towards the two men, taking in the broad shoulders and slim hips girded low with jewel-studded belts and scabbards, the easy grace and sudden laughter. They like each other, those two, thought Eloise, suddenly aware that she would be foolish to tell her father any more of her future plans than she strictly needed to. 'I need only keep out of his way, Mother,' she replied. 'That's all.'

'Yes, dear. That's all,' said her mother, catching Jolita's smile.

Arm in arm, the two sisters chose solitude on the broad walkway along the inside of the battlemented wall that looked out over the town of Handes and the green Derbyshire hills. Though not quite deserted, it provided an escape from the throngs of house-servants, the soldiers, and the guests arriving daily, adding to the inevitable lack of privacy.

Overlooking the part of the wall farthest from the busy gatehouse, they peered down the sheer drop into the satin waters of the River Dove that fed the moat and encircled the castle walls, holding it apart from the rest of the town like an elderly but robust parent wreathed in silver tissue. Below them, a group of young squires washed their masters' horses, flank-deep in water, their coats shining like ripe chestnuts. They looked up and pointed, waving cheekily, bringing a smile to the sisters' lips. An admiring bunch of children watched from the shallows, their toes dabbling in the ripples.

To Eloise, memories of her childhood flooded back with an almost painful nostalgia. Although she was now a guest at her parents' home, this had been hers where the two of them had once been free of responsibilities. They had run barefoot in the fields and flown kites from the hills, shot arrows at the butts, fished for tiddlers in the river and ridden their ponies over logs. But none of that had prepared them for times like this when she herself would be widowed and Jolita, at eighteen, was about to celebrate her betrothal.

Outwardly, the two of them were similar, Jolita being slight and prettily dark with merry brown eyes and a nose that the squires called cute. As a maid, she wore her hair loose, held down by a golden circlet that sat low on her brow, and though she had the same slender grace as Eloise, she had not the same voluptuousness. Her green velvet sleeveless surcoat was worn over a plain green linen gown that skimmed the wide neckline and caressed her creamy skin.

Eloise squeezed her sister's arm. 'Forgive me for that dreadful scene, love,' she said. 'I'll not spoil your festivities. But that man...'

'Yes, I know. It's all right, Ellie. He disturbs me, too.' She sighed. 'I wish Henry would disturb me like that.'

'Tell me about Henry. Is he handsome?'

'No..oo,' Jolita whispered, watching the scene below. 'Not very handsome. Not particularly young. Not bold. Courteous, but not loverlike.'

'Wealthy? Will you like him?'

'Oh, yes, he's wealthy. And I expect I'll grow to like him. Eventually.' She sat in the wide crenellation with the view behind her. 'Ellie, do you mind very much it being on the twenty-fourth? My betrothal? It was not by my choice, and it's not the best time for you to be celebrating, is it?'

'It's all right. It's kind of you to remember, and I can't be a mourning widow for ever, can I? St John's Day has always been a special day for tournaments, and a betrothal without jousting would be a bit of a waste. It's just unfortunate that it's also the first anniversary of Sir Piers's death, but there's no reason why that should concern Henry and his parents.'

'Has it been awful for you this last year?'

Eloise sat beside her sister and smiled ruefully, not willing to give her the details of the last nightmare year in which she had had to fight Sir Piers's relatives tooth and nail for her rights of dowry, dower and jointures, and to pay off his many debts. They had resembled vultures in their avarice, using every strategy and excuse to make it difficult for her, including a refusal to allow her to compile an inventory of his goods, since she had not been named as an executor. She had fought them, but the effort had left her drained and bitterly resentful.

She turned to look over her shoulder at the green hills where, in the distance, another bright cavalcade

of horses and wagons winked gaudily in the sunshine
and snaked its way along the dusty track towards the
castle. Her own manor near Stafford was in a direct
line between her half-brother's home at Coven Hall
in Staffordshire and her father's castle at Handes just
over the border. She had put aside her widow's
weeds for this occasion and, to deflect Jolita's question, brazenly smoothed her hands over the topaz
silken fabric of her tightly fitting bodice. 'First time
I've worn this in a year—' she smiled '—and it still
fits.' It had indeed been made to fit like a second
skin by a tailor who knew how to dart beneath the
bust, over the hips and waist, how to flare the skirt
with wedge-shaped gores, how to set the sleeves into
the tight bodice in the newest fashion and to set tiny
buttons all the way from elbow to fingers. Eloise
needed her maid to lace it down the back and to
attach the long extravagant tippets to each elbow
from where they hung to the ground, lined with pale-
grey squirrel fur, like the low neckline.

Jolita agreed, laughing. 'Not for long, love. I saw
a pair of eyes peeling you like an apricot in there
while you were doing your bit.'

'Let him peel away,' said Eloise, dismissively.
'That's the nearest he'll ever get. Let him see what
he's missed, Jollie.'

Jolita's smile faded. 'As bad as that, Ellie? Truly?'

'Yes. Truly. I've found a dependable man, this
time, all by myself without anyone's help or inter-
ference. Stephen atte Welle may not be the most fas-
cinating of men, but I can rely on him utterly.'

'Your steward? How old is he?'

Eloise hesitated. 'About twenty-eight, I think.'

'That's young to be in such a responsible position.'

'The previous one was old. He stuck to the Gerrards like a leech. I don't think he's ever approved of me, and I was not inclined to keep him on after Sir Piers died, so when the time came for him to renew his ten-year contract, I let him go and appointed the man who'd been bailiff for five years.'

'But why *marry* him, Ellie?'

The reply was evasive. 'Father thinks I'm mad. He says the king won't allow it. He's probably right.'

'The king has sent for you, then?'

'I shall be going up to London with Father after this. And I shall offer the king a fine to release me.'

'It'll have to be a big one, love. Is your steward worth it? You love him?'

'No, of course I don't. Love doesn't come into it. This is a business arrangement, that's all. Look, Jollie...' she saw the bleak expression in her sister's eyes '...they'll find me a new husband if I don't take matters into my own hands. I've had *years* of that and look where it's got me. Two betrothals and a three-month marriage. Stephen is quite content to get on with managing my affairs. He's good at it, the men like and trust him, and so do I.'

'But if the king refuses his permission and finds you a hus—'

'Don't, Jollie...please! I can't think any further

than this.' Her voice suddenly broke and disappeared, her eyes filling with tears.

'Oh, Ellie, dearest.' Jolita placed a comforting arm around her sister's shoulders and hugged her. 'I'm sorry. It's Sir Owain; he's unsettled you, hasn't he?'

Eloise nodded, admitting what she had known since her father had spoken his name. 'I wish I'd known he was going to be here,' she whispered. 'I could have been better prepared. Now he's aware of my anger and I'd have preferred him to believe that I scarce remember him. Indifference is much harder for a man to bear than anger.'

'You can still show him indifference, Ellie. Ignore him, like you said.'

The notion was so absurd that both sisters burst into unladylike guffaws that put paid to the tears. 'I *will*,' Eloise insisted, laughing and wiping her cheeks. 'I will, when he comes galloping up on his great snorting stallion, shaking the ground, I'll pretend I can't see or hear him.' Her voice dropped again. 'It's going to be difficult, Jollie, but I've made my decision and I shall stick to it. It's for the best. And anyway, he seemed content to be as discourteous as I was. He took my insults, and I have plenty more for his sort.'

'No, pet. Don't. You'll not win. You'll be hurt.'

'I will win, Jollie. One way or the other, I will.'

Eloise's definition of winning was not quite the same as her sister's, in this context, for the battles raging within were more complex than the mere sparring to which Jolita referred. The idea was ludicrous that a man could re-enter her life at any convenient moment and expect her full co-operation without a hint of reproach. Not only reproach, but resistance.

As for her being in love with her steward, well, that was the obvious interpretation to be put on an unorthodox alliance. High-born women did not marry their retainers unless there was something unusual involved, like love, for instance, when the matter would be hushed up, for decency's sake. No, Stephen atte Welle was her choice for no other reason than that she deserved to have a man on whom she could depend utterly, a man who would shield her from other men's attentions. And her steward was utterly dependable.

There had been a young lad, a gardener at the lax convent school near Lichfield. She smiled as she remembered. They had had fun, delighting in breaking the bonds of oppressive discipline that threatened to crush their young bones, the frowns, the bells, the rules, the thou-shalt-nots. The idea of running away had occurred to all her friends at various times, but to do it with a young man was an added excitement in a life shorn of any cheer except in talk of what they had done at home, what they would do if they had the chance, what other people did, apparently. The boy had meant nothing to her except as a means of escape. He had been more enthusiastic than adept, and there had been no lovemaking to speak of. The whole thing, taken too seriously by the nuns and her family, had gone disastrously wrong, especially as they had not quite believed the two runaways about the degree of intimacy. Or lack of it. She had had to produce her cloths at her next period, a humiliating come-down from such high jinks. After that, her father had shown an undignified haste to find her a husband, which she had understood, but quietly resented.

Two betrothals had followed, each one more unsuitable than the other, both of them terminated by unpredictable death, neither of them grieved over. But nor did the experience do anything for her self-confidence.

Sir Owain had appeared quite suddenly after having served with the king in France, their handsome neighbour unseen by Derbyshire folk except those men like her father who spent time in London. With only a brief meeting to go on, he appeared to be all she had dreamed of and hoped for. And while she had dreamed on, with more substance than before, he had made an offer and then disappeared, leaving her not only puzzled but bitterly hurt and obliged to pretend that it was of no great consequence, especially as Sir Piers Gerrard made an appearance within days of Sir Owain's sudden departure.

A personal note to her in his own hand would have done, but apparently he believed that she would be like all his other conquests, bowled over by one look and thereafter his for ever with nothing more to do except to wait. Well, she was bowled over, but not confident enough or tame enough to wait for the next snap of his fingers. The knight would have to work harder for his prize than that.

Sir Piers, a tempestuous knight, had left her no time to lick her wounds. The negotiations had been summary, the state of her heart not examined too closely, the marriage itself impelled by her family's relief and by Sir Piers's urgency that was taken for genuine enthusiasm by his adoptive family. But the hurt that Eloise expected to heal did not, nor was it helped by her new husband's coarseness, which had been well concealed until then. To her relief, he had not stayed with her long before a sudden departure to London, but long enough for her to see how he spent money lavishly and wildly, how his jousting came before anything else, even her, how his eyes and hands roamed freely over her few women and how variety in everything seemed more important to him than maintaining what he possessed. The rejection which she had already been suffering now intensified under this new affliction, which was not helped by the strangeness of her new home or by the expectations of Sir Piers's relatives and many living-in guests to whom he gave free hospitality as a manifestation of his munificence.

If she had wondered at the short duration of her previous liaisons, the news of his sudden death at Windsor on St John's Eve only established her growing suspicion that three months was to be the extent of her association with any man. And while on the one hand she experienced relief of a personal nature that she would no more have to suffer his vulgarities, this was tinged by an anger that she had consistently been denied a chance at the kind of happiness she dreamed of, and of which she knew herself to be capable. She had glimpsed it, once, briefly, before it disappeared like another dream. She would not give Sir Owain a second opportunity to wound her: better still, if the chance presented itself, she would wound him just as sorely. Meanwhile, she would make her own arrangements for her security and pray that her determination would persuade the king to let her be.

As for the duration of her next marriage to Master attc Wcllc, it had occurred to her that the three-month curse might only apply to knights, not to men like Stephen. Only time would tell.

Chapter Two

Sir Owain of Whitecliffe was not the only guest at Handes Castle whose company Eloise preferred to evade. Though she and her sister adored each other, there was no such affection from either of them for their elder half-brother Rolph and his sour-faced wife Griselle, a pair they referred to in private as Wrath and Grissle. They were so ill-matched that it became a source of wonder to Eloise and Jolita how they managed to produce a constant stream of infants, a miracle of nature which Lady Griselle lost no opportunity to flaunt before Eloise. The fourth member of the de Molyns's new brood was due to arrive some time in September, but Griselle's pregnancy was not enough to prevent the whole family from travelling to Handes with almost their entire household— nurses, tutors and pets—the promise of a week's hospitality being too good to miss.

Living only a few miles from Eloise's home at Haughton Manor, Sir Rolph had offered to accompany her to Derbyshire, but the thought of being cooped up in the company of her brother's noisy and ill-mannered offspring was unappealing. Nor did she relish the idea of fielding Lady Griselle's less-than-subtle inquisitions about the state of her finances. So Eloise had travelled in relative peace with her own retinue, sure that it would only be a matter of hours before Rolph came to find her.

The castle was crammed with guests, and Eloise had expected to put up with some discomfort. Instead, she and her maid Saskia had been allocated the small round chamber at the top of one of the towers that she had occupied before her marriage. From one narrow window she could see the hills and woodland, but the other side gave views of the market square teeming with people, thatched rooftops and, beyond them, the conical tops of the striped canvas pavilions in the field being prepared for the tournament.

Quietly bustling, the maid shook out garments and placed them over wooden rods to hang in the small garderobe built into the thickness of the wall, and it was during this short period of respite that Sir Rolph de Molyns came to find Eloise soon after his arrival.

He was breathless and red-faced from the exertion of the steep spiral staircase, and it was on the tip of Eloise's tongue to remark that this show of unfitness did not bode well for his success in the jousts. But she bit it back, suspecting that Grissle had probably made similar remarks and that, unless his mission had been vital, he would not have scaled these heights.

True to expectations, his courtesies were barely exchanged before he came straight to the point with no show of finesse. 'D'ye have it, Eloise? My money?' He flopped on to the blue gold-starred coverlet of the curtained tester bed that Eloise herself had embroidered as a child. 'You said you'd—'

'I said I'd look into it, Rolph, but I've had problems trying to get my own dues so that I can continue to run the estate. You must forgive me if I've been tempted to put my own needs first, on this occasion.'

Rolph would have been as good-looking as his father but for the permanent expression of discontent. His downturned mouth drooped slightly open with disappointment. 'But I have more responsibilities than you do, sister, and it's now years since I expected Piers to repay my loans. You must be near winding up his estate by now.'

She was, but she had no intention of letting Rolph know how well her lawyers had done on her behalf, for it was their father who had hired and paid them. 'These affairs can drag on for years, you know. The accountants could find none of the IOUs that you spoke of, nor was I able to find any reference of your loans to Sir Piers.'

'You have my word for it, Eloise. Isn't that good enough?'

There was a note of desperation in his voice that made Eloise wonder whether it was at Griselle's insistence he pursued the matter so relentlessly, or whether the mysterious loans were unknown to her. According to Rolph, they had begun before his marriage and continued until Sir Piers's death last year. 'It may be good enough for me, Rolph, but not for the auditors, I fear. Like yours, they wanted an interim statement at the view of account at the beginning of this month, and my bailiff had to be able to show a profit, right down to the string that ties the sacks of flour. They'd not be nearly as understanding as I'd like them to be if I were to tell them of your loans having to be paid back.'

'But that doesn't come out of the demesne accounts, Eloise, it comes out of Piers's estate,' he wailed, running a hand through his sandy hair. 'Payment of debts is usually one of the first things to be dealt with.'

'Yes, but that is not in my line of duty. I told you that, Rolph. I was not named as one of Sir Piers's executors, and his family would not allow me to take any part in the execution of his will, even though I was the obvious person to do it. They said we'd not been married long enough to receive my dower, or my legitim which gives me one-third of the goods and chattels at home, and it's only recently that I've been given permission to stay permanently at Haughton.'

'There were other properties to move into.'

'There should have been. His family would not move any of the sitting tenants out, so I had nowhere else to go.'

'And your jointures? You could have sold some of your joint property to pay me back.' He swung his legs off the bed with a petulant scowl and went to look out of the window, his hand on his forehead.

As used to his insensitivity as she was, Eloise still found it difficult to keep the sharp edge out of her voice. 'None of my jointures from Father or from Sir Piers's father were due to take effect until we'd been married for a year or until our first child was born, Rolph. As you are probably aware, those conditions were not fulfilled.'

He half-turned, making a gesture with one hand that Eloise took to be either an acknowledgement or an apology. 'Your dowry, then?'

Eloise sighed. 'You might as well know, Rolph, that the cash Father gave me I loaned to Sir Piers to buy a new stallion for breeding and a new suit of jousting armour, among other things. He swore it was a temporary state of affairs, and I too expected to be paid back within the year. I was not. As for the land from my mother that was to form part of my dowry, that's still hers and won't be released until she dies which, God willing, will not be for some time yet.'

His snort of disgust came with a sagging of his shoulders as he leaned back against the tapestried wall from where he regarded Eloise with a mixture of dismay and anger. 'But you've come out of it all right, I see,' he said, glowering at her.

'You see nothing of the sort, Rolph.' Eloise's patience snapped. 'You see a woman of twenty-three who could have had a bairn by now if you'd kept your interfering nose out of my affairs. It was you, remember, who insisted on Sir Piers's suit being con-

sidered before all others, you who assured Father that
you could handle my affairs as well as he while he
was at Westminster. It was you who assured Father
that Sir Piers was solvent. Wealthy yet thrifty, you
said. Well, that was far from accurate, when he'd
been borrowing money from you for years to fund
his extravagances, his newest armour, more horses,
more retainers than Father, almost. Does Father know
of your loans? And why did you continue to lend
him money when he showed no sign of—?'

'No! Eloise…no!' Rolph almost leapt away from
the wall, his eyes pleading for her silence. 'Father
must not know anything of this. Not a word. Promise
me. *Promise* me, Eloise!'

His vehemence took her by surprise, and she trod
carefully through a mire of inconsistencies. 'There's
no need for me to tell anyone of your affairs, Rolph.
But if I were to begin subscribing money to your
loan-fund I'd certainly have to account for it then.
Do you really expect me to forfeit some of my dower
to refund money that you lent to my spendthrift husband before I married him? Do you? When I've had
a whole year of wading through lawsuit after lawsuit
to claw back what is rightfully mine? Does Griselle
approve of your repeated demands, or is she to be
kept in the dark, too?'

Eloise had never known her half-brother look so
forlorn and, at that moment, she felt the beginnings
of sympathy for his obvious wretchedness. He sat
heavily on the bed again and lowered his head into
his hands, mumbling through his fingers. 'If I had

my way,' he said, 'I'd say no more about it. But it's Griselle who's insisting so. It's her dowry money, you see. She discovered by accident—'

'Accident? How?'

'She agreed that we could sell some of her distant dowry properties to buy other land nearer home. Well, that money had just come through at the beginning of June last year, and Piers came over to Cove Hall just before he returned to London to beg me to let him have the use of it. Griselle overheard me agreeing. She went sky-high...flew into a terrible rage...made me promise not to lend him another penny. Then, when he was killed, she demanded I get it back any way I could.'

'From me.'

'Yes, from you. It's hell...sheer hell...she never lets the matter rest day or night. If she knew—'

'Knew what?'

'Oh, nothing. I should never have begun lending him money in the first place.'

'Then why did you? And why didn't you get receipts?'

'He said it wasn't necessary among friends.' He pulled himself up by the bedpost and stood hanging on to it, knowing how unconvincing he sounded. Apart from being neighbours, they had shared little time together.

'Is that why you wanted him to offer for me? Because he was a friend?' she whispered. 'You expected something in return?'

'No...well, no. He wanted you, Eloise.'

'No he didn't, Rolph.'

'Eh?' He swivelled his head to see her face more clearly.

'He didn't want *me*. In the three months of our marriage he spent no more than fifteen days at Haughton Manor, not even enough time to get me with child. So now I've decided to take charge of my own life, at last. I'm going to marry Stephen atte Welle, my steward. You'd best hear that from me rather than from anyone else.'

His expression of bewilderment slowly gave way to utter desperation, and the explosive *'Your steward?'* was forced out like an insult. Lurching towards the door, he yanked it open without another word and headed downwards into the darkening stairwell like a man descending into the underworld.

Saskia emerged from the garderobe where she had been waiting discreetly for Sir Rolph to leave his sister's chamber, her homely face reflecting nothing of the bitterness she had overheard. The two women had been together for over nine years during which the thirty-eight-year-old maid had come to know almost as much about the de Molyns family as they did themselves. Her devotion to Eloise was absolute.

Without comment, she began to unplait her mistress's hair, shaking free the thick auburn silk and enjoying the luxurious sensation rippling through her fingers. She alone was in a position to see what no one else was allowed to see, to handle and care for it as no one else could, and it might have been said that the only thing Saskia did not understand about

Eloise was this most recent decision to marry her steward. She had nothing against the man but, practicalities aside, she alone knew the extent of her mistress's awakening at her first meeting with Sir Owain of Whitecliffe, which had happened with no other, certainly not Master Stephen atte Welle. She began to divide and comb the hair, replaiting it deftly.

'Did I do right, Saskia?' Eloise whispered.

'Now look, love,' said the maid, quietly, 'don't you start feeling guilty about refusing to hand over what you've been fighting for. If it had not been for Sir Crispin's London lawyers, you'd still be wrangling for every penny. These widows' cases can go on for years, you know. No one has a right to demand anything from you after that, and if Sir Rolph wants a repayment of loans, he should file a claim with Sir Piers's executors like all the others have had to do. And if you were to ask me—' She stopped abruptly.

'Go on. Ask you what?'

Saskia's fingers twisted busily. 'No, I've said too much.'

'If I were to ask you? I am doing,' Eloise prompted.

'Well, he didn't go to them because he knew he'd stand less of a chance with them than with you.'

'That's not what you were going to say.'

'No. I was going to say that it sounds more like payments than loans to me. Payments they both wanted no records of.'

'Something illegal, you mean?'

'I don't know, love. But it makes more sense than unlimited unrecorded loans, doesn't it?'

The intricate hair-braiding continued in silence, with Saskia baring Eloise's long graceful neck by looping her plaits back up on to her head and coiling the ends cleverly into a golden cord fixed on top. Eloise would have chosen to wear a fine white linen wimple and a sleeveless brocade surcoat to conceal her contours, but Saskia had ambitions for her mistress. Instead, she suggested a heavy gold chain set with amber, which she knew would lead a man's eyes towards the firm roundness of the breasts beneath the topaz silk. And that was how Eloise went to supper in the great hall, joined by Jolita, Sir Henry Lovell and his parents, Lord and Lady Pace.

Expecting the antagonism between her daughter and celebrated neighbour to continue, Lady Francesca had placed Lord Pace between them at the high table from where the full extent of the decorations could be seen.

'You look lovely,' whispered Lady Francesca to Eloise. 'Feeling a little calmer now?' She noticed with some anxiety how Eloise caught the corner of her lip between her teeth and let it go again. 'There's no reason to worry, child. The men will talk about themselves as they always do, and all you have to do is to smile and agree with them. There now, go along to your place and pretend that all's well.'

The midsummer solstice had now been adopted as the feast day of St John the Baptist and, although the traditional festivities were frowned upon by the church, they were still dished up each year with a strong pagan flavour and celebrated with enthusiasm. By St John's Eve, the hall was dripping with birch boughs and garlands of pine, vervain and rue to protect those within from the spirits of evil. The high table shone with Sir Crispin's most costly glass and silver, reflecting the light from clusters of candles that burned with the sweet aroma of honey.

Placed by no choice of her own so near to Sir Owain, Eloise was made well aware of his popularity, both men and women attempting to draw him into their conversations from several places away, to seek his opinion and attention, to share their laughter with him. Eloise was among a minority who did not, being content to give her attention to Lord Pace whose trencher she shared, and to accept the food he presented to her on the point of his knife. This gave her the perfect chance to study Sir Owain whilst appearing not to, an activity she preferred far more than talking to him.

His teeth were one of the first details she noticed, for it was a wonder that any soldier these days should have a perfect set, especially so white and even. His lips were mobile and quick to smile, and now she wondered unwillingly what his kisses would be like, pushing the thought aside guiltily while watching the keen eyes that she knew had flickered more than once in her direction. Through her eyelashes she was able to observe how his dark hair curled sleekly into his neck and lifted over his ears with no hint of silver, how his face was firmly muscled, fine-lined around mouth and eyes. Hugged by black velvet, his hands were sinewy and strong, his fingernails well manicured and clean, his gestures spare and steady. The gold velvet that skimmed his deep chest was belted low on slim hips with gem-studded enamelled links, and wide bands of gold embroidery on his sleeves winked in the light. Compared to many of the guests his dress was simple, but not one was more elegant.

There had been times, since their first brief meeting two years ago, when she had wondered how her life would have been different if Sir Owain had won her instead of Sir Piers. She had usually consoled herself with the assumption that it would have been remarkably similar in many respects and, as consolations go, that had usually worked quite well. In the peace of the nights, she would darkly ponder about what might have been hers until she was almost able to convince herself that she didn't want it. Never had. Never would. The tragedy that had made a widow of her seemed to underscore that conviction; the man was the same as all the rest and it had only been a girlish infatuation that had made her believe otherwise. But none of this prevented his image from returning to her daydreams more often than was comfortable.

The conversation eventually came dangerously close as Sir Henry, Jolita's future husband, leaned across to speak to Sir Owain whose fame clearly impressed him, declaring himself only partly sorry that he was not being allowed to joust during the cele-

brations 'for obvious reasons'. That had made the
three men laugh, which alone was enough to convince both sisters that perhaps Henry was not after
all as un-loverlike as Jolita had supposed, especially
when he tenderly covered her hand with his own as
she blushed.

His father, Lord Pace, had a reputation as formi-
dable as Sir Owain's as an experienced jouster. Sir
Owain leaned across him to speak to Sir Henry, his
eyes gravely mischievous. 'Can you give me any
words of advice, Sir Henry? Does his lordship's
horse squint, or pull to one side, by any chance?
Does Lord Pace aim high? Or low? Just in case we
should be drawn against each other, you understand.'

Sir Henry wiped his mouth on his napkin, refusing
to catch his father's eye. 'Do you know, Sir Owain,'
he replied, 'that my father put the very same questions to me about you before supper?' With a wink
at Eloise, Henry's droll sense of humour was established, and this time even Eloise was drawn into the
laughter.

Lord Pace was determined to have a contribution
from her. 'And who will be wearing your favour on
his sleeve tomorrow, my lady?' he asked her. 'I wager you'll be begged for both of these.' He picked
up the fur-lined tippets that hung from her elbow to
the floor.

'No, my lord.' She smiled. 'I think not. None of
the contestants will be so short of a maiden's favours
that they need seek a widow's.' She knew Sir Owain

to be listening to this exchange, but not for the world would she acknowledge it.

'Rubbish!' the older warrior snorted. 'There's not a man here who'd be anything but proud to wear one of these in the lists. Here's Sir Owain now. He'll be looking for your favour, I've no doubt. Eh, lady?'

'I do not share your confidence, my lord. Sir Owain's helm and sleeves will be festooned with ladies' favours, but not mine. Men of Sir Owain's reput—er, fame don't need to look so far, or indeed to exert themselves at all in *that* direction. My future champion is one who will gladly devote himself to my affairs rather than to a dangerous sport.' Her reply had begun with a smile, but her last words divulged the reason for her cynicism that threatened to put a halt to what had begun as lighthearted cajolery. Women were, after all, to be begged for favours, and some show of reluctance, even coldness, was an integral part of the sophisticated game of chivalry with which men learned to contend.

'Ah, yes,' said Lord Pace. 'Your steward, your father tells me. A rather unorthodox choice, my lady, if I may say so.'

'Yes, my lord. Unorthodoxy has never concerned me as much as my parents would have liked it to, but my reasons are sound enough.'

'In which case,' said a familiar voice from Lord Pace's other side, 'your lack of convention is in danger of cladding you with a layer of ice. Beware that it doesn't freeze you solid, or your steward will find life at Haughton Manor somewhat chilling.'

'Thank you, Sir Owain. That's the second piece of unwanted advice you've offered me regarding my future, but I'll pass it on to Master atte Welle for our mutual amusement,' said Eloise.

'Do so, lady.'

Warily, Lord Pace looked from one to the other, wondering how best to melt the sudden frost. 'Oh— ho!' he smiled. 'I believe we may have a gentle conflict on our hands. Take no notice of him, my lady. He'll get his come-uppance tomorrow if he's drawn against me, never fear. I'll bring him down a peg or two, eh?'

'I'm sure Sir Owain will understand that far better than anything I could say, my lord, I thank you. And besides all that,' she went on before Sir Owain could respond, 'it would not look good for any man to be wearing my favour at jousting on the anniversary of my husband's death, would it?'

'So your unorthodoxy doesn't extend so far, then?' said Sir Owain.

She was caught out. 'No, sir,' she whispered. 'It doesn't.'

'Gratifying,' he said, leaning back, the contest over.

As the meal drew to an end, the ladies were invited to assemble in the inner courtyard to review the jousters' helms and shields according to their right to make known any objection they might have. Enclosed on all sides by the castle buildings, the small courtyard was already ablaze in the light of tallow torches with the colours and patterns of dozens of shields above which hung the iron and steel helms topped by ornate crests. Heralds wearing the de Molyns green-and-gold livery escorted the procession of ladies around the display, answering every query about each of the contestants and their lineage; their knowledge was exhaustive. For Jolita's sake, they pointed out Sir Henry Lovell's, smiling knowingly as they added that it was there only for show, but went on to indicate his father's helm that still showed a few dents from last time.

'This one,' they said, 'will need no introduction. Sir Owain of Whitecliffe is a winner at every tournament, these days.'

A murmur of approval ran through the women, several of whom giggled and remarked loudly that he could wear their favours any time, and though Eloise told herself that it mattered nothing to her, nevertheless she was drawn to his impressively shining steel helm with its gaudy plume of black-and-gold feathers, and a shiver of fear caught at her throat. Despite her denial that she was challenging him, she knew that the skirmishing had already begun and that, so far, she had nothing to show for it.

As the men came to join them, the draws took place to decide who was to joust with whom on the following day. Tension mounted, and gusts of laughter combined with the usual friendly insult, Owain's laughter as hearty as the rest. Women flocked around him and, from her distance, Eloise was reminded as never before how her late husband had revelled in such moments, drinking it in like a drug as if he was unable to do without it. She looked around her at the knights who would have known him, fought with him and contested him, and she wondered how many of them were bitten by the same madness for personal glory. They were presentable men, well dressed, well mannered and noble; many of them were Sir Owain's personal friends who looked long at her then turned aside to whisper. Others came to talk to her and, in their company, she was escorted to the entertainment in the hall well before he returned.

She had intended to stay close to Jolita to help her with the quiet man they had called courteous but not loverlike, but her assistance in their affairs would have been superfluous, the pair already being deep in conversation in a shadowy corner of the hall. There were other friends who were delighted to keep her company throughout the display of acrobatics, stilt-walking, which they called longshanks, the jugglers and gleemen, and there were others to whom she had a duty, as a daughter of the house, to spend time with. By the time Sir Crispin's chamberlain announced that the village bonfire had been lit, Eloise was certain that Sir Owain had decided to keep his distance, which was a relief, she told herself, eyeing the group that enclosed him.

To the dismay of the village priest, a ring-dance had already begun to circle the huge bonfire that crackled noisily at one side of the river. Reflections zig-zagged across the dark water, and whoops of excitement mingled with the sound of madly scraping viols and wailing pipes to which the village had come alive. Dogs yapped, chanting choruses lost and found the rhythm of the thudding tabor and the nick-nacks of bone that clattered merrily between the butcher's boy's fingers, hitting his knee and thigh in time to the pounding of feet.

It was this period of complete abandonment that made Eloise forget, just for a while, that there was someone whose company she must avoid, for as long as the sights and sounds evoked images of her idyllic childhood, she could recall no feelings of ill will towards anyone. Their return through the castle gates to the great hall was not the mass exodus of before but a slow trickle of weary bedtime guests. After bidding her parents goodnight and then showing a group of six visiting chaplains where they might make their beds in a corner of the large muniment room, she began the ascent to her own chamber in the same tower. Jolita and Henry had long since disappeared.

The heavily-studded door to her chamber was set into the wall on the left of the spiral staircase opposite a man-sized niche with an arrow-slit from where an archer could shoot at an enemy. As she rounded the last steep twist, the flickering glow from a wall-sconce showed her the unmistakable shape of a man leaning inside the niche as a guard might wait for some action. His deep gold surcoat reached almost to calf-length, but the side-slit to the hips showed her one long black-clad thigh and calf bulging with muscle, and a black pointed foot crossed tidily over the other.

Her heart thudded out of control, and the temptation to swivel on the narrow wedge-shaped stair and flee almost overcame her anger. But she knew he would follow, and she would be no better off except for an audience of six astonished chaplains.

Her eyes drew level with his waistline and she hesitated, preparing to turn, knowing that she would have to brush against him to open her door.

'Come, lady,' he said, softly. 'We have some talking to do.'

Again, she felt a perverse tightening in her lungs, and the words she meant to speak with emphasis came out breathless instead. 'I have nothing more to say to you, sir.' She placed a hand on the stone core that ran down the centre of the stairwell, hanging on to its coolness.

'I'm not surprised,' he said without moving. 'You said it all down there in the hall and in the solar, didn't you? Now it's my turn.'

'Ah, of course. So that's what this is all about. I dented your pride, now you must dent mine. You can't afford to be dented too often, can you? Especially by a woman, of all people.'

The smile entered his voice as he ignored the jibe. 'D'ye want to stand there, or are you going to invite me inside?'

'You know I cannot do that, even if I wanted to. It would be most improper, sir.'

In one swift movement like a cat, he coiled and

sat on the ledge of the niche before she could step downwards, putting his head on the same level as hers where she was obliged to see him at close quarters. 'Improper, would it?' he said. 'For someone who publicly protests her unorthodoxy? How so?'

'You know how so. And my maid is waiting for me. And it's late.'

'Saskia? No, she's not.'

'What?'

He pointed downwards. 'She's with my man, in my chamber.'

'Below mine? Your...? How did she...?'

'Yes, just below you, my lady. And Saskia was not forced, I assure you. Now, shall we?' He made a courteous gesture towards the door, waiting for the permission he was sure would follow, however unwillingly, and being far too clever to enter without it.

Still she balked, it being her own unpreparedness that angered her most, for there were a thousand reasons why she could not accept the unnerving closeness of a man to whom, in her dreams, she had often been closer than close. Fuming, she cursed herself for lowering her guard against the one who would see an advantage from a mile away, and seize it. 'I do not *want* to talk to you, sir,' she said.

'I'm not asking you to. I'll talk, if you prefer.' He stood and opened the heavy door, pushing it inside and making the torch flicker wildly in the draught. A cluster of candles shed a warm radiance of wavering light across the tapestry-covered walls like a haven of safety. But while she knew he would not force his way in, the notion of giving in to his request went against every decision not to be one of the dozens of fawning women clamouring for his slightest attention. He had offered for her once and lost his chance, wasting a precious time of her life by his carelessness and losing her husband by some knavery. Against every screaming objection, she moved past him and entered her chamber, knowing that he would follow.

They faced each other from across the room, Eloise wondering if this was how he assessed his opponents from beneath the splendid jousting helm. Provoked by his level gaze, his confident stillness, and by her own capitulation at this early stage, she exposed her own anger even further. 'Well, then, get it over with. I cannot stop you from having your say, it seems, but I suppose it was only to be expected.' With an unconcealed yawn, she sat on the chest and looked about her in apparent apathy, hoping that her rudeness would shake him.

But if she expected him to launch into an immediate explanation for this intrusion, or a dressing-down for her former incivility, she was now disconcerted to find that it was his silence that unnerved her. Furthermore, while she was well used to men's stares, this man's penetrating and steady watchfulness troubled her as no other had ever done.

'Such silence!' His soft laugh riled her. 'Does that come in three-month cycles, too?'

Stung, she lashed out, wildly. 'I am amazed, Sir

Owain, that you have the effrontery to accept my father's invitation to come here at this time when courtesy alone might have forbidden it, in the circumstances.'

'Courtesy alone doesn't stand much of a chance, lady,' he said, placing his hands on his hips. 'There's too much going on here that I intend to be a part of for me to pay much heed to the circumstances, as you call them. You can call it effrontery, if it makes you feel any easier, but I prefer to call it determination.'

'Of which commodity you were remarkably depleted only two years ago, sir, if I remember correctly.'

'Then your perceptions were flawed. It was not determination I lacked then. The king commanded me to be in France at the very time I needed to be at home. I am a soldier. I may not protest that I have a woman to woo when the king needs me.'

'You are a jouster!' she snarled, pouring as much scorn into the word as she could.

'A soldier, lady. A captain in the king's cavalry. The jousting is for practice when we're not fighting, though I can see how your misunderstanding arose when your late husband couldn't tell the difference either.'

'Do not speak of Sir Piers, sir!'

'Why not? Don't tell me you're still mourning him.' His eyes swept over the shining silk and the auburn glory of her candlelit hair. 'And still annoyed, I see, that he took what you had hoped to bestow on me. Don't bother to deny it, my lady. I'm not so inexperienced that I cannot see a woman's interest from the far end of a room.'

'Your vast experience of women is common knowledge, sir, but my *lack* of interest in you was that of a young and innocent maid.'

'Hold it!' He dropped his hands and approached her, picking up a stool on the way and setting it so close before her that his knees almost touched hers as he sat. 'Hold it,' he said, quietly. 'Let's understand this, shall we? Neither of us was innocent, my lady. You ran off with a lover when you were seventeen and still at convent school. Apparently the nuns couldn't teach you all you wanted to know, could they?'

'God's truth!' she yelped, trying to stand.

Sir Owain grabbed her by the wrist and pulled, making her stay, angering her further by his restraint.

'They told you about that, did they?' she continued. 'Is there anything they missed, for your interest? You have only to ask my brother; he'll give you every last detail. If he'd not found us and dragged me back here, I'd still be living happily in a barn, no doubt. Let *go* of me!'

'Whoo…oo, lass!' Sir Owain kept hold of her wrist with enough pressure to keep her seated. 'I don't have to ask Sir Rolph. I made it my business to ask your parents, as any man would. Even a soldier doesn't buy a pig in a poke.'

'Thank you!' she snapped, pulling her wrist free. 'And are you as particular about *every* woman who interests you? Do you keep a stud-book of the count-less women you've covered?'

His head ducked, fractionally, as a smile tweaked at his mouth. 'Er…countless in the sense that I've never counted them. Well…no. I find I can remem-ber all I need to know, as a rule.'

'And you needed to know every misdemeanour of my youth, did you? I was not nearly so interested in yours.'

'I prefer to know if the woman I offer for is a virgin or not. It helps.'

'You are presumptuous. That's something you cannot possibly know.'

'Yes, I can. There was a nail-biting month, so your father says, after your return. What was all that about if not virginity?'

Like a head of steam released, she leapt away from him and across the room in an attempt to escape the humiliating inquisition. 'This is too much!' She pointed to the door. 'Go! Just leave, sir. Insuffer-able…arrogant…'

But Sir Owain was not ready to be dismissed. Boldly, he approached and took her wrist again, eas-ing her away from the wall, back to the chest. 'Sit down,' he said. 'I haven't finished. Now, let's just run through the rest, shall we? I'm sure you'll tell me if I get it wrong, but I have a fair memory for such things.'

'No…*no*, sir!'

He sat before her again, ignoring her protest. 'You ran off with a lad from Lichfield who I don't suppose taught you much you couldn't have worked out for yourself. So that was the end of your education at Farewell Priory and the beginning of another sort. Correct so far?'

Furious, Eloise looked stonily beyond his head.

'Then there was some urgency to get you wed before you got the bit between your teeth again… no…stay where you are…so your father found young Lionel from Carlisle. I knew him, by the way. Nowhere near strong enough for you. He got it in the neck in a skirmish in France, didn't he? So his family released you from the contract as the betrothal was only three months old and not consummated. Which I can well believe. He didn't have much idea about warfare, either.'

'Sir Owain, this is intolerable. Your insults—'

'My insults, lady, happen to be facts, which is more than can be said for yours to me before members of your family. Now, do you prefer this recital to be in private, or in public?'

Again, she was silenced and he continued. 'So, after that fiasco came the next attempt to old Sir Norbert of Essex who got caught by the tail-end of pestilence. And that was another three months gone. I can see how you believe all your connections follow a time span. Strange, isn't it? No small wonder your father was getting desperate, but I was back from Crécy by then and I offered for you, I recall.' His face tipped sideways to attract her scowl, but she avoided his teasing smile. 'But then, after that brief meeting, I was summoned by the king to return to

France without a moment's delay to negotiate the
release of some of his relatives. I sent your father an
offer. It was all I could do, in the circumstances.
Except the letter, of course, which you apparently
chose to ignore.'

Letter? She frowned into his eyes, expecting to
find some insincerity. They held hers without a
flicker. 'Yes,' he said. 'A letter. A personal message
sent to you a few days later from London.'

She could find nothing to say. She had received
no message, yet his eyes told her that this was no
lying excuse.

His lips moved, framing a reply. 'You didn't receive it,' he said, flatly.

'No,' she whispered. 'I received nothing from you.
Not a word.'

'Then I shall tell you what it said.' He took the
shock in his stride, as any jouster would. Messages
sent by hand had been known to go astray, and Sir
Owain was well aware of at least one impediment to
his plan.

'Please...!' She put up a hand. 'Don't tell me.'

'But *you* believed I lacked commitment. Believe
me, I did not.'

'I had no choice, sir.'

'So you allowed your meddlesome brother and Sir
Piers to rig up such an appealing case in my absence
that your father was bound to think that Sir Piers was
God's answer to desperate parents. I don't blame
him. Your father is usually very thorough, very particular, but he was obliged to be at Westminster at

that time and naturally he expected that Rolph would handle things as well as he. But your brother was taken for a fool, lady, as you were. Thank heaven *that* only lasted three months, too.'

Eloise swung her head round to contradict him with the full force of her anger. 'On the contrary, Sir Owain, it was the short duration of our marriage that complicated matters beyond anything you can imagine. For which I have you and your friend Sir Phillip Cotterell to thank. Even if you *had* managed to convince me of your own thwarted interest, you can hardly expect me to be gracious to a man who was involved in my husband's death. Even for you, sir, that would be stretching things too far.'

'I do not deny some involvement, but it was not how you think. Far from it. But nor am I going to attempt to explain exactly what happened at Windsor last year to a widow who has no intention of believing me. You haven't, have you?'

'No.'

'As I thought.'

'You are very sure of yourself, Sir Owain,' she whispered. 'But don't make the mistake of judging me by the standards of your many conquests. I am not of that mould and never will be. You have recited my past as if it explained some irresponsibility on my part, but none of it was my own doing except the first, and that I do not regret even if I don't boast of it. It has nothing to do with you or with anyone else, and if you had it in mind to make Master atte Welle aware of it, don't bother. He knows.'

'Nothing was further from my mind at this moment than your steward, my lady, believe me. Nor have I ever believed you to be of the same mould as the countless other you refer to. If you had been, we would not be having this conversation.'

'Then why *are* we having this conversation, Sir Owain? Do explain.'

'To level the ground, my lady.' He stood, swinging the stool away and replacing it beside the bed. 'You had your say down there, now I've had mine. From now on we're on equal footing, so don't expect to score without a return hit. I shall not be so chivalrous as to be a public target for your barbs. Understood?'

This was plain speaking with a vengeance. 'Oh, perfectly, Sir Owain. Men may suffer another man's hit and laugh it off, but a woman's is a different thing, is it not? Do you know, I didn't even realise I'd scored. Now, isn't *that* strange?'

Laughing quietly, he strolled to the door and paused with a hand on the latch. 'Then you will have to tread very carefully, my lady, in case you score accidentally. The penalty could be particularly humiliating, coming from a man with so many conquests under his belt. Eh? Sleep well, my beauty.' Still laughing, he let himself quietly out of the room.

Eloise was still sitting there, pensive and none too pleased, when Saskia returned a few moments later, ready to explain her absence. However, Saskia's perfectly valid reason for leaving her mistress to face Sir Owain alone, which was because he had asked her to, seemed to concern Eloise less than the knight's conduct, which was not quite what she had expected, if she'd had any expectations at all.

'Are we talking about what he did?' said Saskia. 'Or what he didn't?' She began to unlace the back of the topaz kirtle, harbouring her own thoughts on the subject. When Eloise made no reply, Saskia made it for her. 'Ah, then it's what he didn't do, is it? Well, he's a gentleman, that's for—'

'He's *not* a gentleman. He's an overbearing, condescending, insolent…ugh! I hate the man!'

'Well, that may be so, love, but I'll wager there's not many women he visits at this time of night without ending up in their beds. I'd not have left you alone with him if he'd not assured me he only wanted a few moments to talk. He wants to get to know you, that's all.'

'That's not the impression I got. He seems to think he knows all about me already. Peasant! Well, he doesn't, Saskie. He knows nothing. And if I had any sense I'd let him think what he damn well likes.'

'And do you, love?' Saskia turned her mistress round and sat her down.

'Not enough. I'll teach him how not to speak to a woman who knows what she wants and what she doesn't want, and if he thinks I'm going to step carefully over his precious ego he can think again. Penalties, indeed! We'll see who's humiliated longest, Sir Knight. I can hold the reins as long as you.'

'Whe-e-ew!' Saskia let out a long quiet breath and began to unbraid the auburn hair.

While the candles still burned in her chamber, it was difficult, if not impossible, for Eloise to admit that her perceptive maid was right in her summing up of the thorny situation, so she concentrated on the other source of her anger: his warning that in future she would get as good as she gave. But in the darkest hours of the night, there seemed to be a bewilderment of answers to the vexed question of why, when he could have kissed her, he had not done.

There was another question, too, which he would have answered had she not stopped him. The content of the letter she could almost guess, but who had received it and why they had not passed it on was harder to understand. If it had indeed been sent from London a few days later, then it must have been received first into her half-brother's hand, or in her mother's, perhaps. Lady Francesca would not have kept it from her. But Rolph? Would he have tried to close her heart so forcibly against Sir Owain and keep it open for his own choice, Sir Piers? What devilry had the two of them hatched in those confusing months?

Chapter Three

St John's Day came to Handes Castle in a shimmering haze of peach-coloured sky and a breeze that barely lifted the pennants off the knights' striped arming-tents over on the tournament field. Jolita was an early visitor to her sister's cool chamber, her eyes shining with a new radiance that had been missing the day before.

'What's this?' Eloise took her by the hand and led her to the window, scrutinising the face with a teasing severity. 'Not happiness, surely? One is not supposed to be happy, my child, on one's betrothal day. Now, a sober modest face, if you please.' The accent was distinctly Irish.

They hugged, laughing and squeaking. 'Oh, Ellie! You sound just like Father Eamonn.'

'Well,' the Irish lilt continued, 'I'll let you off the penance for looking happy if you assure me that procreation is uppermost in your mind. Well, child? Is it?'

'Hah!' Jolita yelped, merrily. 'Yes, if you must

know, it is. Oh, Ellie! He's not as we thought, our Henry.'

'*You* thought. So where did you disappear to, last evening?'

'Talking.' Jolita grinned, leaning her elbows on the deep sill, her face illuminated by the day's early glow.

'I saw the talking. What else?'

Jolita blushed, holding her cool hands to her cheeks and suppressing a laugh. 'Oh, just getting acquainted. You know.'

'Jollie…you didn't…?'

'No, heavens, no. Of course not. We're saving that for tonight.'

'So soon? Then he's not unloverlike, after all. And you're going to like him?'

'Oh, yes!' Jolita wrapped her arms around Eloise, vibrating with happiness. 'I was mistaken. He's kind and gentle.'

'And experienced?'

'Yes, oh yes,' she gurgled. 'And he has a lovely sense of humour. Quiet, you know. And he listens, too. He wanted me to tell him what I did and what I liked, and today I'm going to show him—'

'Today, love, you're going to be betrothed.'

'Yes. *Yes*, Ellie!' The squeeze tightened with excitement.

The hug relaxed as Jolita suddenly recalled her sister's situation. Full of concern, she drew her towards the rumpled bed to sit by her side. 'Ellie, what's happened? You're sad. Please don't be sad today, dearest. Is it…is it *him*?'

Unable to lie convincingly, Eloise looked away, sighing before she could stop herself. 'I'm not sad, love. Really I'm not.'

'But?'

'Oh, nothing. It's Sir Piers's year-day and I'm supposed to be a grieving widow, according to Father Eamonn, but for the life of me I cannot be. I've been to say prayers for his soul, and the good chaplain expects me to say how I'm missing him, but I'm not, Jollie. I'm free, and yet…' Her smile took on the colour of sadness. 'Oh, nothing.'

It was not in her nature to be envious of her sister, or indeed anyone, but no one could have been unmoved by dear Jolita's unexpected happiness, her bubbling excitement at the discovery of delights to come, her relief that Henry was, after all, more than capable of making her love him. So far, nothing of that nature had ever come remotely near her own experience, she who ached to give herself, body and soul, into a man's careful and loving hands. At seventeen, she had placed the gardener's lad in this role but had encountered the same inexperience as herself. Since then, her parents had done their best to match her up to worthy knights who had proved to be as insubstantial as snow, for one reason or another. All four of them. Fate was enjoying herself at her expense.

The two sat without speaking as the vibrant sound of a man's singing came from somewhere below them, drifting through the door that Jolita had left ajar.

'Sir Owain,' Jolita whispered. 'Every time I saw him last evening he was watching you. Even Henry remarked on it.'

With a shake of her head, Eloise would have none of it. 'It's only a man's looking at something he's missed, Jollie. Wait till this afternoon, you'll see how things change. He'll have women hanging from each arm and another two waiting to mop his brow. You'll see,' she repeated. 'Now, love. What do sisters wear on betrothal days, then? Green sleeves are not the thing, are they?'

Green was thought to be inappropriate for a bride-to-be as it had often been used to cover up grass stains made by too close contact with the ground.

'No, certainly not. Come and see what Mother had the tailor make for me.'

'Shameless red?'

'No, silly. Maidenly blue.'

Attended by all the castle guests, the betrothal took place under a bower of white roses in the orchard, a large green canopied space that now came alive with splashes of bright colour, men's as well as women's. Eloise, hoping to blend into the background in a soft pink madder-dyed kirtle and matching surcoat, was noticeable for the deep mulberry sheen of her hair that hung past her waist in one thick plait braided with gold. Over this, she wore a gold amethyst-studded circlet, a style that was taken by her family to be a sign of a return to her former unmarried status sometimes reverted to by ladies of rank who could also, if they wished, re-adopt their maiden names.

Lord and Lady Pace, magnificent in gold-speckled blue and red, smiled across at her as she stood on the de Molyns side next to her half-brother, and it was the way their smiles passed over her shoulder that made her half-turn to see who was there. Her heart lurched as she recognised the gold-and-black embroidered sleeve of Sir Owain and felt his warmth at her back and, from that moment, the exchange of betrothal rings and vows took second place to the mad beating of her heart. With the others, she applauded as the ceremony was concluded and tender kisses were exchanged, as they had been for her on three occasions.

Lady Griselle, her sister-in-law, was quick to remind her of this. 'You must be well used to this by now, my dear,' she said to her in a loud whisper. 'Next time lucky, eh?'

Usually so quick to find a retort, Eloise was by this time already rattled by the close proximity of the man behind her, whom she preferred not to hear whatever defense she might have to offer. Nor did she think it appropriate to bicker with Lady Griselle on this happy occasion. She bit back her retort, quietly fuming at the woman's bulging presence but unable to move away.

Help came from an unexpected quarter as a hand rested on her shoulder, turning her gently but firmly away from Lady Griselle's satisfied smirk and manoeuvring her to the back of the crowd towards the low gnarled branches of an apple tree. Ankle-deep in spent blossom, she stood next to Sir Owain while the woman who had tried to provoke her craned her neck to see where she had gone. Her expression as she found Eloise and Sir Owain standing close together with his hand still on her shoulder was more than they could have hoped for. For the first time since their meeting, their shared delight at the woman's vexation brought them briefly together and, though not a word was exchanged, Eloise's smile of thanks appeared to be sufficient reward for her champion, the first he had received from her.

Quickly, they were surrounded by friends as intrigued by this new accord as Sir Rolph's wife was, but Eloise sidled away to seek out her sister and Sir Henry for her personal congratulations, the imprint of Sir Owain's silent protection still warm on her body. Having been through no less than three betrothals in the past five years, she experienced a feeling of *déjà vu* in the hours that followed that came closer to Griselle's cutting remark than even she could have known, and although Eloise tried to steer her mind away from the events in her past towards those in her sister's future, the comparisons were difficult to evade, Jolita's expectations being so much like her own at her betrothal to Sir Piers. Then, of course, Sir Owain had not been present as he was now, though in her mind his image had never been far away, and it was perhaps now more than ever that she recognised her own foolishness and pride in accepting the empty adulation of one in favour of her heart's certainty for the other. Even worse was her present determination to keep him out of her life, despite the steadfastness of her heart's message. Set once more on the wrong course, her nagging doubts kept her heart closed against him, hurting her with the effort of it.

The lengthy feasting and speeching came to an end at last, releasing the wine-weary guests to an hour's siesta and the fitter ones to the tiltyard at the side of the castle walls for some serious jousting practice. The evening tournament would be held in the large field beyond the houses, but here at the practice-tilts, a range of devices was intended to improve the men's jousting techniques that stood them in good stead in times of war. By the time Eloise, Jolita and a large group of their friends arrived, the practice had begun, and though none of the men could have missed the bright colours and bursts of brittle applause from the grassy sunlit bank below the ramparts, few of them were prepared to acknowledge that they were being watched.

Wearing no armour except their shields for protection, the men were easy to identify. Excitedly, Jolita picked out Sir Henry Lovell, who was coaching several of the young squires in the art of bringing their lances down at exactly the right moment in the run and to level the points at a tiny ring that hung from a pole, known as the quintain. The lances were very long, heavy and difficult to control and, though

Sir Henry made it look easy, the young would-be knights found it difficult enough to keep their horses on course without any added complications.

Jolita had said that he was not handsome, but that had been yesterday. Today, she whispered to Eloise, she found his features attractively weatherbeaten and well used, his dark eyes thoughtful and spun about with laugh-lines. Yesterday he had worn a beard, but today it had vanished along with ten of his thirty-five years, to Jolita's delight. They had both suffered the teasing, and now she was eager to praise his every move. 'Watch him, Ellie,' she said, happily. 'He's so patient with them.'

But her sister's attention was drawn to the figure mounted on a large black stallion, his lance held vertically and resting on the top of his foot. Even from that distance Eloise could see that the presence of the women was being pointed out to him by a friend, that he made a brief reply and told the men to take his turn at the quintain. Then, as the man moved away, Sir Owain looked directly across at her, holding her eyes for so long that several heads turned to see her reaction, knowing nothing of the inner turmoil his scrutiny caused her.

Deliberately, he rode forward to his place in the lists and lifted his lance, settling the end of the shaft beneath his arm and spurring his stallion forward. It leapt into a gallop, its mane flying, the rider leaning and lowering his lance, aiming it at the ring his friend had just missed, gathering it with apparent ease on to the point and lifting it high into the air to admiring applause. To Eloise, who had watched his every graceful move, the imagery could not have been plainer or more boldly stated, and when Jolita took her hand in silence and squeezed it, she knew that she was by no means the only one to have understood his message.

An hour later, they left the men to continue their practice, Eloise still disturbed by the knight's directness even though, only a few hours ago, she had almost convinced herself that his attention would be directed elsewhere. And though a part of her continued to deny any interest in him, her most vulnerable and secret heart came alive with a new anticipation.

'Dearest,' Jolita whispered to her as they strolled away, arm in arm, 'he intends to have you. Did you not see?'

'I saw,' Eloise replied. With her sister, the nonchalance was replaced by a more genuine concern. 'I don't suppose that's the first time he's ever sent such tidings to a woman, but he'll not be so used to having a woman refuse him. He must know by now that he'll be wasting his time.'

'That was a challenge, if ever I saw one, Ellie.'

'Don't…please, don't!'

'Why?' Jolita stopped, holding Eloise back. 'You're afraid?'

'That's what I'm supposed to be asking you.'

'But you are, aren't you?'

Eloise looked away, refusing to meet her sister's

eyes yet again. 'I don't know, Jollie, truly I don't. If that was a challenge, then it's a most unfair one.'

'Why so?'

'Because he knows all my objections, and he knows that I've decided on my future. To ignore all that is unchivalrous.'

'Perhaps he doesn't believe you.'

'Then the discovery that it's true will be a novel experience for him.'

'Beware, Ellie. He doesn't give up easily, you know.'

'He did once. He will do so again. Come on, Mother's beckoning.'

'Girls,' Lady Francesca called, 'what is it? Eloise, you're blushing. You talking girls' talk?'

'No, Mother,' Jolita chirruped. 'Women's talk.'

The midsummer crowds from the surrounding villages, hungry for spectacle, poured into the great field on the edge of town for an event that came within their reach only rarely, jousting being too dangerous to be performed without the king's special licence. This was not the way he wanted to lose his best fighting men, yet some practice was essential during the peaceful years, and the suspicion that knights would joust even without his permission was always present.

Dressed in the green and gold de Molyns livery, Sir Crispin's men were everywhere to be seen, with so much depending upon the host's good organisation for the safety of his many guests, their retainers and servants, horses and equipment, none of which came cheap. Swept to one side were the usual acrobats and tumblers, the noisy itinerant musicians, the traders and pickpockets, the whores who plied for trade wherever people gathered. Hoping for a better view from the back row of the stands were those who dressed above their station and slid quietly into the guests' seats. They were soon spotted and moved out.

Wooden tiers of benches had been erected along opposite sides of the open space known as the lists, where the jousting would take place, the scaffolding already providing young lads with a place from which to swing like monkeys until they too were flushed out. A battlemented wooden fence painted in green and gold protected the front row of onlookers from any accident, and it was here, overlooking the heads of the trumpeters, that Eloise sat with the women of her family, Jolita's future in-laws, their ladies, chaplains, their oldest retainers and friends, governesses and nurses, wives and daughters of the contestants.

As Queen of the Day, Jolita sat in the place of honour from where she diplomatically requested Lady Pace, Henry's mother, to identify some of the lesser-known coats of arms, for by this time the contestants were emerging from the bright canvas pavilions and preparing to mount their horses. Clad in shining armour and linen surcoats to the same design as their shields, the knights were attended by liveried squires, young men who would one day be knighted but who meanwhile carried their masters' equipment and assisted them during the jousts. Lack of attention to detail was rewarded with a mailed blow to the body, for a mistake at this point could cost a life.

The women's chatter dropped to an expectant murmur. Torches were lit on the tops of iron braziers. Colours, gaudy in bright sunlight, were now softened by shadows. Here and there was a flash of silver, steel and iron, the ripple of distorted pattern as the horses' caparisons floated around their feet, caught on the evening breeze. Not only did the knights wear surcoats embroidered with their arms, but the horses too. Draped to their hooves in flowing linen in their masters' colours, their heads were hooded, their reins hung with bells, tassels and fringes. Underneath the show were the more serious straps, cords and buckles, paddings and protections, two girths to hold the saddle against the violent shock of each impact, every piece of armour designed to deflect blows, to minimise damage. The men called their own armour 'harness' too.

They carried it effortlessly, even the older men whose skills had not faded as quickly as their stamina. The women watched like hawks, each one seeking out her own man. Some of the knights already wore women's flowing scarves tied around their arms or flowers stuck into the great helms that squires held lovingly in their arms. Lord Pace and Sir Crispin cantered up together to request, publicly, tokens from their ladies, laughing like schoolboys as the scarves tangled with the wind. Eloise had given her token to no one, nor did she expect to.

As the two men cantered away, another knight

passed them with black and gold chequers fluttering through black legs and hooves, a handsome rider with black hair lifting in the breeze, grim-faced and confident.

'He's coming here, Ellie,' Jolita murmured, not looking at her sister.

'No, not to me.' Eloise glanced along the row to see who else was there, but all faces were turned in her direction. Her heart skipped, drunkenly. No. He had warned her, but he would not court her favour.

Pulled to a sudden halt, his great horse wheeled about uncertainly but was brought back to face the stand where Eloise sat biting her lip, her eyes troubled, her mind willing him to move away. It would not do for her to bestow her favour upon a jouster on the anniversary of her husband's death, especially to Sir Owain, of all men. But the decision demanded courtesy, for Sir Owain slowly lowered his lance and rested its point accurately on the ledge before her, and there was no mistaking its request.

Like a thunderclap, his deep voice fell into the silence. 'Your favour, Lady Eloise, if you please, to wear on my arm in the jousts.'

Meeting his eyes with the greatest reluctance, Eloise hesitated, surprised, troubled, and partly defiant. He had no right to ask this of her, nor was this the best way for her to score a point. Only by a refusal could she do that, and that would come at a price.

'Ellie!' Jolita whispered, frowning. 'Ellie, you *must*. You cannot be so discourteous. Please!'

On Jolita's other side, Lady Pace leaned forward, smiling. 'Your tippet, Lady Eloise? Does it remove?'

As if in a dream, Lady Eloise slid the long pink silken tippet down her arm from elbow to wrist and leaned forward to tie it around the point of his lance, bestowing her favour upon the one who was not likely to do anything to deserve it.

I shall take all I came for, and probably more, he had told her, and now he was well on the way to making that prediction a certainty, with her help. Damn the man.

Acknowledging her capitulation, he nodded, curtly, lifting his lance and wheeling his horse away to canter across the field with the pink pennant fluttering above him victoriously. To her embarrassed astonishment, the crowd erupted into laughing applause, even those alongside her, and it was only then that she realised the full significance of what he was parading before the spectators, even more explicit than his feat earlier that afternoon when he had pierced the ring.

To hide her face in shame would have been childish. To maintain a stony mask would have been unnecessarily prudish and, even worse, to laugh would have shown her approval. Instead, she chose a middle way by begging Jolita silently to pretend some kind of distracting conversation. In this way, they kept up a meaningless sisterly chatter until the hubbub had died down but, even with the comfort of Jolita's warm hand over hers, her own were trembling with anger and humiliation at the man's disgraceful tactics.

At the trumpeters' fanfare, the mounted heralds entered the lists preceded by a drummer whose beat echoed that of Eloise's heart. There was no time for more discussion. With one hand raised, the heralds droned out the rules: the winner of each contest to be the one who performed best out of three jousts either by breaking his opponent's lance, unhorsing him, or by bringing down both horse and rider, which would be an outright win. A draw would be decided on grounds of style, a decision the women approved of, for often a contest would continue with swords and axes until one of the men was disabled. Last, they were reminded that all draws had been made and that silence was to be maintained during each joust so as not to distract the contestants.

Well used to brutal entertainments in the form of bear-baiting and cock-fighting, to punishments that were almost invariably public shows, the standing crowds wasted no sympathy on the noblemen and the shattering violence of their favourite sport. To the townsfolk, it was an added attraction that, for once, the aristocracy were getting their deserts, even though they inflicted it upon themselves. Each mighty clash of lance upon shield, helm or breastplate, every crack of lance upon lance, every staggering lurch of the horses as they were stopped dead in their tracks at full gallop was greeted with roars of approval that took no heed of the heralds' commands for silence. Lances were broken and thrown aside, each knight galloping back to his end of the lists to grab another one from his squire before turning again for the next charge, having barely enough time to position himself correctly before the next encounter.

The jousting helms, mostly of iron, allowed the wearers to see through a narrow slit only what was immediately in front of them, making it difficult to keep a horse to the right of the opponent and the lance across the horse's neck to make an assault from the left side.

'They should have a barrier between them,' said Lady Francesca de Molyns. 'Your father's horse seems to know where it's supposed to go, but it doesn't look as if his opponent's does. Who did the herald say he was, dear?' she asked Eloise.

'I don't know, Mother. I don't suppose he knows himself, at this moment.'

Sir Crispin had drawn against a young knight whose borrowed horse had a mind of its own, jousting not being one of its favourite pastimes. A barrier between the contestants would have helped to keep it from swerving across Sir Crispin's path at the critical moment, but this practice had not yet been adopted in England as it had on the continent. As a result, its unfortunate rider was prised out of the high-backed saddle by Sir Crispin's lance, landing him like a fish on the straw-covered ground with a heavy thud while the relieved horse headed for the open field.

To avoid fatal injuries, jousting lances had their

points replaced by coronels, crown-shaped devices with three blunt prongs. Even so, the force of a blow delivered at speed was enough to stop a horse and rider and to splinter an eleven-foot lance against the opponent's shield. Sir Crispin would go on to the next round, but his had been an easy victory. There were others who were better matched.

Still simmering with mortification, Eloise's hurt pride was not about to be eased by the announcement that the next jousts would be between her half-brother, Sir Rolph de Molyns, and Sir Owain of Whitecliffe. Ideally, she would have preferred them both to lose but, as one of them had to win, she laid her weak hopes on Sir Rolph while trying to disregard the pale pink silk now fluttering from Sir Owain's upper arm.

'Well, of course,' said the Lady Griselle, loudly, 'we all know how much time and money Sir Owain spends on his jousting, don't we? My husband is a family man. His estates are—'

'Yes, dear,' whispered Lady Francesca, patting her arm. 'But not now. The heralds have called for silence.'

Lady Griselle pouted, sneaking a glance at Eloise's stony profile and then down at her own fruitful bump. She tucked her hands beneath it, lifting its weight off her thighs. Surprisingly, her husband looked more imposing in armour than he did without it, his gold and green chevrons zig-zagging across every surface and, on his helm, a large papier-mâché water-mill sat firmly upon a mound of blue painted water. At that moment, she was quite proud of him.

Sir Owain took his plumed helm from his squire and placed it firmly over his head, completely obscuring his implacable expression. Without looking, he reached out a metal-plated hand for his lance, tossed it in the air and caught it below the vamplate, the conical guard above the grip. Then he waited for the command.

The fanfare of trumpets sounded. *'Laissez aller!'* called the herald, cutting the air with one hand.

At the prick of spurs, the two horses leapt forward from each end of the lists, increasing their speed with each stride, heads down, necks level, their trappings billowing like colourful sails. The lances, tucked tightly underarm, were lowered to aim immediately before impact, giving the opponent little warning of where it would strike, only that it would, somewhere.

The shock set both stallions back hard upon their haunches, their front hooves pawing the air to keep their balance, the riders flung back into their saddles by the force of the collision. Both lances snapped off halfway, splintering dangerously and denting both shields before the riders could recover, turn, and head quickly back for the next lance.

Grabbed on the turn, Sir Owain's lance danced to the same tune as the previous one before being tucked, couched and levelled at a ferocious speed as the herald called again. Eloise found that her hands were clenched into tight fists, her nails digging into her palms. Her brother was slower this time, his aim late, the collision catching him full-on before his lance-point could make contact, sending it wide away and useless. Sir Owain's lance glanced off Sir Rolph's shield and across his breast-plate, ripping the green and gold chevrons into tatters.

Eloise yelped, then caught sight of Griselle's ashen face, her mouth pulled into a grimace of fear. 'Rolph!' Eloise yelled. 'Come on! Stay up, Rolph!' No one thought it strange.

His horse was strong and agile, able to retain its balance without tipping Sir Rolph off, but their return to the far end was nothing like his opponent's flashy gallop. His squires fussed around him as Sir Owain watched and waited, controlling his horse's impatience to be off again, yet at the herald's third call, it was he who shot away with the clean velocity of an arrow while Sir Rolph's steed reared at the sharp jab upon its flanks.

Again, Sir Rolph's aim was mistimed by a split second and this time the unsettled horse and rider were levered up high into the air on the end of Sir Owain's lance before crashing down backwards, Rolph taking the full weight of the horse on top of him.

Eloise had hoped they might be a good match for each other, but now she saw the difference. Sir Owain's speed, control, sheer strength and accuracy were awesome. Not one of the previous contestants, not even her father or Lord Pace, had shown the same remarkable ability which, albeit unwillingly, Eloise was bound to accept and admire. She heard

Griselle scream and saw her struggle to stand as nearby hands tried to hold her back.

'Eloise,' her mother said, 'shall you...?'

'Yes. I'm going.' Eloise was already pushing past, heading for the wooden staircase that led to the ground. 'You stay with Griselle.'

Her brother was carried into his arming-tent only moments after her arrival there, by which time she had commandeered a trestle-table and covered it with blankets ready for the unconscious and battered body. Piece by piece, men and youths unbuckled his harness and padded gambeson, working to her quiet instructions. They had seen all this before, many times.

Eloise did not look to see who they were but took charge, giving orders to have hot water brought, linen clothes torn into strips, wooden splints to be made.

'Splints, my lady?'

'Yes, splints. There's at least one break here. I don't want any arguments. Do it. And somebody go for my physic-chest. It's in my chamber. And find Saskia. Tell her to bring long bandages.'

'I've brought my physician,' a voice said. 'He can take over now.'

Without looking up from her task, Eloise dismissed the offer. 'No, he can't. This is my brother, and I can do all that's necessary, I thank you. Get him to tend the others.' Her fingers prodded and gently probed, testing the joints with care. 'Collarbone broken. His jaw, too. That'll keep him quiet. And this wrist is bent where it shouldn't be. Tch!'

Not one of her commands was queried by the de Molyns men who knew at first hand her reputation for healing. And of the strangers who did not, none were left in any doubt after seeing how skilled she was at a diagnosis, her setting of bones, the repair of wounds and the salving of bruises, the staunching of bleeding.

'Don't just stand there, man!' she chided one of those who watched her. 'Tear some strips, then hold these splints against his ankle while I bind him.'

A familiar voice spoke gently into her ear. 'That's Sir Owain's physician you're speaking to, my dear.'

'I don't care...what? Father? You here?' She turned, suddenly aware that she had an audience. Next to her father stood Sir Owain, both of them still in harness, bare-headed but streaked with sweat, their hair sticking flat to their foreheads. A trickle of drying blood from Sir Owain's nostril lent an extra cogency to his expression of concern. 'And you, sir?' she said, coldly.

'Will he be all right?'

'Eventually. His brain's addled, but that's sparing him some pain. Bruising. Fractures. He'll mend.'

'Can I do anything? Can my man assist you?'

The physician spoke up for himself, a monk in his middle thirties, darkly tonsured and wearing a grey-white habit that Eloise had not had time to notice until now. 'The Lady Eloise is allowing me to assist her, sir, and that is all I ask. To take instruction from such a master is no hardship, I assure you.' He passed another bandage to her, holding the previous end in place as she continued to bind.

'Forgive me, Brother...?' Eloise puzzled at his accent.

'No need. Father Janos, m'lady. I'm happy to learn from you.' He pronounced it 'Yannosh', but still she couldn't pin his accent down.

Her father laid a hand on her shoulder. 'I'll get them to prepare a litter to take him to the castle as soon as you're ready. Father Janos can go with him, if you want to stay. But we're almost through now. Is there anything you need?'

'No, Father, I thank you. Saskia is on her way. Except...'

'Yes?'

'Griselle needs a litter too. And keep her away from here.'

His hand squeezed her shoulder, and he turned to go.

Sir Owain lingered as if about to say something, his hesitation suggesting to Eloise that he might wish to make some expression of regret. But then, glancing at Sir Crispin's retreating figure, he leaned towards her, whispering, 'Janos Leuvenhoek. Flemish.' Then he was gone, and in his place was Saskia, her arms hung with baskets of bandages, salves and unguents.

The maid saw immediately where her help was needed, as she had done previously on numerous occasions.

'Sir Owain's physician, Father Janos,' Eloise said

to her by way of introduction while taking Sir Rolph's pulse. 'Though I'd have thought his employer would be more in need of a chaplain than a medic if this is his usual St John's Day habit.'

Father Janos looked up from his task with a quick smile. 'I *am* Sir Owain's chaplain, my lady, as well as his physician.'

Eloise and Saskia both stared. 'Then he must keep you exceptionally busy, Father,' Eloise said. 'You are obviously more effective at this than the other. I wonder you've not given up on him.'

The smile lingered over her unconcealed astringency, but he carried on applying a poultice of pounded alder leaves to her brother's bruised and swollen wrist. 'But you must agree, my lady, that if I was not needed, there'd be no reason for me to stay, would there?'

'I wish you'd make that same point to Sir Owain sometime, Father. The sooner the better. Now, my brother is going to have a nasty headache when he comes round. What do you usually prescribe for that? A darkened room and another woman or two?'

'A piece of raw meat applied to the back of the neck often helps, my lady.'

'Yes, of course. Would that be ox meat, or a slice of his victim?'

Accustomed to concealing his thoughts, the priest-physician gave nothing away on this occasion either, although the look exchanged between himself and Saskia might have been interpreted as concern at the lady's rancour.

The lady herself was past caring about her tone. Foremost in her mind was an image of the tall and overwhelmingly powerful creature who flaunted her pink silken tippet on his arm as if he had her approval. Which was very far from the truth. She must retrieve it before he began to believe it himself.

Chapter Four

Eloise's attempt to use her maid and the physician for the unpleasant task of retrieving her favour from Sir Owain's pavilion was doomed to failure, their combined expressions of utter scepticism setting her hopes on the wrong track to begin with. Within minutes, the three of them had returned, Sir Owain flinging back the canvas flap of Sir Rolph's tent just as the litter-bearers were making their exit with his bandaged and prone form.

'Go with him, Janos, if you please,' said Sir Owain, not so much requesting as commanding. 'And Mistress Saskia, have the goodness to wait outside for a moment, if you will.' Without once looking at Eloise's astonished face, he snapped at the remaining servants, 'Out! You can finish your tasks later.'

Left suddenly and unexpectedly alone with him, and infuriated by the failure of the mission, Eloise launched into another attack. 'There was no need for you to come in person, Sir Owain. Neither is there a need for this high-handed treatment of my—'

'Before you go any further, just listen.'

'No! You listen! If you think you can make your victory parade with my favour on your arm after that disgraceful episode…'

'It was *not* disgraceful. It was a perfectly legitimate hit, woman.' He had not changed out of his armour, but it was obvious that he had dunked his head in a bucket of water since their last meeting, for now his hair was wet and combed back, his face clean and damp, giving him the sleek black hard-edged masculinity of a champion fighter rather than a courtier.

Eloise found him alarmingly intimidating. 'I'm not referring to that, sir,' she said. 'If my brother chooses to have his limbs broken by you that's up to him. I'm talking about your flagrant disregard of my wishes not to bestow my favour on any contender today, of all days. You knew of my intentions, and yet you…no!'

His slow advance towards her, which she assumed would not continue, brought him too near for her to evade the lightning quickness of his hand, and he caught her wrist before she could ward him off, bringing her so hard into his chest that she could feel the ridges of his plated cuirass beneath the linen surcoat. Her head was flung back with the suddenness of his embrace, giving him an instant advantage.

'Yes, lady. I knew of your intentions. You made sure I did, didn't you? And now you know mine. Or

shall I make them even plainer?' Without waiting for
her reply, he took the thick base of her plait in one
fist and, holding her head immobile, lowered his
mouth to hers with no more warning.

Having dreamed of a time when she might melt in
his tender arms in the softly scented darkness of a
feather bed, the pain of his fierce grasp and the stuffy
odour of a knight's tent lit only by a smoking brazier
brought the realities home to her in a way no dream
ever would of how a full-blooded male, jubilant and
aggressive after his success, was not the best person
to confront over a point of etiquette even if it was,
to her, an important one.

He lifted his mouth so that she could feel his next
words upon her lips. 'Is that plain enough for you?
Don't ever send messages to me like that again before my friends and servants. I wear your favour on
my arm and that's where I shall keep it for all to see.
Did you think I'd ignore your challenge, woman?'
Giving her no time to answer him, he kissed her
again, holding back her inevitable surge of anger so
successfully that she felt it slipping to the back of
her mind like a receding tide.

He was every bit as skilled as she had supposed,
and as different from the uncontrolled blundering of
Sir Piers as a professional harpist was from a howling
choirboy. She felt herself responding to him while
fighting the voices of conscience that warned her of
the countless others who had gone before. Yet, on
the verge of raising her arms to his shoulders, she
caught the distant echo of his last words.

'Challenge?' she panted, tearing her mouth away. 'You have challenges on the brain, sir! That was done intentionally to humiliate me, though I've done nothing to deserve it, despite your warning last night. Let me go!' She wiped the back of her hand across her mouth, twisting herself out of his arms.

'Humiliate you?' His hands fell to his sides. 'Is that what you believe? That I wore your favour to humiliate you?'

Angry tears welled up into her eyes as she recalled the picture of his lance with its fluttering pink trophy, felt the stares, heard the laughter. 'Are you blind, sir? Deaf? Don't tell me you didn't know how it must have seemed to every one of those people out there,' she pointed. 'You heard *their* response, but have you the smallest idea how shamed *I* felt, on the anniversary of my husband's death, to have one of the men involved parade my favour in such a fashion? Have you? Whatever the penalty you had in mind, sir, nothing you could devise could have been more humiliating than that. If you are quite determined to wear it again tomorrow, then I cannot prevent you. But you'll wear it without me, for I'll not be there.'

To divert her mind from his unwelcome presence, she fumbled impatiently with the knot that tied the bloodstained towel around her waist. Shadows and the moving lights from flaming torches drifted across the walls of the tent, her tears distorting them as they passed. Darkness had fallen. A roar from the crowd wavered across the brief silence between them. Tear-blind, she flung the towel away from her, the day soured and ruined. 'Go away,' she croaked, turning her back on him.

Ignoring the dismissal, he went to stand at her back as he had in the orchard. 'Let me point out to you,' he said softly in her ear, 'that I had no way of knowing what colour kirtle and surcoat you would be wearing today and that, if the spectators saw some significance attached to my lance piercing your—'

'Stop! I shall not listen to this.'

He caught her and held her against him with both steel-clad arms. 'Your pink sleeve-tippet,' he continued, 'then ask yourself whether you'd be quite so upset if you'd been wearing, say, blue or green. Would you?'

'I don't want to hear you.'

His arms tightened across her. 'And think on this, too. Why would a widow intentionally wear her hair in a maiden's style if not to signal that she had reverted to her maidenly status? Unconventional you may be, my lady, but you cannot have it both ways. Grieving widow or available woman. Which?'

With a superhuman push, Eloise released herself and paced across to the other side of the pavilion in fury, though her progress towards the exit was anticipated by Sir Owain's timely manoeuvre. 'I do not owe you an explanation for what I wear or how I wear it, sir. But even a mole would be able to see the obstacles involved when a woman has made her intention to remarry as clear as I have. You cannot pretend to have missed that, too, when I told you myself. That alone should have cautioned you to be-

have more discreetly. And as for your behaviour in
the practice-lists earlier this afternoon, that was
shamefully crude, sir, and unworthy of a knight.'

'Ah…' He smiled. 'You saw, then? And didn't
that warn you of what I intended to do later? It was
meant to do.'

'No, it didn't. It confirmed only what I knew already.'

'Which is?'

'That your mind runs along the same narrow track
as every other male of your pathetic breed. Thank
heaven women have more interesting things to think
about. Now, if you'll excuse me, Saskia and I must
return to the stand. And don't think your mauling of
me will convince me that your feelings are any finer
than the next man, Sir Owain. Any man can learn to
kiss a woman if he practises long enough. In that, it
must differ very little from jousting.'

'An interesting observation, but I believe one must
also allow for some natural ability,' he said, attempting to hide a smile.

A call, muffled by the thick canvas, reached them
from outside. 'Sir Owain! Sir Owain! You're needed
in the parade, sir! The heralds await you!'

'Coming!' Sir Owain called back. 'Bring Dunn
here to me.' He turned to face Eloise, his expression
once more serious. 'Forgive me, lady. It was never
your tears I wanted. Come…' he held out a hand
'…will you allow me to escort you and your maid
back to the stands?'

Determined not to concede any of the ground that

she had won, she held herself rigidly away, shaking her head. 'No, I thank you. Tell your friends how you managed to snatch a kiss from the Lady Eloise, just to show her who's master. They'll love it.'

The call came again, more urgently. 'Your horse, sir!'

'Damn!' he muttered, under his breath. He strode quickly away through the triangular opening towards the dark silhouette of his horse, vaulting in one swift leap into the saddle and clearing the high back as if it had been no higher than the garden gate. The stallion snorted and bounded away, scattering a group of servants, his squires chasing after him with helm and lance in the direction of the lists where the parade was already forming.

Trumpets blared a medley of fanfares as the day's winners paraded in triumph. Tomorrow they would joust together for an outright winner.

Meanwhile, in the deserted silence of her brother's pavilion, Eloise clung to Saskia and wept for all that had happened and for all that would never happen, for her courage as well as her frailty, for her pain and for the secret spark of forbidden pleasure she had experienced in his punishing embrace.

He had handled it badly, he knew. To blame the conditions, the lack of time and the lady's anger was tempting, but none of these could excuse his clumsiness. She had every right to be angry. Sir Owain of Whitecliffe lifted one arm mechanically for his squire, ignoring the jolting as the buckles were loosed and the metal plates removed, upper and lower vambrace, the cop to protect the elbow, the ailette laced to his shoulder. He should not have embraced her wearing this stuff. Not even in anger. His half-annoyance alerted the young squire.

'Sire?' said the lad.

'Nothing. Get on with it.'

'Will it please you to sit, sire?' The lad was not as tall as his master.

Sir Owain sat on the rug-covered chest, allowing access to the buckles that fastened the plated and padded cuirass over his chest, seeing the events of the day in a more critical light after Lady Eloise's volley of resentment. To be honest, he told himself, the whole palaver was fraught with double meanings that few would be able to ignore, one way or the other. Lances piercing rings, the giving of favours, colours, conquests and yieldings: no small wonder that any combination of these was enough to raise her hackles again after that earlier first smile of peace. He had seen the problem as soon as she tied the pink tippet to his lance, but by then there was nothing he could do about it. He smiled.

'Sire?' the lad said again.

'My hauberk.' He raised his arms above his head.

'Yes, sire.' The shirt of chainmail was hauled up and off and passed to another squire. He nipped round to Sir Owain's back to unlace the quilted gambeson, hearing a 'Tch!' and seeing a slow shake of his master's head. 'You are not happy with the result, sire? You should be. It was the best today.'

'Wait till tomorrow, lad. Never count your chickens.'

That was, of course, exactly what he had done when he'd arrived, believing that she might be inclined to look favourably upon him after her marriage to that disgusting little upstart, Gerrard. But although he had realised at their first meeting that this woman was different from the rest, he had not understood until now by how much, nor had he known anything of the lasting anger his sudden departure had caused her. And, of course, if he'd had the slightest inkling that Gerrard and her brother were ready to leap into the breach with such alacrity, he'd have made more sure that his bid had stuck. As it was, he had believed that time was on his side, with her father's approval and probably hers, too. Now, he had not only her anger to contend with but her resistance to jousters, to his reputation, and to his unfortunate association with her late husband who, if any man did, got what was coming to him. It was a pity that he himself was not the one who should have the telling of it, but that was Sir Phillip's task, and he was on a pilgrimage of absolution to Rome, poor chap.

So, with a lady who would neither be impressed nor intimidated, what was to be his next line of attack? He pulled off his damp linen shirt and threw it at his squire. Then he allowed his linen chausses to fall to the floor as he strode across to the bath of steaming water. Taking the sponge in one hand, he sat its heavy wetness on top of his head and pressed.

* * *

Father Janos and the Lady Francesca de Molyns halted their conversation at the patient's bedside as Eloise and Saskia entered the low-beamed chamber where the walls danced with the moving shadows of silent servants.

'I came as soon as I could,' Eloise whispered. 'How is he?'

Neither her mother nor the physician missed the tearstains and swollen eyelids, even in the dimly lit room, and both of them guessed that Rolph was not the cause.

Her mother enclosed her, tenderly, as Saskia had done. 'Coming round slowly,' she said. 'Drifting in and out of consciousness at the moment.'

'That's a good sign. Has he spoken?'

'Nothing intelligible, dear. You've done well.'

Eloise saw now that the monk was of medium height, that his habit was clean and in good repair, his strong sympathetic hands ever ready to dive away into wide sleeves when not in use. His eyes were dark and steady, and she knew instinctively how difficult it would be to hide anything from him. Perhaps that was why he was also Sir Owain's chaplain.

'And Griselle?' Eloise said. 'Has she been to see him?'

Lady Francesca smiled, wryly. 'No, her ladies took her to her rooms. I'll go and see her now you're here. Don't stay long. You look as if you could do with some rest yourself. It's been a long day.' She kissed her daughter's cheek and brushed away a lingering tear with one finger. 'Courage, child,' she whispered, smiling. 'You're not alone.' Then she left.

The door closed, and Eloise caught sight of the chaplain's gentle eyes. 'I'm sorry I sent you...' She reached out a hand to touch his arm, then thought better of it and withdrew before it made contact.

Father Janos shook his head to stop her apology. 'No matter,' he whispered. 'Think no more of it, my lady. Better two who understand than two who don't.'

'Thank you, Father. I think your understanding must be better than mine, in this case.' At the prickling sensation behind her eyes, she turned her head away, though not before the priest-physician had seen a bright teardrop glisten in the reflected light. 'And thank you for your help with my brother. You were far more than an assistant, and I was impolite. Please forgive me.' She turned towards the bed where Rolph had begun to move his head upon the pillow. Kneeling beside him, she caressed his brow, and he opened his eyes at her tender touch.

They searched her face, unfocussed. 'Marie?' he whispered.

'It's me, Eloise,' she said. 'You're in the castle, Rolph. Quite safe. You did well.'

To their consternation, his eyes welled with tears, his bandaged jaw working to speak but forming only one word. 'No.'

Again, she caressed his forehead but this time he frowned impatiently, and Eloise turned her attention to Father Janos. 'A fever, as usual. I generally give powdered willow-bark with honey, Father. Is that what you use?'

'There's nothing better, my lady. That will ease the pain, too. What about a sedative?'

'Yes, Saskia makes a useful infusion of mullein. I know Mother grows it in the herber. I'll have some gathered immediately.'

'Excellent. Do you carry your physic-chest on all your visits, my lady? You're remarkably well equipped.' He glanced appreciatively at the range of wax-covered pots, phials and stoppered bottles all neatly labelled, the tools, tweezers and scissors, silver knives and spoons, the tiny hand-held balance and weights.

'Always. There'd be little point in going abroad without it, nowadays, when there are so few reliable medics to be found. Now, I think it's time for a sample of urine as soon as he's fully conscious. His birth sign is Capricorn.'

'I'll make that my responsibility, if you wish.' He smiled. 'I have my flasks here, and my charts. Do you use arnica, my lady?'

'For bruising? Yes, do you have some?'

'I prepared a new tincture just before we left.'

A sound from the bed made them both turn. 'Eloise.'

'Yes, love. I'm here.'

Rolph's voice was faint, but calmer now. 'I'm sorry,' he said. 'And thank you. I think I can recall…'

She dabbed at his forehead, wiping away beads of sweat. 'Shh! A slight fever, that's all. We can fix it.'

'What's the damage?'

'Jaw, collarbone, wrist, ankle, some bruising. Not too serious, considering the weight of that brute. You'll be up and about in a few days.'

'My horse?'

'Fit as a fiddle.'

'I'm no match for…ouch…Whitecliffe.' His face contorted with pain, but with one finger he touched her cheek that still bore the stain of tears. 'Did he unhorse you, too, sister? Those were not for me, surely?'

'Yes, love,' Eloise said, keeping her voice low. 'They're as much for you as for anyone. Griselle's very upset.'

He frowned. 'Is she? Well, don't let her c—'

But he was too late. The door opened to admit Lady Griselle, accompanied by Sir Owain of White-cliffe, this time wearing a calf-length silver-grey bliaud luxuriously furred at the hem and wide sleeves. A violet cloak was fastened on one shoulder with a large silver disc that shone with amethysts. By contrast, the lady's surcoat of figured red brocade did little for her sandy hair and blotchy pallor. A troop of women followed them in, most of them in Griselle's household.

Eloise stood to make way for her sister-in-law, but already Rolph had escaped into a pretence of uncon-sciousness and, by the time Griselle reached the bed, he had put himself beyond her interrogation.

Crossly, Griselle turned on Eloise. 'They told me you were caring for him, but you've only just got here.'

Before Eloise could defend herself, Sir Owain came to her rescue far more effectively than she could have done. 'Lady Eloise was the first to tend him, my lady. You have her to thank for such promptness.'

Ignoring the suggestion, Lady Griselle lowered herself on to the stool by her husband's side. 'Rolph, dearest...oh, Rolph! What have they done to you? Where does it hurt?'

Father Janos and Eloise exchanged glances. 'Everywhere, I should think,' he murmured to her, lifting one eyebrow.

It was impossible for Eloise to avoid Sir Owain in the now overcrowded room, and his question was directed as much to her as to his physician. 'He'll recover, won't he?'

The sincerity in his voice left her in no doubt of his concern, but it seemed to her that, though Father Janos could easily have allayed Sir Owain's fears, the monk remained silent, allowing Eloise to answer while he watched and listened for the tone of her response.

'Yes, he'll recover,' she whispered. 'He's strong enough, though not as fit as he once was. He's already recovered consciousness, sir.'

'But...?' Sir Owain looked over his shoulder. 'He's *shamming*?'

'Well, not exactly. Almost.' The last word was

spoken in unison with Father Janos. 'Father,' she said, 'I must leave to prepare myself for supper. I dare say Lady Griselle will want to stay with my brother awhile, but Saskia will prepare the willow-bark and the mullein, if you wish.'

'And I will gladly administer it, my lady. We can attend to the arnica tomorrow when the dressings are changed. I carry an unguent of comfrey, too.'

'And we grow the leaves for a poultice.'

Griselle's whine broke into their conference. 'Are you discussing him? Didn't I ought to be consulted? Have you bled him yet?'

Patiently, Father Janos spoke for them both. 'No, my lady, we have not. Sir Rolph has lost enough blood down his sister's front in the last two hours.' He touched Eloise on the arm. 'You go, my lady. Sir Owain will escort you.'

'Oh, Sir Owain can stay—'

But the silver-grey knight was already turning her towards the door, disregarding her objections. 'Yes, I intend to, Janos. I'll have some food sent to you. We'll return later, before bed.'

'Will we?' Eloise said, in the passageway outside the door.

'Yes, lady. We shall. That, among other things.'

Too weary to ask what he meant by that or why she needed an escort at all, Eloise walked by his side in silence through a hive of torch-lit passageways where the rich aroma of roasting meats was carried on the draughts. Echoes of clattering dishes, shouts of men and the discordant tuning of musical instruments assailed their ears at every turn until they reached the stairway that spiralled upwards to their chambers.

Eloise went on ahead, but when Sir Owain passed his own doorway and continued up to hers, she halted, leaning against the wall to look down at him.

'Go on,' he said. 'It's all right.'

She hesitated, unable to see his expression in the shadows, but feeling his hands on her waist, moving her on. Resigned, and unable to argue, she climbed the last few steps and opened the door, making no protest as he followed her inside and closed it behind them. The chamber was lit only by one candle on a tall iron stand, its flame already guttering in the gust of air from the door.

'Wait,' he said. He took another candle from its sconce and lit it, then another, instantly returning shapes to their places, adding faces to their voices, meanings to expressions.

'Thank you, Sir Owain,' Eloise said. 'I can manage now alone.'

He stood looking at her as the distant wail of a hurdy-gurdy was caught on an uplift of night air. Slowly, he held out his arms. 'Come on,' he whispered. 'Come on, lass.'

She had no need to ask what he meant, but her resistance to him was now well rehearsed and she was unwilling to trust her impulses as often as she had in the past. Her legs refused to obey either his command or hers, yet her eyes could not hold back the messages of compliance as they watched him unfasten the silver brooch, lift his cloak off his shoulders and toss it on to the bed. Without releasing her from his careful watch, he came to her, reaching out and drawing her carefully into his arms, tilting back her head, angling it into the soft candlelight.

His thumb brushed tenderly over her eyelids, wiping away a fringe of dampness that remained. 'No more tears, my beauty. No more fighting. The skirmishes are over for today. You've had enough, haven't you? Now it's time to call a truce.'

She could have stopped him, pushed herself out of his embrace, but this was nothing like the previous harsh capture of steel-plated arms, nor was it the stuff of her dreams, downy and insubstantial. It was rock-firm, comforting and, for the first time in her life, everything she wanted. This time, his lips lured and enticed, nudging her into the response to which she had been so close before, tenderly leading her deeper into surrender, masterly and persuasive. He gathered her closer in to him.

She reached up at last to hold his head, to cling and touch and fill her fingers with his hair, with the cool skin of his neck and the width of his shoulders. The strength in her legs left her, weightless, spineless. 'No,' she whispered, heeding some aimless, pre-planned, age-old response.

'No,' he agreed. His mouth explored the long satin sweep of her throat, hungrily tasting while she breathed in the heady aroma of male success.

'No,' she said again. 'You forget.'

He lifted his head and regarded her seriously. 'No,

lady, I do not forget. I know of your plans to remarry.
You told me yourself. I do not accept them. Nor will
the king. Nor should you pursue them. They will fail.
Forget them.'

Wearily, she shook her head. 'Please, don't try to
persuade me. I'm too tired to argue.'

'I know. This is no time for decisions. You've had
a damnable day, haven't you? And you've dealt with
it all as I knew you would, superbly. But there's the
rest of the evening to get through, and I've decided
we'll do better to get through it together, in each
other's company, without the hostilities.'

She began a protest. It would be misunderstood,
misinterpreted, and anyway her family knew she
didn't like him, and it would appear disloyal, and so
on. But he stopped her with another skilful kiss that
made her forget the rest.

'Yes,' he said, slipping the gold and amethyst circlet off her brow and smoothing the mark of it with
his fingers, 'I know all that, too. But people will believe what they like, and a truce is merely a breathing
space, not the end of the battle. There, does that reassure you? Come, lass,' he whispered, touching her
lips like a butterfly with his own, 'trust me. I'll take
good care of you, I promise.'

To his credit, he had shown her, directly and in-
directly, how it felt to have his protection. With him,
she need not fear that dreadful half-existence or the
effort of pretence that dogged each of their public
encounters. The suggestion was a consolation for a
day of intense mental effort that had kept her barely

on the edge of normality. She nodded, closing her eyes and resting her cheek upon his silk velvet-covered chest. 'A truce, then. A temporary one, mind.'

His quiet laugh bumped at her cheek. 'All truces are temporary, lady. They also have rules. Neither party may reopen hostilities within the time period without giving the other fair warning. Is that agreed?'

The distant blare of a trumpet overlapped his words.

'That's the hall-steward's trumpet for supper, and I'm not ready,' she said.

'We should go down. Come.'

'I cannot go like this. Saskia...'

The door swung noisily open. The maid's assessment of the situation was reliable and skilled. 'Supper!' she said, carrying Eloise's physic-chest sideways through the door and depositing it into Sir Owain's waiting arms. Without batting an eyelid at his presence, she took charge. 'No time to change. Have you washed? No, you haven't! Tch!' With the untiring efficiency of a nurse with a tardy child, she sat Eloise on the bed, tidied her hair, dabbed at her face with rose-water, then accepted the use of the violet cloak to cover the stains on Eloise's pink surcoat. The effect could not have been bettered.

If Saskia was puzzled by the new accord between them, she gave no sign. Yet, of all those in the hall who noted it, it was she who understood the real reason for Eloise's most unusual docility in the company of the one she privately claimed to loathe.

As plans go, it worked well for both of them, being a great source of relief also to Sir Crispin and Lady Francesca de Molyns who had begun to fear the worst for the already problematical relationship. They need not have worried: to the outward eye, all was at peace between their victorious neighbour and their daughter and, if she was somewhat more sub- dued than usual, it could be due to one of two things, either his discipline or her tiredness.

To Eloise, the immediate effects of being in Sir Owain's company were at first comfortably ill de- fined, his kisses having acted like a drug, the effects of which were potent and lengthy, sedating her as effectively as any mullein infusion of Saskia's. He must have known, for his hand occasionally took hers beneath the white-covered table, holding it on her knee or his own while talking to others, not showily as if to boast, but possessively.

Even so, his quiet attentions to her did not go unobserved, and more than once she noted his friends watching them, smiling and commenting below the level of the general clamour in the hall. Cynically, it crossed her mind more than once during the evening that Sir Owain had insisted on their truce to add some credibility to the fact that, to all intents and purposes, he was her champion on whom she had bestowed her favour. Any continuation of their former hostility would have been hard for him to explain after their private talk in Sir Rolph's pavilion.

That she was the object of some envy from the women did not escape her either, especially as he made no attempt to disguise his interest throughout the splendid supper, the plays and mumming, the disguisings and the dance that followed. Coming from the one who had shown such outstanding prowess at the jousts, who was by far the handsomest, the one on whom men were laying their wagers to win outright, his attentions were all the more valuable. But by far more meaningful to Eloise was the unexpected thrill of knowing that, for whatever reason, she had the power to make their truce last as long as she chose.

Unaware that Sir Owain was also the cause of some envy amongst the men who had harboured their own secret hopes, Eloise felt a sporadic sense of confusion at her own inconsistency in the matter, not so much for the way it might look to others but at the way it felt to her. The tormenting dread that she had taken the first steps towards becoming yet one more of his 'countless' conquests was never far from her mind, nor was the perverse reminder that she had sworn never to allow a repeat of the hopes she had had once before. Worse than anything was her chaplain's nagging advice that she should keep this day quietly alone, in prayer, and what was the good of employing the man if not to take his advice? If Father Eamonn had known of her desires at this moment, he would probably have dismissed himself from her service for having failed in his duty.

She had time, during the evening, for a few words with Jolita, whose newly betrothed had been prised from her side for some vital men's talk. Full of excited anticipation, Jolita could hardly help but notice her sister's new bond with Sir Owain of Whitecliffe.

'A truce, love?' Jolita said, delightedly. 'Well, that's a good start.'

Eloise might have disagreed, but this was no time for such a discussion in the face of Jolita's happiness. 'Before you disappear again,' she said, smiling, 'does Mother know what you intend tonight?'

Jolita's eyes sparkled. 'Heavens, no! She'd not disapprove, but we'll tell the parents afterwards or they'll embarrass us with advice. You know what they're like.'

Yes, Eloise did. Consummation had been at the forefront of Sir Piers's mind at her betrothal too, yet the experience had not been for her one of life's more exalted moments, especially as he had publicised his intentions well beforehand to anyone who would listen, robbing it of any delicacy or spontaneity. Eloise shuddered at the memory, suppressing a dark shadow of envy at Jolita's light-heartedness while they hugged, willing her to be treated with more respect than she had been.

'Tomorrow,' Jolita said, 'I'm staging an archery contest. Men versus women. Sir Henry doesn't believe women can do better, so I told him we'd beat them hollow. You'll be there in my team, won't you, Ellie? I dare not lose my wager.'

Eloise didn't ask what the wager was. 'Of course I will. In the morning?'

'At the butts, as soon as we've broken our fast. Tell Sir Owain. And don't be too late to bed!'

Loaded with meaning, the warning came out in a loud whisper as she danced away to meet Sir Henry.

'You're under a misapprehension, my love,' Eloise muttered sadly.

Towards midnight, after the dancing and singing, after the wine and the young men's usual horseplay, Eloise and Sir Owain made their way, as they had promised, to the chamber where Sir Rolph was being tended by Father Janos and a gently snoring Griselle. Her two ladies sat in one corner by the brazier, talking in low voices.

Father Janos laid down his book and rose to meet them, approval showing plainly in his face at the sight of Eloise wearing his master's violet cloak and brooch. 'He's coming round nicely,' he whispered. 'And you two?'

Sir Owain kept a straight face. 'Yes, we're coming round nicely too, I thank you.' He placed an arm around her shoulders and drew Eloise to his side. 'Very nicely.'

Eloise explained. 'You may as well know, Father, that we have called a truce for Jolita and Henry's sake. It's only a temporary one. It won't last.'

The physician's face betrayed nothing. 'Ah, a temporary one. Those are the best kind.'

'They are?'

'Oh, yes, my lady. Permanent ones never last, in my experience.'

Coming awake to the sound of voices, Lady Griselle busied herself with the bedsheets in an attempt to convince them that she had not been sleeping. Her ladies came forward to help her rise. 'I *do* wish he'd wake,' she complained. 'Are you sure you're giving him the right medication? What about a little verjuice in water, Father?'

'My lady,' Father Janos replied, 'we are trying to get him to sleep peacefully rather than to wake him up. Now, you've done more than a wife's duty here. Perhaps you should allow your ladies to take you to your rest. It's important, you know. Come, ladies. Your mistress is ready to retire.'

As they had suspected, the door was no sooner closed upon the three women than Sir Rolph cautiously opened his eyes with a sigh and caught sight of his audience's amusement. He tried to grin at Sir Owain but managed only a frown at the pain in his jaw.

Sir Owain went to his bedside and crouched on the warm stool. 'How are things, old chap?' he said. 'You take some knocking over, I must say.'

Their subdued conversation, though lopsided, was a comradely and detailed one in which their contest was dissected, move by move, before edging on to those that Rolph had missed. Seeing their involvement, Eloise saw a way of taking her leave at last without Sir Owain's attendance.

'I'll come first thing tomorrow,' she told her brother, smiling at him. She laid a hand on Sir Owain's hunched shoulder. 'Please stay with him,' she said. 'Rolph is enjoying your company.'

He turned, taking hold of her hand before it could

be removed. 'Yes, I'll stay here awhile, but I think our good doctor should leave now. Shall you escort Lady Eloise, Janos? Two of Rolph's men will be here soon to take the night watch.' He lowered his voice for Eloise alone. 'Goodnight. Sleep well, my beauty.' Holding her hand for a moment longer, he kissed her knuckles and let it go.

'Goodnight, Sir Owain. You'll be at the butts tomorrow?'

'Certainly I will, if only to prove Sir Henry right.' His handsome face stretched into a grin as he turned back to Sir Rolph with an explanation, and Eloise felt a flutter of excitement vibrate around her heart as she left the room with Father Janos.

'Who is Marie?' he asked as soon as the door was closed.

Eloise had half-expected the question at some stage, aware that he had heard her brother's first word on regaining consciousness. 'Sir Rolph's eldest daughter,' she said. 'She's almost eight. She and her father are close.'

'Ah, then I shall suggest that she visit him tomorrow.'

They reached the muniment room at the base of the tower where the flock of noisy chaplains were merrily disputing the bedding arrangements, clearly having taken every advantage of the good wine that evening. Inevitably, Father Janos was hauled into their midst to adjudicate whilst Eloise took the opportunity to slip back to the hall to see if Jolita and Henry were still there.

Loud and over-merry, the sound of men's shouts and laughter was funnelled through the passageway perforated with openings that led downwards and upwards into shadowy tunnels. Ahead of her, the light from the hall cast a glow already being dimmed by the hall servants, then by a straggling crowd of men whose intention to seek their beds was being hampered by the need to continue their rowdy gossip. They hung around the entrance, presenting an unattractive obstacle to Eloise's progress, so she waited in the shadow of an archway for them to pass. But they were slow, and she had almost decided to go back when the sound of her own name grasped her attention with a sickening jolt.

They sauntered nearer, arguing and laying bets.

'I'll lay you any odds,' one of them yapped.

'Too late, lad. He'll be in her bed at this moment. He doesn't waste time with a woman, you know. I've seen him get to work.'

'Rubbish! You saw Lady Icicle tonight. If she'd been with me I'd have thawed her out for him.'

'You!' The laughter burst like a floodgate opening, turning Eloise's blood to a slow crawl in her veins. The hair on her arms prickled under the violet cape, and she drew back further into the darkness at their unsteady approach.

'You...and Lady Eloise... Hah!'

'She's a rare beauty all right, but he'd be daft to wed her.'

'Not when he can bed her without it, eh? I like that. Bed but not wed. Bed but...'

'Shuttup! You know her form. Anyone would be daft to wed her with a reputation like hers. She's been through two husbands...' Too much wine had disturbed his memory.

'One.'

'Argh! Who's counting, anyway?'

'She was betrothed to them, you fool.'

'Well, only for three months or so. Somebody ought to warn him.'

'Argh! He knows what he's doing.'

'He knew what he was doing when he had his lance through her pink sleeve, didn't he, eh?' They laughed. 'Cheeky sod. And her not knowing where to put herself.'

'I'll bet she knows now though.' More laughter.

The opinion was put forward again. 'Somebody ought to warn him. We might lose him after three months if he doesn't watch his step.' The laughter at this was so riotous that the hall steward approached them with some authority.

'Gentlemen...gentlemen! Come now, the hour is late and there are good people in the hall seeking their rest. Enough, now! Move on...move on.'

Still arguing and laughing, they passed the place where Eloise stood shivering and wrinkling her nose at their combined stench of wine and stale sweat. She saw the faces of those nearest her and the bile rose in her throat, making her sick with anger and shame, for she had heard in the basest possible terms what was also the darkest of her fears, that no man was ever to be hers for more than three months.

With the farmyard talk still ringing in her ears, she stood for a long time breathless with shock and cursing herself for her most recent weakness. At the same time, she was able to contradict that guilt with an irrational urge to exploit her non-conformity to the full, to take everything that lay within her grasp, immediately and without reserve. With a three-month curse hanging over her head, what did scruples matter? All her long-term plans would be doomed anyway.

Numbed and cold, she made her way back down the passageway, past the snoring chaplains and up the stairs. Father Janos would have assumed that she was safely in her chamber. There was no sound from Sir Owain's room. Saskia, turning down the linen sheets of the bed, began a smile of welcome that faded in mid-air as she saw her mistress's ashen face. But there was no conversation that night. No tears, either. Only a deep pain and a terrible need for revenge.

Chapter Five

Eloise tilted the mirror that Saskia held before her, studying the pale reflection for any outward sign of the tight knot of bitterness that had enclosed her heart so painfully all night. Beneath the twisted band of gold that sat low on her brow and the single turquoise on her forehead, no sign of distress was visible. In the low morning light, her eyes reflected the pale leaf-green of her fitted kirtle and the deeper green and gold of the loose sideless surcoat she wore over it, its silken sheen changing to bronze as she moved. A gold-and-turquoise buckled girdle held the garments close over her hips, and again she had chosen to wear her hair in the ambiguous maidenly plait that Sir Owain had apparently found so confusing. It was braided with gold, decorated at the end with a bunch of green popinjay feathers from her mother's pet parrot.

She swung the thick auburn plait back out of sight. 'Well, at least that shows some consistency,' she murmured.

'What is it, love?' whispered Saskia, watching the examination. 'Is the truce to be ended so soon?'

Eloise spoke to the mirror. 'I should never have accepted it. I was a fool.' And that was all she would say on the matter.

'I'll go and get the boys to empty the bath.' Saskia sighed.

'And bring a posset up from the kitchen for me.'

'You'll not go down and break your fast with the others?'

'No, I'll have it up here.'

'You don't want to see Mistress Jolita?'

'I'll see her at the butts in a while. Hurry, Saskie.'

Saskia was not always obedient. Laying the mirror aside, she sat beside her mistress on the clothes-chest and took one of her hands on to her lap. 'You must not let her happiness get to you in *that* way,' she said. 'Try to be happy for her, love.'

'I am.' The back of the other cool hand was pressed beneath her nose as a sudden heat rushed to her face. 'I am, Saskie. Truly.'

'And we'll try to be extra kind to Sir Rolph's lady, shall we? She's had a nasty shock, and she probably knows as much as anyone that the only advantage she has over you and your sister is her ability to breed like a rabbit. She envies you at times. Did you realise that?'

'Yes.'

'So, today's going to be better?'

'Yes. Go, Saskie, before I start blubbing.'

'I'm going. And if you're going to shoot, wear

your glove.' She patted the hand and laid it back on the green lap. 'It's over in that trunk.'

Eloise's first duty, however, was to her brother who, although still showing signs of a slight fever, was recovering enough to sit up and listen to the chatter of his daughter Marie who sat on his bed. Eloise took his pulse and examined the sample of urine that Father Janos had saved to show her. He was not happy with its pinkish tinge, but when Eloise smiled, his puzzled frown was turned upon her. 'Lady?' he said.

'Beet,' said Eloise. 'Our cook uses the roots of the red kind as well as the white. Rolph loves it. Very nutritious.' She took the flask from him and tipped it gently. 'Ruled by Saturn, Father, if that's any comfort to you, but beets do tend to colour the urine. Don't be alarmed. Still, he should be drinking more barleywater to clear all this sediment. That's also ruled by Saturn.'

The expression of concern on the physician's face was replaced by total admiration as he removed the flask from her fingers. 'Amazing!' he said, with some reverence. 'Why did I not ask myself what he'd been eating? Where did you learn your skill, my lady?'

'From Saskia's father,' she said. 'He was an apothecary in Flanders but he had to leave because he was accused of practising medicine without a licence. He and Saskia came over here, and my father took him into his service as physician. He taught me what I know, but sadly he couldn't cure himself of a terrible cancer. He died three years ago.'

'A most learned and gifted man, obviously. It was your good fortune, my lady, that he was not appreciated in Flanders. Whereabouts was he?'

'In Louvain. His name was Antoine Borremans.'

Father Janos's eyes widened. 'No! I cannot believe it!'

'You knew him?'

'Indeed I did. I studied theology at Louvain before I went on to do medicine at Bologna. He was the apothecary we used to call on as students when we needed advice, or a physic.'

'Advice?' Eloise looked sideways at the monk's sheepish grin.

'Students,' he whispered. 'Yes, even theology students needed advice from an apothecary from time to time, and Messer Antoine was never judgmental. A fine man, and very clever. We all thought highly of him.' He lifted the flask to eye level and gazed reflectively at its contents.

'And so did I. Steeped in common sense. Here's Saskia. Why not tell her?'

'Tell me what, my lady?' said the maid, glancing at the flask. 'Sir Rolph been at the beets again?'

By the time Eloise and Saskia reached the shooting butts, the flat ground between the castle and the bailey wall was transformed by the brightly coloured garments of young men and women ready to take sides in defence or repudiation of Jolita's claim. Large straw-plaited targets had been set up some distance away in front of a cluster of trees, while an audience of guests sat in the sunshine on the grassy bank below the castle wall.

A bevy of smart young squires assisted the master-at-arms to choose the best bows for the participants. 'I've kept this one back for you, m'lady,' the burly soldier told Eloise, handing her a bow and quiver of arrows. 'And I fletched them myself, too.'

She took them, rewarding him with her best smile. 'That was thoughtful,' she whispered. 'I'll not let you down.'

But her thoughts were less on her performance than on a tall familiar figure whose fine legs were now visible beneath a short blue-and-red embroidered cote-hardie with a red velvet shoulder cape. It was belted with blue leather with a matching pouch, his pointed shoes of finest calf already darkened with the dew. Her heart leapt at the sight of him, but purposely she steered herself away from the men and towards her sister.

Jolita and Sir Henry Lovell were laughingly debating the distance their teams should shoot when they caught sight of Eloise. 'Ellie! Come over here, if you will, and explain to Sir Henry that we don't need a shorter distance than the men.'

'Dearest one,' Eloise said, 'if Sir Henry wants to make it easier for us, then let him, by all means. Go ahead, Sir Henry, be gallant. Give us a head start, if it pleases you.'

The debate was joined by the others, and soon Sir Owain came to stand by Eloise, despite her evasions. He smelled clean and fresh and looked as if he had slept like a child. 'Well met, my lady,' he said, low-voiced. 'Our truce is still intact, I take it?'

'No, sir. Not any more.'

There was a pause, then, 'So soon? Why?'

'There's been a development. A setback. I cannot explain further.'

The argument about distances having been settled, Jolita broke into their conversation, saving Eloise from having to find further excuses, but not before Sir Owain's parting shot in her ear. 'Not good enough, my lady. I shall insist on an explanation.'

Youthful contests with their father's squires had made Eloise and Jolita as efficient as any of the men at archery, which could not be said for the rest of the women's team, many of whom had not handled a bow for years. From the men and spectators, there were noisy shouts and much teasing laughter as arrows went wide into the trees or fell short of the target, and it began to look as if, in spite of the two sisters' high scores, the men's lead would be maintained to the end.

A group of scoffing young men went to stand at the receiving end of the shoot, taunting the last contestant to aim at them so that she might hit the butts by accident rather than by design. One of them, the most vociferous, was one of those who had so reviled Eloise in the passageway the previous night. He leaned against a nearby tree, straddling its roots, folding his arms mockingly and unwittingly making himself a target that Eloise knew was well within her range, not to wound him but to scare him out of his stupid wits. The temptation stole up on her and, without thinking, she slid an arrow from her quiver and fitted it to her bow, moving forward to stand some way beyond the contestant's shoulder. She could see the girl shaking with nerves.

A large strong hand closed over Eloise's wrist as she drew back the string, making her frown with annoyance as her chance was ruined. The archer let her arrow fly and, while all eyes were on the target, Eloise was pulled firmly away, her resistance making not the slightest difference to Sir Owain's unrelenting force.

'Let go of me!' she muttered as sidelong glances noted their progress towards the space behind the contestants. 'Sir Owain...let me go!'

He stopped and faced her, keeping hold of her wrist. 'Now, you can tell me what's going on,' he said. 'What has that young loudmouth done to deserve an arrow through him?'

'I was not going to—you *saw*?'

'Well, of course I saw, lass. You were watching him like a hawk. My, but you're a fierce one to cross, aren't you? Would you really have used an occasion like this to wing somebody you don't like?'

For the first time since her impulsive intentions, she realised how it would seem to Jolita's guests, how it would ruin the contest, draw attention to herself and her anger, upset Jolita and Henry. 'No,' she whispered, shamefaced. 'I shall have to find another way.'

'Another way to what? Kill him? What's he done

to offend you? Has he insulted you?' His keen eyes darted across the crowd to the young man, then back to her. 'One of your brother's lads. Almost as indisciplined sober as he is drunk. I'd flog him oftener if he were mine, but not before a crowd this size, I think. Does he have something to do with our truce?'

When she made no reply, he slid a hand beneath her arm and propelled her gently towards a door in the adjoining garden wall. 'In here, I think,' he said, ushering her through into the green and secluded vegetable plot. 'If he does,' he continued, 'I think I ought to be told. Don't I? As part of the agreement?'

'There was no agreement,' she ventured, imprudently.

He smiled at that. 'Lady, there is always an agreement or there'd be no truce. I can see I shall have to introduce you to some rules of war, one of these days. Or should it be rules of peace?' He removed the bow and arrows from her hand and eased her back against the high wall, imprisoning her.

'Sir Owain,' she said, 'can we forget all about this truce business? It's giving everyone the idea that there's something between us, and you know as well as I that that is very far from the truth. It's foolish.'

'It's not nearly as foolish, my lady,' he whispered, bending his head to her, 'as pretending that there isn't. And who is everyone? That lad you were about to punish?'

Again, she was silent. How could she expect him to understand her dilemma? He was a man who would do what all such men did when faced with a woman's problems. He would argue, try to change her mind, talk her round in circles, persuade her that there was no foundation to her concerns. He would put aside all her objections as if they were fantasy. He would show her the advantages of forgetting them while he was there, after which they would reappear and leave her racked with guilt. And that was something she could do without.

Brutal directness was the only course. 'All right, I'll tell you, since that's the only way to make you understand. They said—'

'They? Who?'

'That crowd. That lad was amongst them. I heard them as they passed me in the passageway. They were tipsy.'

'Ah!'

'Yes, sir. They were tipsy enough to speak their minds on the subject of your intentions towards me.'

'Which are?'

'They said someone ought to warn you. Well, I'm warning you myself that no man who shows an interest in me lasts more than three months. *They* know that, and I've already mentioned it. It's true. And they said that...no...I cannot say the rest.' She turned her head away, suddenly afraid of the words and of his reaction to them. It was too personal.

'Said what? That I should take you to bed? That I could do that without any further commitment? That you'd be as easy as all the others? Is that it?'

A wave of heat flooded into her face and neck as if a brazier had been set before her, bringing back the shame of last evening when such opinions had been accompanied by lewd laughter. Except that Sir Owain was not smiling. Eloise held the cool palms of her hands to her cheeks, nodding her agreement of his guesswork. 'If you must know, yes,' she whispered. 'And that, sir, is not the kind of thing any woman wishes to have said about her, especially when there are but a few months to her wedding. I was shamed, sir, and angry. And if you had not interfered just now I would have taught him how to keep his mouth shut. I could, you know.'

'I don't doubt it, my lady. Your scores showed me that. And you have every right to be angry. But there's a better way than that to silence such gossip, you know.'

On the verge of losing her temper, she believed she could read his mind and, pushing herself out of the enclosure of his arms, rounded on him in fury. 'Yes, a man's way! Don't take me for an idiot, Sir Owain. I know well enough how you would silence the gossip, but it's not the way I would choose. I have a reputation, and so do you.'

'I do?'

'You know you do. As a womaniser. And God forbid that my name should be linked with yours in *that* department.'

'I thought it already had.' Mentally, he kicked himself for a fool. 'I mean….'

'I know exactly what you mean,' she snarled. 'And that is as far as it goes, sir. I want nothing to do with your sort. I cannot afford to have my name tarnished with the name of Whitecliffe, nor can you be so short of women that you must seek me out for your attentions. Now, leave me alone, Sir Owain.'

Blinded by fury and unable to see that she was heading towards a compost heap, she turned away from him, only to be caught before she reached it. His handsome face was set hard in an anger more dangerously under control than hers. His hand linked with her upper arm, slewing her round in midstep and bringing her body hard into his restraint.

'Not so fast, my lady.' He held her punishingly hard against him. 'Now, just remind me of something, will you? I kissed you last night, remember?'

'No,' she snapped. 'I forget things that do not interest me.'

'I see. Then you will not recall how you responded. How you softened.'

'No. Let me go!'

'Or how you would have given yourself to me.'

'I would *never* give myself to a White—' She stopped in mid-word, knowing that she had gone too far into perjury, that she would have given herself to him whatever his name had been. As she would now, despite her resentment of him.

His arms were like bands of steel pinning hers down in an embrace far from loving: his eyes challenged hers as they had done before. 'Yes, my lady,' he whispered. 'That was well done, for if you had used my name as target practice a second time I would have taken that as a declaration that our truce was indeed at an end. You've not seen a Whitecliffe defend his honour against a lady, yet. Let us hope you don't. Guard your tongue more closely, woman, for your safety's sake.'

It is not my tongue that needs most guarding. 'There is an easier solution to that problem, Sir Owain. You remove yourself from my line of fire. A mile or so should be adequate.'

'I seem to recall that that kind of solution makes you even angrier. Perhaps the opposite would work better.' He gave her no time to query his intentions but, as he had done in the lists, moved so swiftly that the opponent was given no chance to evade him. It was the same for Eloise, the kiss that followed being meant to show how close to her he intended to stay and how ineffectual was her advice to one as accomplished as he. As it was, it did far more than that for both of them.

This time, there was no interruption from Saskia or the herald to call them to supper, and whereas Eloise's exhaustion of last evening had made her compliant, this time her anger was channeled dexterously by Sir Owain into a response that took her so far beyond her objections that they might never have existed. Understanding more about her complex emotions than he had previously, he purposely goaded her into releasing them, taking her fierceness in his stride and fuelling it with ever deepening kisses that gave her no time to recover. This time, he used his hands deftly over the green bronze of her surcoat, slipping them into the open sides to feel the smooth curves of her back, the oval roundness of her buttocks.

Starved of the loving she had craved for so long, of the loving she had stored and damped down in the deepest vaults of her heart, Eloise found that the ensuing release was immediately beyond her control, sweeping her away into an inferno that blazed white-hot with sensations. His mouth, his hands, the hard warmth of his body, his unnerving male aroma and the texture of his skin and hair under her fingers filled her mind and took it over, closing it to everything outside. No thoughts. No reservations. She would have done anything he asked of her.

Far more experienced than she, Sir Owain sensed her capitulation and slowed, having proved the point both to himself and to her. Holding her closely against him, he cradled her head and felt the trembling, the ragged shaking of her lungs, the aimless wandering of her hands whose shameless curiosity had now been exposed. He took one of them in his own and kissed the knuckles, noting the long delicate fingers and the plain gold wedding ring. Thankfully, he said nothing.

'Why?' she whispered, breathlessly, watching the kiss.

'Why what?'

'You know you cannot do this. You cannot simply walk back into my life and take things up from where you left off. It's too late. I've moved on now.'

'Have you?' he said, touching her lips with his warm forefinger. 'Well then, perhaps you've moved on in a direction you didn't know you were taking. Perhaps what you believed was the end is actually the beginning. Perhaps…just *perhaps*…I've made you confront something you've been keeping hidden all this time. Eh? Would you dare to admit that, even to yourself?'

'If I did, what would it matter to you? There's no shortage of potential wives or mistresses for a man of your standing. You have no need to turn your attention to widows, Sir Owain.'

'You said as much before. Is that what rankles? That you think I might be dallying with you? Just for something to pass the time?'

'Such an assumption would be understandable, sir. It's what you're known for as much as for your jousting skills.'

'So you're fond of telling me. Thank heaven men usually place my skills in the reverse order, but no matter, I still have to tell you that you are mistaken in your assumptions, understandable or not. You obviously have an opinion of me that makes it impossible for you to take me seriously. But believe me, my lady, when I say that I do not yet have a reputation for seducing unwilling women or those whose hands are promised to others.'

'Yet.'

'This is the one and only occasion when my good record may suffer, but I have two excuses, you see. First, I offered for you before Gerrard did. Second, I refuse to recognise your relationship with Master atte Welle, your loyal steward. And I have told you, and so has your father, that the king won't recognise it, either.'

'That doesn't make it any less valid, sir. I mean to go ahead with it.'

'Then until you are stopped there is no point in my telling you how you fit into my plans, is there? I can wait. Meanwhile, it is futile for you to continue to fight me as if we were sworn enemies.'

Disengaging herself from his arms, Eloise stood before him with her hands flat on the red velvet of his shoulder-cape, reminding herself of the insurmountable barrier between them. 'Then what fancy name would you prefer to give it, Sir Owain, if not enmity? Am I suddenly expected to disregard your making a widow of me? Have you given any thought to how it might appear for me to give my friendship freely to the one whose best friend killed my husband? It was a year ago, sir. One year. Scarce time for the memory to fade, I'd have thought.' Her voice was dark with passion as she spoke.

Without warning, he pulled her back into his arms, closing his mouth over hers with a ruthlessness that she had no time to prepare for. Each time was different, this being more like retaliation for a wound just delivered than persuasion. His voice was husky with an emotion Eloise could not identify but which, she thought, came perilously close to hatred. 'Memories!' he growled, his lips close above her. 'Tell me not of your sweet memories of him, woman, or I'll have to brand you a liar. You are loyal but he did nothing to deserve it, and you well know it. Yes, I

can say that even though you cannot. But don't tell
me how you swooned in his arms as you just did in
mine. Don't tell me how you enjoyed his loving, how
you longed for his embrace, his—'

'Stop! Please…stop!'

'I will stop because it does no good to continue,
but don't pretend to miss that whore-begotten fleshmonger, my lady. Not with me. I knew him, remember.'

'Fleshmonger? You mean he—?'

'Enough. I've said too much. God, woman, I've
never known anyone stir me as much as you do.
Have you slipped me a love potion?'

'No, sir. I have not.' She hid her smile well. Was
there love, then? 'But I have one for a man who has
lost his reason. Daisy, sage and southernwood in
wine. It works quite well, as a rule.'

'You believe I need that, do you?' His arms released her. 'Well, that may be so, but I still have
enough reason to see that you cannot plead time and
association as an excuse to keep me away while telling me in the same breath how little you care for
convention.'

'It was not in the same breath.'

'Trust a woman.' He smiled. 'All right, but my
argument stands, lady. You cannot have it both ways.
And if you cared about convention you'd not be here
but on your knees on the cold stone floor of a
chapel.' He caught her as she turned sharply to walk
away. 'Now, shall we forgo the pretence and allow

some honesty between us? At least give me some credit for knowing the difference.'

'Sir Owain, I'm sure you do, but you are not a woman, nor were you there to hear the base talk I heard last night. A man could have laid the lot of them out cold; a woman cannot do that. She has to pretend it doesn't matter, but it does. Especially when they cannot be the only ones—'

'To think as they do? You're talking about your three-month terms again, I can tell. Well, all I can say is that any man who allows himself to be put off by such a set of coincidences, my lady, was not so keen in the first place, in spite of what I said the other night. Forget it. It means nothing. It means less than nothing to me.'

She looked into his eyes, daring herself to ask, 'Then what is it you want, Sir Owain? A taste of what you thought you'd missed? Revenge?'

He shook his head, letting his eyes roam over her face and hair. 'So beautiful, and yet so cynical. There's going to be a lot of gentling needed here, my beauty, isn't there, before the harm is undone? Eh?' He smiled, holding her arms. 'No, nothing of revenge or of tasting either. If I wanted revenge, his death was that, but I didn't. Nothing so ordinary. What do I want? Your friendship will do nicely for today. Could we re-negotiate the truce, d'ye think?' His hands caressed her shoulders, softly, tenderly.

What more was there for her to say? She looked along the gravelled pathway towards the orchard where yesterday they had stood ankle-deep in blossom, he with his hand protectively resting on her shoulder. She recalled the euphoria of being safe at his side last night, being released from continuous explanations concerning her past, present and future. It had been a short-lived bliss, well worth the concessions.

'Yes,' she said on a sigh. 'Yes, I suppose so. Temporarily.'

'Temporarily, of course.' He smiled. 'Twenty-four hours, this time?'

She nodded, accepting. That was safe enough, for by this time tomorrow she and her father would be well on their way to London.

He reached down to her waist and hauled up the end of her plait, calmly removing the ribbon and the bunch of green feathers that bound the end. These he placed in the leather pouch at his belt. 'Thank you,' he said, grinning.

Bemused, Eloise did nothing to stop him, nor did she protest when he combed his fingers through the loosened hair, undoing half of her plait, carefully placing it behind her to make sure that it hung well. No man had ever done so much for her, and she wondered how many times he had done it before and how many maids had watched him.

Her wariness must have showed, for he took her chin in his hand and held it, watchfully. 'You're like a badly broken filly, lass,' he whispered. 'Distrustful. And no wonder. You're ready for a kinder master now, I think.' Before she could find a reply, he swept his hand slowly downwards over her throat and the wide neckline, continuing over her surcoat and on to the proud swell of one breast. Briefly he held it, weighing it with a cupped hand before moving down to her waist, all the while watching her eyes change from green pools to dark mossy depths, heavy-lidded with desire.

'Come,' he said, 'before I do some damage of my own.'

Kneeling on the window-seat, Jolita craned her head as far as she dared to breathe in the cool night air that still vibrated with sounds of activity below, men preparing carts, the muffled yelp of a hound. She left the window ajar to accommodate a bewildered moth and turned to watch her lovely sister whose half-nakedness still fascinated her, even after years of familiarity. Clasping her hands behind her head, she glowed with happiness. 'Oh, Ellie! Did you ever know such a day?'

The rhetorical question did not disturb Eloise, whose reply came with a smile. 'No, love. I never did. I doubt anyone could have packed more into it, and you were the loveliest Queen of Hearts I've ever seen. Or anyone else, for that matter. Did you see Mother's face?'

'Yes, and Father's.'

'And Grissle's!' The duet was accompanied by a rising scale of laughter, not entirely charitable.

Eloise pulled her face back into a mask. 'She's so sad, Jollie. I didn't see her smile all day. Not once.'

'Well, I don't suppose she was too pleased with Father, for one thing.'

'Why ever not?'

'Didn't you hear? He sent six of Rolph's men home in disgrace at noon.' Jolita slid down over the cushioned seat and came to sit on the bed that Saskia had turned down for the night. Its blue coverlet now revealed a light linen sheet and a grey fur rug, with embroidered pillows, one of which Jolita took and hugged to herself, lovingly. 'Bad behaviour, Henry said. Serves them right. They'll probably be flogged.'

Eloise controlled her voice with difficulty. 'What did they do?' she said.

'Insulted one of the guests, apparently. That's all I know. I expect they'll be more angry at missing the jousting than getting a flogging. But Ellie, were you not *so* excited by Sir Owain's performance? Isn't he the most amazing man on a horse? I knew he'd win. Everybody did.'

Predictable or not, Sir Owain's demolition of three men's opposition, one after the other, had been nothing short of incredible, particularly as the last contestant, the redoubtable Lord Pace, was by far the most dangerous. His experience was greater than Sir Owain's but his vigour and skills were no match for the younger man and, though the contest had run for three rounds, Sir Owain's last lance knocked Lord Pace's clean out of his grasp and sent it flying across the lists into the wildly cheering spectators.

He had not sought Eloise's favour on this second day, but had tied her green ribbon and popinjay feathers around the pink tippet on his arm, which everyone knew had held her hair that morning. As he had intended, her hair stayed loose, falling around her shoulders in thick auburn waves like a cape. Saskia combed it and gathered it up ready for the nightly plait.

'Leave it, Saskie,' Eloise told her. 'It's late. I think you should go now.'

Saskia laid down the ivory comb. 'We have to make an early start in the morning, remember. I shall have to rouse you before dawn.'

'I know. I'll be ready. Goodnight, love.'

'Say your prayers. Rub your teeth. Snuff the—'

'Saskie!' the sisters chorussed, laughing.

The door closed behind the maid, guttering the candle flames. 'Did you know that Henry's father had to forfeit his horse to Sir Owain?' Jolita said, squeezing the pillow. 'But Sir Owain gave it back. He kept the others he'd won, though. He must be immensely wealthy by now, Ellie, and I'm so glad you've decided to—'

'Jollie, I haven't decided anything except to hold my peace for a day.' Eloise pulled at the length of linen with which she had dried herself, tucking it beneath her arms and hiding the corner between her breasts. She lifted her arms, scooping up her hair and holding it back in a loosely tied cord made of plantain stems, then came to sit cross-legged opposite her sister. 'And that gives me good time to make my escape before he's astir in the morning.' She grinned, mischievously. 'Gone!' she said, spreading her hands. 'Just like he did.'

Jolita, whose mind was racing ahead, missed the connection. 'And now I can tell you my news,' she said. 'Henry and I are coming to London with you. We're to stay on the Strand in his parents' house. Isn't that wonderful? It's not so very far away from you and father at Sheen.'

After almost a year of separation, the news brought a smile of relief to Eloise who had not entirely been looking forward with enthusiasm to the days ahead. 'You'll be with me?' she whispered.

'Of course we will, love.' Jolita reached forward to lay a tender hand on her sister's arm. 'Whatever the outcome, you'll have us there. Try not to worry.' She had it in mind to offer further platitudes, but knew that these would be of little help when the outcome was not likely to be in Eloise's favour. The king was notoriously hard to bribe unless the remuneration was irresistible.

'I'm so glad you're happy,' Eloise said, caressing Jolita's hand. 'Your Henry is not what you thought, then?'

Jolita grinned at her over the top of the pillow. 'I cannot believe how mistaken I was,' she said, twisting her betrothal ring. 'I think I'm in love, Ellie.'

'And what about losing the archery contest? Have you paid your forfeit?'

The pillow flew away as Jolita leapt off the bed in one bound, her hair swinging like a brown sail changing tack. 'Saints' alive! My forfeit! He'll be waiting…oh, my lord! 'Night, Ellie. Sleep well.' With a quick peck on her sister's cheek, she was away through the door like a rabbit down a burrow, her feet making no sound on the stone steps.

For a few moments, Eloise listened to the sounds of the night, to the cry of the night watch in the town who assured everyone that all was well, an opinion that failed to take into account the state of at least one confused heart. The pictures of the tournament that Jolita had drawn returned to her in full colour, slowed down for analysis, every expression recalled, every move, word and gesture. Owain's performance at the jousts had thrilled everyone, but only she could claim, though she did it silently, that the champion wore her favour on his arm. He had received from Jolita a wreath of flowers for his head and then presented it to her, Eloise. She had worn it all that evening and then hung it on the bedpost where she would see it last thing and first thing. That, of course, was not his only prize for, during the evening's dancing, he had been awarded a magnificent diamond. If only Sir Piers had been so successful, Eloise's financial worries might have been less.

Sir Owain had been attentive to her, courtly and gallant, but not overtly affectionate so as to embarrass her or draw extra attention to them as a pair. Sir Crispin and Lady Francesca had watched but said nothing, though Eloise knew by their faces that their concern was not wholly to do with the success of the festivities. For their sakes, and for her sister's, she had not regretted the truce: for her own sake, she was glad of the excuse to enjoy his company.

She slid off the bed and replaced the stray pillow, smiling at her sister's joy and wondering how many forfeits would be as gladly rendered as hers. She, Eloise, had gone with Sir Owain to see her brother before retiring, her fourth call of the day, and found him recovering well, considering his injuries. As before, Sir Owain had stayed with him to recount the action while she had bid them both a courteous but formal goodnight, concealing a pang of wistfulness that that would be the memory of him to which she would have to cling for the foreseeable future. A kiss for her knuckles was to be his last touch. Another episode of her life over and done with.

Her arms encircled the flower-adorned bedpost as hot tears stung her eyes, closing them against the fractured and crazily dancing candle flames that should have steadied by now. A draught of air breathed over her back. The door had opened silently and closed again. She half-turned, expecting to see Saskia with a last piece of advice for her well-being. But it was not Saskia.

He stood by the door as if conjured up by her longings; tall and taut with sinew and muscle, a scattering of dark hair below his throat, his narrow loins wrapped round with a linen cloth, as she was. 'Eloise,' he said.

Speechless with disbelief, it made no sense for her to long for his presence and then to protest at the fulfilment, but such an immediate response to her needs took the wind out of her sails, and the bedpost to which she had been clinging as a substitute a moment before now became her support.

The first word that sprung to mind was no, which emerged as a whisper but had no effect on the apparition except to make him smile. That gave her courage. 'No...no, you cannot,' she said, while a spark of wickedness flared at the back of her mind to show her how, once and only once, she could wound him as he had once wounded her, how she could give herself to him and then leave him to starve for a lifetime afterwards. Tomorrow, she would be gone. The spark flared and faded. 'I cannot do it,' she said, suddenly afraid.

'Can you not, my beauty?' His smiled faded as he reached her, his strong hands around her wrists opening her fingers like flower petals and peeling them away from the bedpost. The woman was a smouldering mass of contradictions, hard, brittle, and raging with an anger so fierce that she would wound herself in the process of wounding him, yet inside she was still vulnerable and fearful of emotions which he himself had released years ago without knowing it. He could feel her trembling, pulling away from him, making him realise that the origin of her fear was the memory of another less accommodating lover. Her late husband.

He released his hold of her and went to stand in the pool of candlelight that illuminated his body, showing her the bruises where the impact of his shield had caught his chest and shoulders, where his arms carried red weals, where the slam of the high saddle had marked his thighs. He had said nothing of them all evening, nor had he intended to, but now her natural concern overcame her initial shock, and he used them as a key to unlock her limitless loving. He saw her attention refocus on his bruises, propelling her slowly towards him as if walking through water, her face still tear-stained.

She touched the red-blue marks on his shoulder with gentle fingertips, her eyes full of pity in the candlelight.

'Salve me, Eloise,' he whispered. 'Tend me, as you did for Rolph. Reward me. Do what you will.' He reached to the back of her head and snapped the plantain stalk, loosing her hair in a silken flood down her back.

She placed her lips where her fingertips had been and saw him flinch as if she had applied an astringent lotion. Searching tenderly, she followed the path of her hands with kisses, wondering at the magnificent body and tasting the warm firmness of his skin, breathing him in through her mouth and aware of a new situation in which, instead of being flung on to a bed and forced to endure the molestation of a clumsy husband, she was now being led with care along her own path. And when she found that her hair was falling around her face, she pushed it aside and whispered through its veil, 'I'm not dressed for this, am I?'

'No,' he said. 'You're not.' His hands were deft where the linen clothed her, and she heard his gasp of admiration as it fell away to reveal the luscious landscape of her skin, its sheen and shadows. Again, for the first time, she was allowed to savour the indescribable caress of a lover's eyes before his hands touched, to see desire open his lips before words did.

Her inexperience brought her to a standstill and, looking at the swirl of dark hair upon his chest, her words stumbled out. 'I think…I believe…er, that my own wounds may be of a different nature. Not so visible. Not earned, either. Would it be possible…?'

'For me to tend them, my lady? Yes, I can heal you, if you will give me time. And I can help you to forget. Which is why I came.' He took her arms and, linking them around his neck, carried her across to the cool linen-covered bed where he placed her beneath him and let her feel his full weight spread over her without a hint of menace. Reaching down, he pulled at the linen that covered him and flung it aside, causing her to quake with anticipation at the intimate heat of his body. 'Let go,' he whispered. 'I know where your hurts are.' His kisses lured her into forgetting and, long before the first of them was finished, his hands had begun a seductive path of the sweetest healing her body had ever known.

It did not enter her head, as it had before, to wonder how his expertise had been gathered in the arms of others or whether this was his best loving, or perhaps second-best. Nor did she spare a thought for her own contradictions, for the mad inexplicable surrender at which she would have scoffed only that morning while rejecting a truce. And if she had thought, even for a second, that he would be the one to suffer most by her flight on the morrow, she might also have realised with a terrible sense of dread that the reverse was just as likely.

Lying sated in his arms with her head rising and falling rhythmically on the great swell of his chest, she had time to recall how he had controlled his undeniable passion so as to give her time, whispering to her as he would to a wild creature, gentling, stroking, reassuring her, calling her his beauty, his woman, the one he had waited years for, almost despairing. Stealthily, she slid herself over him and resumed her salving of his bruises with her hands and lips, bathing him with her hair while he lay as if sleeping, which she knew he was not.

Chapter Six

The comfortable brown cob picked its way carefully over the dust-filled holes in the track, ignoring the excited hounds around its hooves, their yapping competing with the tinkle of bells that hung along the edge of its green and gold rein-guards. The neat ears swivelled to catch the muted chatter of riders, the first eloquent song of a blackbird, but the horse's own rider was silent, deep in thought.

Riding pillion behind one of the Gerrard grooms, Saskia put her mistress's silence down to a certain heaviness of heart and tried a cheery word to lighten it, clutching at the groom's belt as the horse lurched gently beneath her. The remark was not wholly effective.

Eloise glanced at the pink sunrise and smiled dutifully, her thoughts firmly bedded in the dark warmth of a man's arms, the imprint of his body still on hers, his expert kisses still searching over previously unexplored surfaces, luring her into an abandonment she had never known before and making

her realise how little she knew of loving. Their mutual rewards had lasted for hours until exhaustion
claimed her in sleep, and she had woken to Saskia's
urgent call to find no sign to show that he had been
there except for the linen towel he had been wrapped
in. Hers was missing. He had obviously picked up
the wrong one in the dark.

Puzzled by his silent departure, she had lain for
some moments trying to recapture not only the events
of the night but also her vaguely revengeful intention
to leave him without explanation, as he had once
done to her. She recalled how, in a brief respite between loving, she had dismissed the idea at last as
being unworthy, only to find at the end that he had
again disappeared with neither explanation nor farewell. Saskia had told her that the chamber below hers
was empty and that he and his party had already left
for Whitecliffe, twelve miles away. Eloise experienced first disbelief, then an anguish so searing that
the pain almost crippled her. Now it had turned to
numbness that left her unable to find an explanation
for this second cruel abandonment other than that she
should have expected it from a man of his reputation.
It was her own fault. She should have known better.

Yet, try as she did, she could not negate the hap-
penings of the night as if they had been of no consequence, nor could she believe that she could so
soon join a long line of conquests when his loving
had been fashioned to her personal needs with such
care.

The discovery of a leaving present did not help in

any way to resolve the question. She had found it under her pillow in the small blue velvet bag in which it had been presented to him that evening. The diamond, the largest and most brilliant she had ever seen donated, apparently, by Lord Pace as his contribution to the tournament. She had held it for some time, trying to understand its message. Was it a reward? A bond? A token of esteem? Payment? God forbid—not *payment*, surely? A palliative to soften the blow, perhaps? What, then? She had placed it deep within her girdle-pouch for safety, resolved to return it to him at the first opportunity.

His linen towel had been placed with her own personal belongings in her saddlebag, a precious but most unglamourous remnant of an unforgettable night in his arms that had far excelled the fabrication of her dreams and had helped them both to forget their injuries. She almost smiled at last, lingering over the thought that few if any of his previous lovers would have known how to soothe his aches as well as she, how to massage him, even if her attempts had ended in a predictable tangle. The pain returned as sharp as ever.

Jolita and Sir Henry drew level with her, eager to talk, to share their happiness, not realising until later what it cost her to join in, nor what pain their gentle teasing caused at the mention of Sir Owain's skill in softening a lady's heart. If only they had known the truth of it.

Sensing that all was not well, Jolita sent the

slightest of signals to Sir Henry to say no more. Had Eloise seen Sir Rolph before they left? she asked.

Yes, she had seen their brother to say farewell, noting the absence of Father Janos and the appearance of a new man who had already been primed by the monk-physician in their method of healing. Attempting to draw some conclusions from the fact that Father Janos had mentioned neither his own impending departure nor Sir Owain's, Eloise was still at a loss as to why she had been left with no word of explanation. Had Sir Owain known of her plans to start for London at dawn? Discussed them with her father, perhaps? To ask her father would seem strange, in the circumstances.

Poor Rolph's excursion to Handes Castle, however, had been every bit as disastrous as her own except that he would be immobile for at least another week before he could travel. His disconsolate expression wrung her heart and, in a spontaneous surge of pity, Eloise had tucked a bag of gold coins into the sheet folded over his chest. 'To be going on with,' she said. 'I'll see what else I can do. Meanwhile, this'll help to make Griselle happier.'

That had caused a wry smile which, on later reflection, might have been a grimace close to tears. She had not hung about to see, but had responded to the tug on her hand with a quick kiss to both cheeks and a whispered farewell.

'Good luck,' was all Rolph said, and she believed he meant it, though it was both a vain hope and a meagre return for all her efforts.

*   *   *

By the end of the second day, Sir Crispin's party had reached the prosperous town of Coventry where, not far from the church of Ṣt Michael, the magnificent new guildhall and a large private dwelling stood side by side, ready to take on the joint hospitality of the King's Deputy Keeper of the Wardrobe and his daughters. Eloise shared a chamber with Jolita and their maids, their first chance to talk coming in the semi-privacy of a cosy bed, the curtains of which they closed against the noise from below.

By this time, Eloise's unhappiness was obvious, her supper only picked at, her eyes shadowed by tiredness. Little by little, Jolita drew out the crux of the problem which was that her dearest sister was in love, though that was the easy part. The rest was unbelievably complex, being to do with Eloise's inexplicable capitulation which, they both agreed, verged on madness, Sir Owain's record of absconding at critical times, his association with Sir Piers's death and Eloise's insistence that to be seen as his newest lover was too near the bone, even for her. That both sisters were sharing a physical experience for what seemed to Eloise like the first time was their only common ground, apart from love, which was almost irrelevant in its simplicity. Jolita had little to offer except a sympathetic ear, which was better than nothing, and Eloise's misery continued as far as Thame in Oxfordshire. Here, both sisters were in complete agreement that prolonged riding and prolonged sexual intercourse did not make the best of partners, though this *did* have the advantage of making them both laugh. On this topic, dear Sir Henry was left out in the cold as spasms of giggles overtook them throughout the next day for no obvious reason.

It was dusk by the time they reached the deep curve on the River Thames where the king's favourite palace of Sheen stood on the water's edge within easy distance from the city of London. King Edward and the Flemish Queen Phillipa spent as much time at Sheen as they did at their other palaces of Eltham, Westminster and Clarendon and at Windsor Castle, and though Sir Crispin could easily have been accommodated in the palace complex, he had a house of his own that nestled within spacious gardens outside the eastern wall.

As the sun set, the light from the river bounced off the windows, setting them ablaze and flooding over the whitewashed pattern of stonework and timber. But the palace itself took on a fairy-tale unreality, taking their breath away. Towers and turrets pierced the pink-streaked sky with shafts of silver and gold while streaming pennants waved to the last malingering rooks seeking refuge around the chimneys. Windows winked like jewels in a crown.

With the last of the daylight came the closure of London's city gates, too late for Sir Henry's large retinue to reach their house on the Strand that night. He sent two mounted messengers on ahead with his warrant to herald the morrow's arrival, while here at Sheen House the pack-horses and carts clattered into the cobbled courtyard, and guests staggered wearily into the comfort of well-prepared rooms.

Savouring their last evening together for some time, Eloise and Jolita strolled arm in arm through the extensive gardens where, in the soft Surrey climate, the fruits were already forming on trees and bushes, the vegetables inches higher than in Derbyshire. Above them, swifts scooped up beakfuls of insects over the rooftops, and Eloise mused on her two days' respite before she would be snared by the king.

'Tomorrow and Sunday for rest,' she said, quietly, 'then Westminster on Monday to plead my case. Shall you and Henry meet us there?'

'We'll be there,' Jolita promised. 'But, Ellie, tell me something.'

'What, love?'

'Well, you must have thought of it. What if...?'

'What if I'm breeding? Yes, I had thought of it.'

'What will you do? Did you think it might let you off the hook?'

'It might. But that's not what I had in mind.'

'What *did* you have in mind?' They stopped at the wicket gate to scratch the sleepy head of the donkey in the next field.

'To be honest, my mind wasn't functioning at all.' Eloise smiled. 'Later, when I could think, I suppose I was glad that, if I bear a child at all, it will be his. That'll be the next best thing to marrying him, which I could never do, of course. With a bit of luck—no, a *lot* of luck, I might be able to pass it off as my next husband's. But then again, I may not be breeding anyway. Who knows?'

Jolita returned her smile. By what Eloise had said about her night of loving, it would be surprising if she were not. 'But it's sure to complicate matters, isn't it?' she said.

Eloise was silent for a time, her mood once more melancholy as they turned along another pathway. 'I can't help it, Jollie,' she whispered. 'I can't think of anything else. Only him. I can scarcely believe he'd do this to me after...' Her voice cracked and faded.

'Does he know how you feel about him?'

'No, I could never tell him that. Besides, he'll have heard it all before *ad nauseum*. I swore I'd never be added to his list, and here I am, within a couple of days, mooning about like a lovesick calf. What's happening to me, Jollie?'

'Ellie, you're missing something out, love. He *offered* for you once, didn't he? And how many other women has he offered for, I wonder? None, or he'd have been married long before now. Has it not occurred to you that he might really want you and no one else? That he might even be in love with you? That he accepted Father's invitation to the tournament so that he could get to know you again, to start afresh? Why else would he have singled you out if not for that? It makes no sense, does it, to insist that he cannot be serious?'

'Then why did he leave so abruptly again?'

'Isn't that what you said you'd intended to do?'

'I thought of it, briefly. I decided I couldn't.'

'Well, you've put yourself beyond his reach just

as effectively by coming down here, love. I assume he knew the king has sent for you?'

'He knew, but nothing was said about my leaving Handes so soon. And by the time I return home it will all have been decided. As for his being serious about marriage, I've no way of knowing what his intentions are. I suppose I made it difficult for him to tell me. He knows more about my intentions than I do about his.'

'Then perhaps it's your insistence on doing things your own way that's made him keep quiet about the alternatives.'

Eloise broke off a twig of rosemary and held it to her nose, breathing in its pungent aroma. 'That's how it has to be,' she whispered. 'There are too many reasons why it cannot be any other way, Jollie. And while I'm here in London I shall make it my business to find out what happened this time when Sir Piers met his death. Perhaps when I discover the truth, things might begin to simplify.'

'By which time it will be too late to matter.'

'Then nothing will have changed except my peace of mind. Sir Owain admitted to me that he was involved, but I don't want a one-sided version. I want the truth.'

'Even if it hurts?'

'It cannot hurt me any more than it already has, love.'

Jolita persisted, in spite of the finality in her sister's voice. 'Ellie, wait! Are you telling me that you *want* Sir Owain to be implicated, as well as Sir Phillip Cottcrell? Do you *really* think that the truth will simplify matters between you, even if it's what you fear? Surely that's taking things to unnecessary lengths, love. Why not let it be?'

'Oh Jollie…for pity's sake! I thought you'd be the first to understand. I'd not have told you otherwise. Of *course* I don't want him to be guilty of anything concerning Piers's death. Quite the opposite. For my own peace of mind I want him to be entirely innocent, don't you see? How can I allow him to stay in my life without knowing? I'm not blaming him for disliking Piers. I'd begun to dislike him, too. But I'd like to be given the chance to clear my mind of this barrier they're all creating by not telling me. You cannot blame me for wanting to find out for myself. I pray it's not as serious as they're making it out to be.'

Jolita's sisterly embrace satisfied her that the intention was understood. 'Tread carefully, love. Men have their own reasons for doing what they do, and we don't always agree with them, or understand. Think only the best of him, dearest.'

'I do, Jollie,' Eloise whispered, her eyes welling with hot tears. 'I do. Why is it that my younger sister is wiser than me, d'ye think?'

Her sister's smile was concealed by darkness, but she felt it on her cheek. It had been as well for Jolita to ask, forcing her to look harder at her reasons for doubting Sir Owain, for her anger at the way her marriage had been curtailed so abruptly. True, she had begun to dislike, even fear, her new husband, as would any woman plunged into a permanent relationship which changed so suddenly from congeniality to a shocking crudity, even before the wedding ceremony. Then, she had accepted with blushes what passed for the eagerness of a bridegroom, believing in her innocence that it was all for show and not for real. She had been quite mistaken. The real Sir Piers was worse, far worse. She had wept bitter tears in the privacy of her chamber, too proud to allow her parents or family to see her bruised heart, or her arms and thighs, her bleeding tender parts. There had been enough of her problems to concern them in the past without adding more.

But none of that was reason enough to want him killed, whether by accident or design. Like many other wives before and since, there were methods of keeping out of the way, setting up a cushion of friends around one whose love would be an antidote to the husband's neglect. It had not quite happened in Eloise's case, Sir Piers's relatives and hangers-on being difficult to bypass. But she'd had hopes and plans, her own home at last, and a certain amount of freedom during Sir Piers's absences. She had adopted a superficial contentment that appeared to satisfy most people, deluding even her parents. She had not expected anything to worsen after the first few months, though looking back she had seen the money dwindling as fast as his respect for her.

His sudden death had numbed her, severely testing her resilience. In one fell swoop he had gone, leaving her free but with problems of property and debt that she had no idea how to handle. Her parents had rushed to her aid, helping her through the nightmare created by her husband's avaricious relatives who did their best to prevent her acquiring anything. No one could have blamed her for being angry at that, angry at the added catastrophe, angry at the mountainous indignities of having to fight tooth and nail for what was rightly hers, angry at yet another failed attempt to do what other normal women did, to be wifely and motherly to somebody. And if Sir Owain had had a hand in that, however reluctantly, well then, yes, she could be angry with him, too, and then some more for being the one to set her heart aflame. Now, as if that were not enough, when she had been given her freedom with one hand, the king was intent on taking it away from her with the other, for he granted women permission to keep his property only if they had a man to render his dues, as a tenant-in-chief must. In other words, she must marry. The penalty for refusal would be a fine of crippling proportions, or a forfeit of the tenancy and all that went with it. Widows of child-bearing age were expected to marry after one year; holders of his estates must vacate within three months; holders of castles must vacate immediately. Eloise's father had pulled strings for her, but most widows were not so fortunate. And Eloise herself thanked the heavens that Sir Piers had not received permission before he died to add the crenelations to Haughton Manor which would have made it into a small castle. Yes, that had been a blessing, but a small page of relief in a catalogue of anger.

With Jolita's departure next morning, the two days that followed stretched interminably through the warmth of late June which Eloise tried to fill with any activity that would keep her mind away from her forthcoming meeting with the king. She did not find it easy, for the problems of a possible refusal squeezed into every gap between household discussions, whether of beds, mattresses and linen, silver and kitchenware, checking the garden or instructing the stewards and chamberlain. A constant stream of visitors arrived as soon as it became known that Sir Crispin had returned to duty, and invitations crowded into the weeks ahead as if Eloise's visit would last as long.

She dressed for the great occasion in a deep mulberry-coloured kirtle with a sideless surcoat of mulberry silk shot with green that changed colour as the light caught upon its folds. Saskia braided her mistress's hair in an intricate nest of plaits which she crowned with a gold circlet sitting low on her forehead, glinting with garnets. The effect was of rich mulberries, red wine and copper-beech, ripened peaches, hints of green-shadowed foliage and moss-lined pools. She wore no other jewellery but, because the river journey was cool, she threw a soft woollen cloak around her shoulders, two tones paler than her hair and trimmed with strips of fox-fur that her father had obtained for her.

The wide river was cooled by a breeze that skimmed the surface, but the elegant barge sped easily down the current with the merest dip of eight oars towards the city. Even now, Eloise could not cease her rehearsal. 'Your Majesty, is it?' she whispered to her father. 'Or is it your Grace?'

'Relax,' Sir Crispin smiled. 'You know what the form is by now. He's not going to eat you, love. Not with me there, anyway.'

'All I ask is that he listens to my plea.'

'Oh, he'll listen,' her father assured her, restraining the unhelpful opinion that that was probably all the king would do to please her.

Her fingers closed over the soft leather pouch at her girdle where, deep inside, a blue velvet bag nestled with its priceless contents. Whatever Sir Owain's reasons for leaving it with her, it could never be put to better use than as a fine with which to buy her release. If the king was not impressed by the sum of money and the lands she intended to offer him, then this would surely make a difference. And for the hundredth time, she wondered if that was what Sir Owain had intended her to do, after all.

They came to the Palace of Westminster from the riverside steps where boats were tied up at the wharf and where, even at this early hour, men had already begun their business of the day. Beyond the sprawling complex of hall, apartments, government offices, gardens and yards, the great abbey towered over the site in a confection of flying buttresses like a tangle of delicate scaffolding, carved stonework, white, elegant and massive.

Through swarming crowds of market traders heading for the selling area within the abbey walls, it was only a short walk to the North Gate and past the amazing Clock House and another courtyard with a large circular fountain intended, Eloise suggested, to calm one's nerves.

'No,' said her father, smiling. 'It's used by most men to cover up their private chatter. Look at them.'

Tonsured clerics stood clutching at bundles of papers, deep in conversation with their clients and lawyers while, all around them, red-liveried servants escorted others through archways, down steps, along passageways, through courtyards.

One of them caught up with Sir Crispin, breathlessly. 'Ah…sir! There you are, sir. They told me at the wharf you'd arrived. You're not in the Court of Common Pleas, sir. His Grace wishes to see you and the lady in his apartments.'

Heads turned to stare, and Sir Crispin flicked one eyebrow which, for him, was a sign of surprise. 'Has his Grace not started yet?' he said.

'No, sir. He's waiting for you.'

'Father,' Eloise said, 'we were going to meet Jolita and Sir Henry here.'

'Don't worry, m'lady,' the man told her. 'I'll come back here and tell them. They'll no doubt be waiting for you when you return.'

There was no time to admire St Stephen's Chapel

as they passed across its western end, nor to stop and pass the time of day with Sir Crispin's many curious acquaintances. The atmosphere was quieter where the red liveries mingled with the occasional blue and white of Lancaster, the voices lower, the pace more leisured.

At the top of a flight of wide steps, they were halted at a large door which their escort opened quietly, ushering them into a tapestried antechamber with a view across a private garden where ladies strolled.

Nervously, Eloise turned to her father. 'Do I look all right? Am I tidy?' She smoothed her kid gloves over her fingers and twitched at her girdle.

'Stunning,' he said, kindly. 'You can remove your cloak if you wish.'

She hung it over one arm. 'I wish Jollie had been here.'

'Got all your papers?'

'You've got them.'

'Ah, so I have. Good luck, love.' The door beyond them opened.

There had never been the slightest chance of Eloise being able to conduct her business with the king in private; such matters usually came before the Court of Common Pleas in an atmosphere of public scrutiny. This private audience was a privilege few could expect and due only, she supposed, to her father's special place in the king's service. But even as they entered the spacious and colourful chamber, her privacy had already been diminished by the presence of several noblemen who stood together at one side. A group of ladies stood near the king, and a bevy of cleric-monks from the abbey hardly lifted their heads from their scribbling at a nearby table piled high with rolls, books, ink pots and quills, seals and caskets.

Unexpectedly, the king left the group to meet the pair with both hands outstretched towards Eloise, giving her no opportunity to examine faces other than his own. He was as he had been at their last brief meeting many years ago, tall, good-looking and brown-haired, wearing quantities of gold over a mid-length gown of red and blue woven with rampant leopards. His manner was gracious, though she was not deceived into thinking that this would make him any less covetous where money was involved.

His blue eyes expertly absorbed every detail of her appearance. 'Lady Eloise,' he said, supporting her as she rose from a deep curtsy, 'we have had progress reports on all your doings.' He glanced at her father and winked. 'Sir Deputy Keeper of the Wardrobe, so you are getting your daughters off your hands at last, thank heaven. But this one merits some special attention, I believe. Time we had a chat about it, then.'

Sir Crispin bowed. 'Your Grace is too kind.'

The king kept hold of one of her hands, swinging it to one side as if about to dance. 'And your reputation as a beauty has not helped you in this, lady?'

'I know of no such reputation, your Grace,' Eloise replied, keeping her eyes suitably lowered. The floor was of patterned tiles, the walls richly painted with scenes of a distant king's coronation. 'I believe my problems are more to do with Fate than with anything else, Sire.'

'Fate! Ah, well now, I believe in that, too. Come, Lady Eloise, I'd like you to meet the Princess Isabella. She is only a few years your junior.' He beckoned to a graceful fair-haired young lady of nineteen whose smile was as alluring as her father's. Her shimmering gown was a riot of primary colours that would have swamped her delicacy except for the softening effect of white fur that trimmed every edge of the surcoat. Her fingers sparkled with jewels.

The princess waited for Eloise to rise, and pouted prettily at her father. 'My gracious father takes some persuading,' she said, 'that we women know the state of our hearts better than men do. But we are given little choice in the matter, Lady Eloise.' Surprisingly, she took Eloise by the shoulders and placed a light kiss upon both her cheeks, whispering close to her ear, 'Trust him.'

It was meant to be reassuring, but Eloise had come here to insist on her own choice of husband and to persuade the king that she was the best one to say what she required. Surely he would see the difference between herself and his daughter.

'I thank your Highness,' she said.

'Well,' the king said, looking from one to the other, 'you two should have plenty in common, being so choosy about husbands. But there are more matters at stake here than preferences, lady. Your father has been more indulgent than most, and your brief marriage to Sir Piers Gerrard was not entirely his first choice but yours, so I understand. It's tempting to see that tragedy in terms of Fate, but a more realistic view of it might be appropriate, in this case.'

'Yes, Sir. But it is hard to be quite so realistic when tragedy strikes from a hundred or more miles away. So I have come to the opinion, if I may be forgiven, that my future would be best served by heeding my own advice rather than others, however well-meaning. I hoped you might allow me the chance to prove it, this time.'

With the change in tone, the hushed murmurings of the men stopped, turning them towards the serious exchange of opinions. Princess Isabella glided gently backwards, leaving the three to debate alone but with an audience of attentive ears.

'And what about your Sovereign's advice, my lady?' said the king, releasing her hand. 'Isn't it my turn next? You are still young to be given a free rein in this, you know.'

'I am young, Sire, as you say. But I am not in-experienced, and I can do as well as any to keep an estate in good order.'

'Is that so? Then you'd do even better with a husband.'

'Yes, Sire. I have a good man in mind for that position.'

The king smiled, tolerantly. 'I might have known it. You have come well prepared. Who is this man?'

'His name is Master Stephen atte Welle, Sire. He has been my steward for the past year.' She looked directly into his eyes, hoping to read his response, but he gave nothing away. This man was used to dealing with kings and high churchmen; a mere woman would find no easy path through his mind. 'He is a good and reliable man, as well able to care for your property as the noblest knight. He has my good intentions at heart.'

The king's mouth stayed in an obediently straight line, though his blue eyes twinkled. 'I'm sure he has, my lady. But then, so have I, and my intention has never been to pass my lands into the hands of estate stewards, however reliable. I have to be sure, you see,' he said, not unkindly, 'that my tenants-in-chief marry nobly. I need men who can fight with me and lead others in time of war, who can pay me knight-service and, in your case, who can breed more of his kind. You must see that that does not include low-born men. The title you bear and the lands you hold must remain in my gift, Lady Eloise, and that includes you. You are far too valuable to me to lose in the way you suggest.'

She had fully intended, at some point, to tell the king what she had told her father: that there would be no children to complicate matters of property after her death. Now, however, things had happened that made any denial impossible, and now she was left floundering in the face of the king's obvious determination.

'And what,' said the king, 'do Sir Crispin and Lady Francesca have to say about this decision of yours, lady?'

'I have been made aware of their disapproval, Sire.'

'Then it's time someone took a firmer hand in the matter. You have been given a twelve-month in which to grieve and to sort out your affairs, and now it's time to take up your duties according to my wishes. As a titled lady of wealth. As a wife. And as a mother. Your assets are valuable. There are many noble knights who have already shown an interest in a connection with the de Molyns name. Your father has an excellent record and his son's wife is about to provide him with a fourth grandchild. Isn't it time you did the same?'

The room became suddenly oppressive; its raftered ceiling of green and gold stars began to bear down upon her. Her case was slipping inexorably through her grasp, her control of her future disappearing before her eyes. She passed the warm woollen cape to her father, stripped off her gloves and removed the bundle of charters from under his arm, avoiding the pity in his eyes. She had played a lonely game. She had known it would be difficult.

She held the charters towards the king. 'The charters to my most valuable lands, Sire. I understand that you have occasionally allowed widows to buy their freedom to remarry. I would not wish to do so without your approval, and so I have—'

'Lady Eloise, one moment, if you please.' The king made no effort to take the charters or to have one of the clerics remove them from her, but took a deep breath, looking at her with eyes as hard as flint.

'Are these the properties your late husband held in dower for you? The ones you have fought for the past year to regain control of through the courts?'

'Yes, Sire. They are.'

'And now you are willing to forfeit them? For your…your steward? Forgive me if I sound incredulous, my lady, but this man must hold some special place in your heart to be worth so much to you.'

'Then I fear I must have expressed myself badly, your Grace. Stephen atte Welle is of an ancient and loyal Staffordshire family, but he holds no place in my heart, only in my bid for a say in the running of my own life. It is that freedom which I prize above all, which is worth all this to me, and more.'

'More?' His eyes of flint sparked, greedily.

'Yes, Sire. More.' Her hand was ready to open her pouch, to show him, but he stopped her before she could undo its buckle.

'No, my lady. This has gone far enough. Stop. I do not need to know what more. Give those charters to your father and listen to me.'

Her heart sank, dragging her well-prepared case with it. Perhaps it had never stood a chance. Perhaps it had all been decided beforehand. Shivering with panic, she did as she was commanded, touching her father's arm for a last vestige of comfort. 'Is there nothing else, Father?' she whispered. 'Nothing?'

Sir Crispin pursed his lips. 'It's for the best, love,' he said.

Eloise had never been short of courage, but this was her life they held like dice, tossing it to win a point for their posterity, and her courage came close to dissolving at that moment. As she turned back to the king, she caught the tail-end of his signal, the shortest eye-contact to one of those in the group of men whose firm footsteps and the sharp clink of spurs approached and then stopped at some point behind her left shoulder. She would not turn to look. The king spoke directly to her. 'Lady Eloise Gerrard, I have had numerous applications for your hand since the unfortunate death of Sir Piers. The first of these is here now, a man of the highest integrity whose offer is being made for the second time, so I understand, and who I see no reason to refuse. Would to God he'd been more successful on the first occasion or we'd not now be going through this performance to get you wed after all these years. You know each other well enough.' His bald statement wrapped around her heart like a sheet of ice, numbing her response. She turned to look.

'You! No, Sire!' she whispered, half to herself. 'You cannot mean it!'

Sir Owain's expression, arrogant and unrelenting, was easier for her to read now than it had been only a few days ago, for she had discovered how to interpret the steady grey warning in his narrowed eyes as a cover for something deeper. He stood tall and apparently unconcerned by her denial, looking down at her, and far removed from the naked lover who had spent a night in her arms only recently. He would have stood out in any group had he not been keeping himself well concealed, for his gown was of the finest pale gold silk-velvet trimmed with grey squirrel. His cloak was the same that he had lent to her one evening, violet, clasped with gold at one shoulder.

The room swayed. 'There is…has been…must be a mistake,' she said to the king. 'Sir Owain knows I cannot…Sire. With respect.'

The king was never one to bluster. Indeed, he appeared almost to expect her objection. He looked from Sir Owain to her father with a wry smile. 'I can see the problem,' he said. 'The lady has ever been a handful, I suspect. Time for a change of ownership, Sir Crispin, eh?' To Eloise, he said, 'Sir Owain tells me, my lady, that he believes you *can*, with a little persuasion. If you are referring to what took place at Windsor a year ago, you need not be concerned by Sir Owain's involvement. I have accepted his explanation of exactly what happened on that sad occasion, and Sir Phillip Cotterell's also. I have no doubt that they will explain it to you in due course.'

'Nevertheless, your Grace…' Eloise found her voice from somewhere '…I regret that I cannot accept your recommendation.'

Trying hard not to smile at this continued intransigence, the king glared at the curious clerks whose hands had been stilled this last five minutes or more. 'Then I have a solution to the problem that might ease your conscience, lady. We have a tournament planned for tomorrow, a late celebration of Princess Isabella's birthday on the sixteenth. I suggest that we decide the question there. You will take Sir Owain as your next husband if he wins the contest. If he does not, I shall choose one of the other applicants for you. There, that's settled then. Do you think that fair, Sir Owain?'

'Indeed I do, Sire. Nothing could be fairer.'

'Then you'd better win, lad, hadn't you?'

'Yes, Sire. I intend to.'

'So take her off somewhere quiet and start your taming of her now, or you'll have bought more than even you can handle. I suspect her father is all set to put her into a nunnery.'

'By your leave, Sire,' Eloise said, blushing at his stinging remarks, 'that's where I would prefer to go.'

He swung back to her, clearly unused to being answered back by any woman except the Queen. Taking her chin in his hand, he spoke quietly, though all the room could hear. 'No, my lady, that you will not do, either. This time you will marry whom I choose. I want to see a pride of Whitecliffe cubs with dark red hair and courage to match their parents. Be at the tournament tomorrow. You will be the guest of the Princess.' Lifting her chin up higher, he kissed her on both cheeks and then on her lips, ignoring the tears of anger that glistened, ready to fall. His message to Sir Owain was much less ambiguous than Eloise supposed it to be, consisting only of a murmur of approval and a thoughtful glance at his favourite jouster. But Sir Owain had seen the look before and knew its significance as well as Eloise's father did.

Chapter Seven

Unable to trust herself to utter the polite and accepting words of a noblewoman, Eloise had intended to keep her lips tightly sealed until she was well away from the royal apartments. But on this occasion, the training of her noble youth counted for nothing in the face of this latest episode that had culminated in the upsetting of all her well-laid plans. Anger, reproach and indignation, humiliation and bitterness spilled over and found targets in both her father and her erstwhile lover who, to those watching, appeared to be guarding her against some self-imposed injury.

She rounded on them, spitting with fury and turning to walk off in the opposite direction so that they were forced to catch her on the rebound. 'You knew!' she snarled. 'You knew, both of you! Since it was settled well before this, why not simply send a message? It would have saved me a journey and it would have saved you having to...ah, no! Of course. You'd not wish to forgo that pleasure, would you,

Sir Owain? The applause...the...' Her arm was wrenched round, swinging her back into her previous stride.

'Enough! *That's enough!*' Sir Owain held her, his eyes like cold steel. 'Sir Crispin, would you forgive me if I asked you to give us a few moments in private? We'll be in the garden sir. Thank you.'

Sir Crispin was already yards away, eager to escape, a wave of his hand dispensing with fatherly courtesies.

'Father!' Eloise whispered, her face contorting with tears.

'Come, my lady,' Sir Owain said, gripping her arm. 'This way.'

Tears now flowed, choking her, preventing even thoughts from presenting themselves in an orderly fashion. Her eyes swam through a blur of arches and stone steps into a green-lit enclosure that chirruped with birdsong and the water from a fountain. A stone bench hit the back of her knees, and she fell with an undignified thud on to its cold slab.

'At great risk to my best velvet cote-hardie,' she heard him say, 'I am prepared to soak up your tears upon my chest.'

Taken into his arms, her mental and physical resistance were at odds. 'I don't...don't want you,' she sobbed, relaxing against him.

'What you want is no longer an issue,' was the unsympathetic reply. 'It's now down to what the king wants and what I want. And what your parents want, for that matter. You'll get used to the idea.'

She found that any reply she might have made was stopped at source by a kiss so effective that her tears were halted.

'Well?' he said, holding her face in his hand. 'When are you going to stop trying to resist, woman? Can you not see even now how your intransigence merely makes things more complicated than they are already? Or do you relish the idea of men fighting for your hand? I could have managed without it, you know, in spite of what you think.'

Eloise frowned and wiped away a tear with the back of her hand. 'You believe I wanted that?' she croaked. 'Of course I didn't. I wanted him to reconsider, to see that I meant what I said. But if I'd known it was all decided beforehand…'

'Well of *course* it was! What d'ye think your father and I have been trying to tell you for the past few days? You wouldn't listen, would you? And now look where it's got you. And me, too.'

'That's *most* unfair!' She leapt away from him in fury, hurling the mulberry-coloured cloak at him to stave him off. 'It's you who won't listen to me! If I were a man my wishes would be heeded and none of this…this nonsense would be happening. But because I'm only a woman I can be passed on to whoever makes the best offer, sold to the highest bidder. So it appears you got your bid in first, Sir Owain, though why you could not have told *me* remains a mystery.'

He caught up with her well before she could see through her tears how to evade him. 'And what good would it have done to tell you,' he snapped, placing himself in front of her, 'when you were so set against any plans except your own? Would you have listened to mine? I gave you the chance, remember, but you turned it down. God, woman, but the king was right. You *do* need a new master.'

'No, I would not, sir. Nor do I want to speak to you again. Ever!'

'Yes, and I expect you were just as determined you'd never sleep with me, weren't you? And that you'd never accept a Whitecliffe. But you'll do that, too. Do I make my point, or have I missed something?'

'Oh, indeed you do, sir. Clearly. Did you win your wager, too?'

Angrily, he took her by the arms. 'My wager?' he whispered. 'And what does that refer to, exactly?'

Regretting it immediately, Eloise looked away, refusing to show him how his grip pained her. 'I don't know,' she said, 'but you hurt me sorely when you left again without a word, so why should I not take the chance to hurt you?' Her words lost themselves in new tears. 'It was unforgivable!'

His hands slid across her back, pulling her into his arms. 'Shh!' he said. 'No more tears, sweetheart. It was not done to hurt you. Never that. The very fact that I was here before you is the reason I had to leave so soon. The king had sent for me as well, you see.'

'Why didn't you tell me, then? You said nothing of it.'

'No. I was as intent on keeping my movements

from you as you were on keeping yours from me. If you'd known, you'd have done all you could to stop me, wouldn't you? I didn't want to take that risk. I've waited too long, sweetheart.'

'Not as long as I've waited for my plans to work, sir.'

He smiled at that and led her back to the stone bench, taking her hands in his and kissing them, recalling where they had been only a few nights ago. It was time to tell her of his waiting. 'Listen to me. My plans may not be quite as controversial as yours, but they are far more mature. I was first to offer for you as soon as you were widowed last year. July, to be precise. I wanted you before Gerrard did, and I was angry when he won you and I wasn't going to let that happen again. So I bypassed your father and went directly to the king. It was his doing that put me out of the running the first time, so he was hardly surprised. What's more, I've had a rather surprising confession from your half-brother, Rolph.'

'How so? Did you threaten to break another rib?'

He grinned, melting her knees. 'Not exactly. He told me that it was he who intercepted my letter to you when I went away. He asked my forgiveness. Oh, yes, I asked him why,' he said, answering her silent question, 'but he said it was something to do with his loans to your late husband. He didn't seem to want to go into details and I didn't press him, poor chap. Perhaps we'll find out more one day when he's up to it. But you can see why I put my bid in without consulting you, can't you, and why I didn't want you to know that the king favoured my offer? I tried to warn you, as your father did, but that's as far as I dared go, my sweet.'

'So when did you tell my father of this?'

'Only a few days ago, at Handes.'

'And it didn't occur to you that I might have made plans of my own by that time?'

'It's true that I hadn't anticipated the depth of your anger with me, but your plans never stood much of a chance, did they? You have to admit that even you had doubts. Why else would you have brought the diamond along if not to boost the bribe?'

She tried to pull her hands away, but he was prepared for her and held on to them. 'Let me go,' she said. 'If I'd known—'

'Yes, if you'd known I was going to be there, you'd—'

'I intended to return it to you, sir, in the first place. I still have that intention. If it was meant as some kind of reward, I cannot accept it.'

He pulled her hands on to his chest to make her look at him. 'Reward, woman? Nay, never that. It was to remind you. Didn't you understand?'

His eyes held hers in a combination of reproach and hope, failing to hide the admiration which had once been mistaken for arrogance. He was a superb creature whose character she had only just begun to understand and who was now saying that his interest in her was far greater than she had guessed. Their night together had been, for Eloise, a unique experience, but how unique had it been for him? And did this interest have anything to do with genuine feelings of regard or did it have more to do with winning? He was, after all, fiercely competitive. And determined.

She watched his thumbs moving over her skin. 'I need no reminder,' she said. 'My memory is quite reliable on such matters. But I shall insist that you take it back.' Slowly, she leaned towards him until her forehead met the damp patch upon his chest. 'I need no reminder,' she repeated, 'and I want you to win. God knows that I do. But I never wished for this to happen. If I could go back in time for a while, I would. I'd make him understand that it's not the way it appears to be, that my objections are deeper than mere whimsy. But I do not see how I can accept you as my husband, despite all the scheming. I've not been consulted, only told what I can and cannot do, but why should any man tell me who to share the rest of my life with, who to obey in all matters, sleep with and bear children to, share with other women or lose in a man's game?

'I made mistakes before, I know, but I would rather live with them than with someone else's. No one has yet given me the truth of what happened to cause the last one and, until they do, I am unwilling to commit myself to the same kind of marriage contract. Not even to you, Owain.' She raised her head to look at his face, the steady eyes, the mouth that had done so much to heal her wounds in one glorious night. 'Yes—' she placed a soft hand over those lips '—I know that I gave myself to you the other night, but that was my decision, freely given, and I don't regret it. My body is mine to give. And that's why I've chosen this arrangement with my steward, not because of any tender feelings towards him but because he expects nothing from me except security and I want nothing from him except respect and loyalty. It's simpler that way.'

She removed her hand and, because she felt tears ready to start again, laid her cheek against his chest, hiding her face from him. 'Besides, if he should meet with some tragedy after the allotted three months, which he undoubtedly will, my heart will not be broken as it would be for you. Safer not to tempt Fate. There, I've said it.' The tears had already begun to flow, her body to shake at the terrible bleak picture she had painted of her future: the confusion of her reasons hung like droplets of rain between them, too fragile to hold.

He rocked her until the shaking ceased, smoothing her back with one hand and holding her to him with the other. 'Yes,' he said, eventually. 'I understand why you think that way, but after tomorrow's events, the king will expect us to plight our troth and you will not be allowed to refuse. You must prepare yourself for that. A betrothal is an agreement to marry at some time in the future, remember, and it cannot easily be broken except for a very good reason. The marriage ceremony finalises it in the eyes of the church but, since we have already been intimate, and shall be so again, our bond will be well-nigh irrevocable.'

'I should know, I'm an expert at it, except that in my case there appear to be built-in impediments. Yes, I know I shall have to accept his decision but… Owain?'

'What, my beauty? More doubts?'

'Don't expect me to leap into marriage immediately, will you? Give me some time to get used to the idea. I shall have some explaining to do.'

'To your loyal steward? Yes, you will. I'd not like to be in his shoes when you do, but we'll keep him on if it's only security he wants. Eh?' His arms tightened around her as he smiled, teasingly, though he was not deaf to her deeper concerns. 'As for the three-month thing, sweetheart, put it out of your mind, once and for all. It's not going to happen. Now, anything else worrying you?'

'You will win tomorrow, won't you?'

He tipped her into the crook of his arm and studied the tear-stained face, the long dark eyelashes spiked like daggers, the lovely mouth that had not laughed enough in recent years. 'I shall win,' he said, grimly. 'Don't doubt it, woman. And then I shall make you pay.'

A tightness caught at her reply, holding her breath. 'I shall tend your bruises,' she whispered, 'until they are gone. Shall you wear my favour, Owain?' Releasing herself from his arms, she slid the long mulberry silk tippet past her elbow and wrist and tied it round his upper arm over the pale gold velvet. It hung there, looking in the bright light of day like a blood-soaked banner. A shiver of fear ran through her as she glanced into his eyes, but she saw nothing except pride softened by something else which she could not name. 'There,' she said, trying to smile. 'If I have to accept someone, it had best be you.'

His kiss was intended to be gentle, but Eloise had had only memories to feed on for days and, despite her reservations, her need of him was wild and undisciplined. There, in a quiet haven in the centre of Westminster's thronging palace, his lips and hands reminded her of their night together, and predicted those to come.

The arrival of Sir Crispin de Molyns's two beautiful daughters at Westminster, one of them Sir Piers Gerrard's widow, was not to stay a secret for long, though why the latter should have refused Sir Owain of Whitecliffe's offer of marriage was more than most women could believe. Eloise and Jolita and their escorts soon became the centre of attention, for both Sir Henry and Sir Owain had a wide circle of friends, all of them eager to show the ladies round the abbey chapter-house, St Stephen's brightly painted chapel, the murals, the carved and painted beams and the gaudy tiled floors.

The most extrovert of Sir Owain's friends was Sir Walter de Mauny who had accompanied the queen from her native Hainault in 1327. His former role of Official Carver and his relationship to the counts of Hainault soon projected him like a shooting star into the king's service where he had distinguished himself as one of the best military commanders. Now in his mid-forties, he was still unmarried for reasons similar to Sir Owain's, though he was more outspoken about it. 'Beauty and youth, great wealth and nobility,' he said to Eloise without hesitation, though his blue eyes laughed with mischief that belied the seriousness of his reply. 'Anything else comes as a bonus, my lady. That young whipper-snapper made a bid for you before I did, damn him, which is often the case, but I've put mine in, just the same, so all is not lost. We have tomorrow to get through yet.'

Eloise looked up sharply from the goldfish that had come to nibble at her fingers. 'Sir Walter? Are you being serious?'

He took her dripping fingers in his own, gently, his eyes still merry. 'The king doesn't publish his list of offers, but I'm on it, believe me.' He was larger than life, well proportioned and dashingly handsome with a reputation as a fine athlete and an almost suicidal courage that went far beyond most men's. Her father had often mentioned his exploits, adding that, in his opinion, he ought to have been one of the original members of the Order of the Garter, having more ability in his little finger than some he could mention.

Disturbed by this newest development, she said nothing of it to Sir Owain, but put it to her father up in the Great Wardrobe, a suite of chambers set on the south side of the great hall at the palace. Here he presided over a team of tailors and furriers, silk-women and artificers, clerks and carpenters. They found a relatively private corner lined with shelves where grotesque masks grinned at them in rows above rails of exotic gowns used at the king's ceremonies.

'Princess Isabella's birthday tournament,' he said to her, taking her arm and leading her towards an archway almost blocked by wooden crates. 'Her Highness wants gold everywhere,' he mumbled. 'Just like her mother. The brighter the better.' They sat together on the crates. 'Beads, spangles, gold-foil, jewels.' He tapped the space between them. 'Now, what's this about de Mauny?' he said. 'Yes, of course I knew.'

'Isn't anyone going to tell me the whole of it?' Eloise snapped. She was instantly contrite, and took Sir Crispin's hand in hers. 'I'm sorry, Father. About what happened earlier, too. It was not my intention to embarrass you, but his Grace cannot pass me from hand to hand like that.'

Sir Crispin sighed, patting her hand. 'I've told you before, lass. He can. You're in his gift and he can marry you any way he wishes. And the only thing you can do about it is to take yourself off to Farewell Priory and let him take the whole of your estate back into his own hands which...' he pulled her hand into an expressive gesture with his own '...which he will *then* sell to the highest bidder. Which is what he is doing already. The king doesn't lose, my dear. Well rarely, anyway.' He sighed again, watching the sadness in her eyes, still puffy from weeping. 'Look, lass,' he said. 'I suppose I was expecting too much by hoping that this business would be settled by now.'

'On my record, Father, I suppose you were, though for the life of me I cannot believe I deserve to be kept in the dark about things that concern my future happiness. Is there anything else I ought to know? You seem to be aware of those who've made offers to the king. Did I not ought to know of them, too?'

'More importantly, my dear, you ought to be aware that, unless Sir Owain is put out in the first round, which is most unlikely, the rest of this list is academic.'

'Academic? You mean…the competition?'

'I mean…oh, dear…there's no delicate way to say this. Didn't anyone ever develop a special language for fathers to use to daughters?'

'I'm twenty-three, Father, all but a few months,' she reminded him.

'Tch! Yes, well. His Grace kissed you this morning.'

'Yes, but there's nothing so unusual in that, Father.'

'No..oo,' he agreed, not looking at her, 'and to those of us who know him well, there was nothing unusual in his expression to Sir Owain, either.'

'What do you mean, his expression? What expression?'

'To put it bluntly, lass, the king wants you for himself. It's as well that you should know of this so that it doesn't come as too much of a shock at the end of the tournament. He intends to take part, you see.'

Slowly, Eloise withdrew her hand, feeling its clamminess against her father's warm palm. 'How do you know this?' she whispered.

'I know this,' he said, gently, 'by experience and because his Grace has chosen to use this tournament for such a purpose. Sir Walter de Mauny will be hard to beat, but the king will be even harder. If he should win instead of Sir Owain, your immediate future will be here in London, my dear, between the palaces of Westminster, Woodstock, Eltham, Sheen…'

'No!' she cried, hoarsely. 'Don't go on, Father. This is too much…too much!'

'You asked if there was anything else you should know.'

'Yes. But this is dreadful!'

'You want Sir Owain, then? After all?'

Pressing both palms beneath her breasts, she tried to steady her breathing. 'Yes…yes…oh, my God… yes, I do. Please God,' she whispered, 'make him win!'

'It's as well to go straight to the top in these matters,' said Sir Crispin, wryly. 'Now, since you have to be at Smithfield tomorrow, you'd better stay overnight with Jolita in London instead of returning to Sheen.'

'What about Saskia? My things?'

'I've already sent for her.'

'And you? Will you stay there, too?'

'No, love,' he said, rising and dusting himself

down. 'I shall be here till late, getting to grips with this lot. Heaven knows what they've been doing in my absence. I shall sleep at the palace, as I usually do.'

'Father,' Eloise said, joining him, 'you'll be there, won't you?'

He took her face in his hands. 'Of course. One way or the other, I shall have to be there, won't I, with their gowns to deliver? Eh? And stop worrying; Sir Owain's good. The best.'

'Except the king?'

'There's always a first time, lass.'

'Does Sir Owain know what you've just told me?'

He nodded and let her go. 'Yes. It's not so very unusual. It doesn't last. His Grace has had most of the queen's maids. She knows.' He led her back into the bustling chamber and the piles of fabric, the tables next to the windows on which tailors sat, cross-legged and stitching furiously.

'Doesn't she mind?'

'Hm! She's the queen,' he whispered. 'She's given him a large brood and they adore each other. She knows he's a man like any other.'

That was not by any means the first time Eloise had come across that sentiment, but it was the first time she had heard it from her father who she had always supposed to be unsympathetic towards erring husbands. Until now. His instruction for her to stop worrying was, however, doomed to failure in view of the serious predicament in which she found herself, And if her father's laconic acceptance of the

king's behaviour had startled her, she was even more
perturbed by his obvious lack of outrage that his
daughter was already on the receiving end of the
king's attention. Far from suggesting that they should
return home immediately, he had even declined to
offer her any advice that was worth having on how
to deal with the unwanted complication, preferring
to accept the king's interest in her as being well outside his terms of reference.

Late that night, with Jolita sleeping deeply beside
her, Eloise held aside the hero-worship reserved for
her father to investigate areas previously taken on
trust, finding a remarkable consistency of detachment
that could not entirely be attributed to fatherly in-
dulgence. There were questions difficult to answer
with any degree of charity. Was this latest example
of unconcern the result of the previous years when
all his attempts to find her a mate had come to nothing? Had he given up on her? Was he finding her
attempts at independence too baffling to deal with?
Was this the cause of his dour remark that he should
not have expected things to be settled so easily that
morning? This, from one who had recently accused
her of cynicism?

The investigation sharpened. He had left her third
set of marriage plans in the bungling hands of his
eldest child, Sir Rolph, while he himself had returned
to his duties in London, refusing to delegate his work
for the king for the sake of his eldest daughter's future. He had done his best to remedy the situation

by making his lawyers available to her and, to be fair, they had won back her property from Sir Piers's relatives. But why, when he had personal daily access to the king, had he not allowed her to be given the full details of what had happened to cause Sir Piers's death? To insist that it would not help to know was an insult to her intelligence and yet, in the light of today's revelations, her father's attitude seemed like another example of his dwindling commitment.

Guilt crept in like a snake. Was she being unfair? Mistaken? Seeing things upside-down? Dawn appeared long before she was ready for it, bringing a new wave of fear that the pattern of her life was being repeated, over and over, way beyond her control.

The air inside Sir Owain's arming-tent smelled warmly of leather as the knight watched his squire's nimble fingers buckle the steel knee-cop over one knee.

'Shin-guards, sire?' the young man whispered. Sir Owain would not allow squires' chatter before a joust: it spoiled his concentration.

He shook his head. 'No, leave them off.' His hand caressed the breast-shaped cop until the tent-flap was pushed aside. 'Walter!' he said.

Even fully harnessed, Sir Walter du Mauny rarely looked serious. 'So!' he said, with traces of clipped Flemish still lingering in his voice. 'This is an amusing situation, my friend, is it not?'

Sir Owain did not return the smile. 'No, Walter. It bloody well isn't amusing, and well you know it.'

'Doubting? Surely not.'

His friend heaved a sigh of disgust and stood, raising his arms for the padded gambeson and lifting his chin above the high rolled neck. He had had leather patches sewn to each shoulder, but would make no reply until his silk shirt had been smoothed down under the quilted linen. 'The whole thing's ridiculous,' he said, looking down his nose. 'His Grace knows exactly why I made my offer so early, yet he's still putting me through this palaver, Walter. And now he's putting his oar in, too, which is one oar too many, in my view. Heaven knows I'm as ready to joust as he is, but to put a woman in such a position lacks chivalry, and that's putting it bluntly. Especially a woman who's been through all that. She thought it would have been settled by now, as we all did.'

Sir Walter quirked an eyebrow at the young squire who laced up his master's back, but Sir Owain reassured him. 'It's all right. Michael won't speak out of turn. He values his position too much. Eh, lad?'

'Well, we're drawn on the same side, Owain, so that should take us both into the next round, thank goodness. But that means one of us will be against his Grace at the end unless something goes drastically wrong. It seems to me, my friend, that we could do worse than to put our heads together about his Grace's tactics, since I shall need all the help I can get, even if you don't. What d'ye say?'

'I beat him only once, and I've never been sure whether that was due to my own prowess or simply a fluke. I suspect the latter. Bring us some parchment and charcoal, Michael. Two heads are better than one, and we *both* need all the help we can get. I have to win this one.'

Sir Walter straddled a stool and drew the parchment towards him. 'Look, I've observed him doing this so often…it's so clever…when he turns… always on the right leg, not the left…'

'And especially on the grey he takes a longer run-in…'

Words overlapped and became muffled as the chain-mail hauberk was slipped over his head and, piece by piece, his armour strapped to his body. The handsome knight combed his hair and stood to attention, smiling at last. Without a word, Sir Owain and Sir Walter hit each other's right hand in mid-air, grasping and supporting. Then, as if at a signal, they bowed their heads in a prayer for their mutual safety, success and, in Sir Owain's case, a woman's smile.

He adjusted the mulberry-coloured fabric on his left arm, grinning at his friend as the tent-flap was held open, and the two emerged, side by side, into the bright sunshine.

'He's there,' Jolita said. 'Look, Ellie! With Sir Walter.'

But Eloise had already seen the two shining figures, one of them in a surcoat of gold and black chequers with a dark red tippet bound around his arm. Then they were obscured by their great caparisoned horses and, along the front row of the stand where Eloise sat, necks were craned to untangle a kaleidoscope of colours as horses, knights and their squires wheeled about and re-formed for the parade.

The tournament field was many times larger than the one used at Handes for Jolita's celebrations. The 'smooth field' now known as Smithfield was just outside the city walls near the priory of St Bartholemew whose monks administered the nearby hospital which Eloise had passed at Aldgate. The smooth plain teemed with spectators, as it often did for the public executions held there, and with horse-traders who relied on these events for their contacts, the showy beasts parting the distant crowds with flashes of brown, black, white and cream.

Pennants, banners and bunting fluttered gaily from post to post, scooping up the blue sky with jewel colours that echoed the bright garments upon the tiered stands. Along the front row at one side of the lists sat Queen Philippa with her ladies in a blaze of gaudiness and gold that shimmered in the sun. Well known for her extravagance, the queen spared no expense on such occasions, her wave to her daughter on the opposite side sending reflections of blue-white light across the space, drawing every eye to her splendour.

Imitating her mother's preference for showiness, the Princess Isabella sparked with gold, her hair bound in nets that quivered with diamonds, emeralds and sapphires, pearls and aquamarines. She had been gracious to Eloise and Jolita, insisting that they sit next to her, eager to hear of their doings and even more eager to tell them about hers. She sympathised with Eloise: her father was in a hurry to marry her off, too, but so far the princess had rejected all suggestions.

The heralds' fanfares split the air with piercing and discordant blasts, making the horses rear and fidget. They led the procession of eight mounted knights past the queen's stand, saluted her, and proceeded round to the opposite stand to salute the princess. Led by the king himself, all the contestants were bareheaded, though few were smiling, wrapped in their own thoughts, meditating on tactics, summing up the opposition and showing off their own magnificence, their superior horses, armour and squires.

'Here he comes, your fine knight,' Princess Isabella said to Eloise. 'So handsome. He *must* win today, Lady Eloise, mustn't he?'

'Indeed he must, your Highness,' Eloise replied, watching Sir Owain control the glossy black Donn with one hand. 'But his Grace the King is almost impossible to beat, so I'm told. Sir Owain will have to fight extremely hard this day, I fear.'

The princess leaned towards her, confidentially. 'You have changed your mind since this morning, my lady?'

'My mind is the same as it has always been, your Highness. Sir Owain has always known it.' She could say no more with so many ears listening, eyes lip-reading. She sent Sir Owain a smile and knew he had received it.

'Then he will not fail you. My father is not invincible, you know, and today I have the power to bestow the victor's crown where I wish if the contestants should be too evenly matched for an outright win. So...' she patted Eloise's knee with a jewel-laden hand '...you'd rather take Sir Owain than my father, would you?'

Astounded by this outspokenness, Eloise stared, barely able to believe that this seemingly innocent young woman of nineteen should understand more about her father's doings than she herself did about hers. In an instant, it emphasised the absurdity of the situation in which she was now unwillingly involved, of the times she had sworn never to be associated with another jouster as long as she lived. The contestants had passed; the princess's question remained unanswered, and Eloise's father, who sat behind with Sir Henry Lovell, would no doubt accept the outcome with his usual equanimity.

The heralds began their proclamation. To begin, there would be four contests of three jousts each, the four winners going on to the next contest, then the final two. All contestants had agreed to abide by the rules and by the judges' decisions. All lances would be blunted by coronels at their tips. Swords also would be blunt.

'Swords?' Eloise whispered to Jolita. 'Not swords, too?'

'Shh...listen!'

The contest would be awarded to the knight who broke two of his opponent's three lances, or scored a hit on his opponent's helm, unseated him, or brought down both horse and rider. In the event of an equal score after three lances, the joust would continue with swords on horseback and then, if there was still no score, on foot.

The heralds sounded the fanfare again as the first two contestants rode to the far ends of the fenced space they called the lists, donned their helms, took lances from their waiting squires and weighed them, tucked the long grip beneath the right arm and waited for the call. *'Laisser allez!'*

The squires let go of the bridles. The jousting had begun.

Telling herself that these men enjoyed it, were taught from the cradle how to fight and defend themselves, that they were honoured to be there, did nothing to add to Eloise's enjoyment of the next few hours. It had been reasonably safe to predict that the king, Sir Owain and Sir Walter would win their first contests and that the king and Sir Owain would win the second, though all the men were better matched than they had been at Handes and the afternoon sun was fiercely unrelenting.

But the final contest was by no means as predictable, both men appearing to be invincible and equally determined. Eloise felt sick with fear, not for herself alone but for the man she loved more than she dared to admit. She gripped Jolita's hand to curb an unladylike display of agitation within the royal presence.

But the crowd had no such inhibitions; they were wild for Sir Owain's success.

The first three jousts were ferocious in their speed and accuracy, each broken lance being thrown aside and replaced by the next, each with the same shattering result. Buckles were tightened, horses changed, helms removed and replaced, swords drawn. The two men rushed at each other, each man eager to strike the first crippling blow and to anticipate the other's, Sir Owain fending off the king's heavy battering with his shield and by the skilful handling of his horse, placing a mighty blow of his own across the king's right arm in a back-hander that his Grace clearly had not expected. The clash of steel upon steel could be heard above the crowd's roar as each man redoubled his efforts, dodging, swerving, pulling the restive horses closer into the combat. The heralds consulted and rode between them, calling them to stop and dismount. They must continue on foot.

Squires ran forward to assist their masters, to remove the horses, to exchange the long swords for shorter ones, the official pause before starting merely a courtesy before facing each other again.

Eloise offered a silent prayer. *Courage, my love. Beat him!*

They circled each other while waiting for an opening, beginning with the formalised thrust-and-parry manoeuvres they had been taught as youths as if sharing some private jest. The crowd yelled, recognising it. But Sir Owain was prepared for the ploy to turn with typical lightning speed into a savage attack with swing after swing of the broad sword seemingly from every direction which, for a man who could see his target only through a narrow slit in his jousting-helm, was anything but easy to achieve. Although he took some blows to the body, Sir Owain soon rallied, changing his defence into an assault that pressed the king ever backwards, time and again, giving him no chance to regain his balance before the next onslaught. The noise from the crowd was deafening.

Eloise and Jolita sprung to their feet, yelling like country-bred wenches, 'Yes…yes!' and, to their delight, Princess Isabella did the same. 'Come on!' she called. 'Come on, man!' Then, catching her mother's eye, she sat down again, blushing.

But it was as if Sir Owain had heard their cheers, for no one could have withstood the punishment he was dealing out to the one man who could take from him what he had set his heart on. The king held his ground, but only with great effort, his blows now weaker and less accurate. His shield was not raised soon enough to block a devastating blow to his shoulder, and his arm dropped, powerless, allowing the shield to slither to the straw-covered ground. He staggered, lowered his sword and swayed on straddled legs from exhaustion, too dazed to think.

Sir Owain, however, had already begun to savour this moment when the heralds and squires would rush in to support the king and lay him carefully on the straw while they removed his helm and dashed water on to his face. Half-blinded by sweat and gasping for breath, the victor looked towards the stand where Eloise, laughing and crying, was again on her feet, though it was not until his helm was lifted away that he was able to see her tears of joy, and she was able to see his blood.

Chapter Eight

Unwilling to tempt Fate, Eloise had given little thought to what could happen afterwards, win or lose, so the inevitable delay to any sort of privacy had to be borne with no sign of impatience on her part. Sir Owain had been less long-suffering, though his obvious eagerness to take his hard-won prize home and enjoy it in peace caused merriment as well as envy, and not a little perverse obstruction. And if anyone at the evening feast at the house on the Strand had thoughts about the reputations of either Sir Owain or Lady Eloise, they were far too happy, relieved and circumspect to say them out loud until after the two had made their exit from the scene. By which time, they were on their way to Cold Harbour.

'Where?' Eloise asked, running to keep up with him and dragging Saskia behind her.

His hand pulled her along to where their horses were being held by yawning grooms and a retinue of men to protect them along the shortest route past the Savoy Palace, past the tolling bells of St Clement

Danes, along the Fleet Street with only moments to spare before the Ludgate was locked against them.

Sir Owain's dwelling was a substantial part of a vast stone-built property owned by the mayor of London on Upper Thames Street, set back behind the church of All Hallows-the-Less, its impressive gateway alongside the steeple. It was known as Cold Harbour, but by now it was almost dark and Eloise could see no obvious connection to either cold or harbour as the party poured into the wide inner courtyard where the sound of the city curfew bells was muffled by stone walls, windows, doors, the calling of grooms and liveried servants, the gleeful whooping of welcome for the victor and his lady.

Sir Owain eased her out of the saddle and scooped her into his arms, kissing her before them all, laughing at their applause and sharing with her the heady euphoria of success.

'There are chambers prepared for you and Mistress Saskia,' he whispered.

'They knew I'd be coming with you?'

'They never doubted it, sweetheart, any more than I did.'

Whilst not exactly doubting, there had been moments after the contest when her concern for Sir Owain's wounds made her wonder how he had carried on as long as he had, for the king had not spared him and the day had taken its toll. His nose had bled profusely, causing her to ask Father Janos, 'Does this usually happen?'

'Yes, my lady,' the physician said. 'He's strong,

but this is a weakness. His nose was damaged with
his eye and jaw a year ago, and now it's a recurring
problem. The helm is a very cruel head-protector,
and the heat doesn't help.'

'Powdered nettle leaves,' Eloise told him. 'In-
haled. Usually works.'

'Alas,' Father Janos said, searching his medicine
chest.

'Then I'll send Saskia for some fresh yarrow
leaves. Turn his head to one side.'

Between them, they had stopped it by carefully
inserting plugs of yarrow leaves into each nostril, but
the evening celebration that followed had been an
extra ordeal Eloise would have preferred him to be
spared. She was aware that he had other injuries, but
Father Janos had tended him and neither he nor Sir
Owain would elaborate.

Hardly able to contain her excitement, Saskia
knew that it would not be long before Sir Owain
came to join her mistress. 'Shall I leave your hair?'
she said, scattering a handful of fresh rose-petals between the linen sheets on the large bed.

Open-mouthed, Eloise watched the ritual with
amused astonishment. 'Saskie! What on earth are you
up to? We're not *married*! We're not even betrothed,
yet.'

Saskia went on scattering. 'No, love. But two people of your temperament are hardly going to spend
the night in chaste beds after all that, are they? Why
d'ye think he's brought us here? Everyone here
knows why and everyone at Sir Henry's inn knows

why, too. Why pretend?' Briskly, she cleared away the remnants of the disrobing and snuffed all but one of the candles, closing the window against what she called 'river smells' and ignoring her mistress's pained expression. 'There,' she said. 'Goodnight.' They kissed. 'I'll go and tell his man.'

'Don't you dare!' Eloise said, tying her robe at the waist.

But the door was already closing.

Whether Saskia carried out her intention or not, Eloise had just enough time to open the window again before Sir Owain entered, closing the door without a sound as before, but this time wearing a silken gown that reached his ankles, which she knew was to cover his bruises more than anything else. He leaned against the door and held out his arms to her, and she went into them as a bird finds its nest, snuggling into the warmth of him.

His kisses were urgent, which she had expected, though she sensed in them a desperate tiredness that he would never have admitted and, even now, was determined to overcome. 'This is what I fought for,' he whispered with his hands in her hair. 'I would have killed him...anyone...for this.' He held her away, studying her eyes in the dim light of the single candle, searching them for a sign. 'You knew?' he whispered.

'Yes. I knew. Father told me.'

His eyes closed, briefly. 'Oh, God. He should not have.'

'I'm glad he did. There has already been too much

secrecy. I need to know.' Her fingers were undoing
the leather thongs of his gown, her eyes already preparing themselves to be shocked. It slid to the floor,
revealing a magnificent nakedness marred by red and
purple injuries which, in spite of chain-mail, padding
and plating, were the result of the continuous assault
of three contestants, the last of whom had taken
longer to beat than the other two combined. 'You
said I must pay,' she whispered, 'and I will. Will you
accept any coinage?' Her fingers smoothed tenderly
over him, feeling him flinch beneath their touch. 'I
think you should,' she said. Even as she spoke, her
robe was being parted, eased off her shoulders.

For some time he made no reply while his gaze
roamed over her as if in a dream, his hands touching,
verifying what he saw. Then he sighed. 'I had something in mind,' he said with an unsteady voice, 'of a
more specific nature.'

Smiling, she slid her hands to his buttocks. 'I
know. And so have I. But I can make it even better,
if you will allow it. To please me?'

'To please you, lady.'

She led him like a child to the bed and lay him
upon Saskia's rose-petals, and there she fed him with
the tenderest kisses for each and every one of the
many hurts he had suffered to reach her. Twice,
when she touched a vulnerable spot, he fought off
the heavy waves of exhaustion to respond greedily
like a man reminded of his starvation, but she eased
him back again, cradling his head and lying half over

him with her breast against his mouth, watching sleep reclaim him.

Then, as her tears were released, she wiped them softly away from his brow and gave herself up to the pains of her heart that warned her against loving too much, against commitment, against everything she had found and would have to forfeit, one way or another, by autumn. No longer responding to the nagging question of why he had gone to such lengths to win her, men having a hundred different reasons for wanting things, she set her mind towards the immediate future, which was the only future worth considering.

The candle flame had long since died when she half-woke to find that their positions had been reversed and that his lips were now exploring her as expertly as he had been. Gasping at the sweetness of his touch, she held his head and opened herself to the quest of his hands. 'Payment?' she whispered. 'Is it payment time, then? So soon?'

'The balance,' he said. 'Every last jot. With interest.'

For what was left of the night, Eloise gave herself to him without reserve, merging rewards, payments and gifts into a boundless exchange of pleasure that ebbed and flowed on an endless tide. He called her name during the most intense peaks of bliss, dispelling the last vestiges of her doubts, if any remained, that whatever his past truancies had meant, they did not signify indifference. And with that, she responded to his needs, tapping into the loving she had hoarded especially for his use, discovering a new joy in her learning which, in its own way, was as great a craving as his.

As dawn appeared through the open window, Sir Owain was able to see her loveliness in a different light, though it also revealed the exact extent of the payment he had been offered.

'You wept?' he said, penitently, touching her eyelids. 'There were tears? Why, sweetheart? Did I hurt you? Oh…I was selfish.'

'No, no…Owain, it's nothing. While you slept, that's all. It's gone.'

He lay above her, seeing how the mossy greenness of her eyes reflected the day's early light, the dark lashes, the shadows of fatigue. And something else. 'There has to be a time,' he whispered, touching her cheek, 'when Fate wearies of the game she plays. Whatever it is that makes you weep, sweetheart, and I believe I know what it is, lay it to rest now. As long as you're with me, you're safe; and now I have you, I intend to keep hold. Forget all that's happened. This is now. Today, we shall plight our troth to each other as the king has commanded, and by this time next year we can still be holding each other and a bairn as well. Think of that and believe it.'

'Do you have any bastards, Owain?'

His eyes flickered at the directness of her question. 'Sweetheart,' he said, 'you have credited me with a certain degree of activity in that department that I don't wholly deserve. So have others, for that matter.

Most men have a bastard or two somewhere, if the truth be known, but unless one keeps a mistress, which can be an expensive exercise, it's hard to be sure about one's offspring. I do not have a mistress, nor have I ever had one for more than a few weeks. And you are the only woman I have ever offered for. Twice, remember. And I've fought like hell to get you. Those *were* tears of joy I saw yesterday, weren't they?'

'Joy. And pride. And relief.'

'Then let's move forward. *Can* you move?' He laughed. 'I used you mercilessly in the night, my sweet. Forgive me.'

Together, they found plenty in their mutual weariness to amuse them which they were sure their friends would notice, Saskia being the first to confirm their predictions as soon as she entered with food on a tray to break their fast.

'Oh, my God!' she said, plonking the tray down and staring at the bed. 'It looks like a battlefield. So much for my rose-petals.'

'And so much for two people of our temperament,' murmured Eloise.

Sir Owain turned to look at the bed. 'She's right, you know. Crécy was nothing to this.'

It had been too late, last night, to take much notice of Sir Owain's London apartments at Cold Harbour nor, to be truthful, was its situation of paramount importance to Eloise after such a day. But the new day awakened her interest to see how close the River

Thames was, smooth and expansive at the end of a long sloping garden that ran between high walls and trees. Beyond the rose-covered trellis, the thriving river swarmed with boats and skiffs, large trading vessels heading for the wharves, and the well-appointed barges of wealthy noblemen and city officials. The water sparkled, almost blinding her, littered with traffic and the dipping of oars.

'Now I see,' she said, 'This is a harbour, isn't it?'

'Known as Dowgate.' Sir Owain pointed down-river to their left. 'And up there is Ebgate, see? And there's the bridge, and just beyond that is Billingsgate. You might just be able to see the Tower in the distance over the tree-tops. There...see?'

'And across there? Is that Southwark?'

'Yes, on the Surrey bank. There's the spire of St Mary Overy, called Overy because it's over the bridge. See all the orchards?'

Gardens and orchards softened the edges of every cluster of buildings, green, luscious and secluded, like the one in which they stood which had a private landing-state at the river's edge.

Father Janos came to meet them. 'Ah, they said I'd find you here.' He smiled warmly at Eloise. 'Does the garden meet with your approval, my lady? I tend the herbs myself when we're here, but I'd be glad to have your advice.' He looked around him, yet his superficial examination of the scene was, Eloise knew, the preliminary to another matter, and she had no heart to pretend innocence.

'Heartsease, Father? You grow that, too?' She smiled at him, tipping her head to one side.

The priest was as open to her charm as any other man and, looking down at his sandals, laughed softly at them. 'Heartsease? Yes, lady. And is your heart eased now? More accepting, perhaps?'

'The truce had to end, Father, and now we have to face another more permanent agreement, and there is really no point in my not accepting it. I tried that, but it got us both into deeper problems. For Sir Owain's sake and my own, I have to obey the king. If that's heart's ease, then so be it.'

'Good. Then you are ready for the betrothal, both of you?'

Standing behind Eloise, Sir Owain recognised the formality. Janos knew better than the rest of the house what they had given and received from each other. He laid his arms across her so that her chin rested upon them. 'Yes, we are, Janos. But we both feel that this celebration must be private, this time. Totally private.'

'Not even family?'

'No. Let them hear of it afterwards, by all means, but Lady Eloise has been through all this before, as you know. This one must remain different in every sense, as it has been from the start.'

'Then why not now, sir?' Father Janos said, quietly. 'You both wear rings. Why not simply exchange them, here and now?'

'Before you?'

'Before me. Do you wish it, lady?'

'Yes,' Eloise whispered. 'That is how I wish it to be. Here and now, in private.'

So there, in the Thames garden at Cold Harbour on the second day of July in the year 1351, Lady Eloise Gerrard and Sir Owain of Whitecliffe formally plighted their troth with no other witnesses except Saskia, a curious peacock, and the physician-chaplain, Father Janos Leuvenhoek, whose dark eyes were awash with tears as they exchanged rings, neither of which fitted well, and then a formal kiss.

They chuckled as he wiped his cheek apologetically. 'I do beg your pardon,' he said. 'I can face any illness, but this is…oh, dear. I'm so relieved that things have come to this after…oh, dear.'

Sir Owain bellowed, pulling Eloise possessively to his side. 'After being on the sharp end of the lady's tongue, eh? Is that what you meant? Well then, so am I relieved, my friend, believe me. Never was a woman so unwilling.'

But Eloise said nothing to contradict him, for it would have spoiled the magic of the moment which, even she had to admit, had all the hallmarks of inimitability.

She and Father Janos had tried to persuade the great handsome creature to allow her to apply a leaf or two of red cabbage to his worst wounds, but he would have none of it.

'Well, then…' she had held out some pills of dried herbs to show him '…perhaps we can persuade you to take one of these morning and evening in a little ale. You'll not taste it.'

Like a small boy, he had questioned their content, full of scepticism.

'Tansy, hemp, red nettles, raspberry,' Eloise told him.

Father Janos continued. 'Plantain, avens, madder...'

'Argh! You really think that stuff will—?'

'Yes, and so do Father Janos and Saskia. Anyone would think we were trying to poison you instead of heal you. Come on now, drink it up.'

To please them, he had obeyed, but in private he had insisted that her more intimate therapy had done more to salve him than anything that Janos could prescribe. And then she knew that, like all patients who begin to question their medication, he was recovering well.

The problem of their ill-fitting rings was soon overcome by a search of their combined jewel collections, Eloise not wishing Sir Owain to continue wearing one so dangerously poised on his first knuckle or to wear one herself that might fall off at any moment. And used though she was to living in some style, the magnificence of the apartments at Cold Harbour gave her a taste of what she might expect at Whitecliffe if ever they got so far. Used only for Sir Owain's stays in London, the chambers, though not large, were unusually well furnished after a man's taste, lacking nothing of silver and precious tableware, glass from Venice, colourful tapestries from Flanders, tiled floors and painted woodwork with expensive gold leaf and ultramarine. The small chapel was a jewel of a place where they celebrated mass with the senior members of Sir Owain's household and where Eloise tried desperately to dispel her fears, not entirely with the success she had prayed for.

Perversely, her original plan to make enquiries about her late husband's death and, by implication, Sir Owain's involvement, surfaced again as soon as the day began to swing into action. Naturally, she had said nothing of her intentions to anyone except Jolita and Saskia, who now agreed with her that this barrier must be overcome.

'Well,' said the maid, licking a finger and smoothing Eloise's arched eyebrow, 'since you ask, I'd say that the place we went to yesterday would be one of the best places to enquire. Smithfield. That's where Sir Piers bought some of his horses from, isn't it? The horse fair there.'

'You're probably right. I expect he had friends there who remember.'

The friends were more numerous than she had thought, and of both genders, according to the informants who had obligingly told Saskia all she needed to know about her late master's popularity in exchange for an arm about her waist. Eloise had recruited the companionship of Jolita and Sir Henry for their visit to Smithfield, Sir Owain having business with the king to attend to that day, and Sir Henry was happy to escort the two sisters to find suitably well-bred and good-looking palfreys for their use.

It was not difficult for Saskia to find dealers who recalled Sir Piers Gerrard's performances in the lists as well as his reputation as a pursuer of women. 'Aye, he loved danger, did Sir Piers,' one gap-toothed horse-dealer told her. 'You one of his ex-mistresses, then?'

'Do I look like an ex-mistress?' Saskia snapped, pertly.

'Well, you could look like mine if you come to stand a bit closer,' he said, grinning, 'and I could tell you what you want to know, couldn't I?'

So, for the price of a little harmless familiarity, Saskia had gleaned from more than one source some of the shameful details that made Eloise begin to understand why she had been kept in the dark for so long. Her husband had courted danger. His death could not have been accidental.

'*Many* mistresses?' she said to Saskia, back in their shared chamber in the house on the Strand. Jolita had insisted on her sister's company, and Eloise could see the practicality of being free from Sir Owain's watchful presence while her enquiries continued. She sat on the large comfortable bed and stroked the green brocade coverlet. 'I assumed Sir Piers must have had somebody else or he'd not have been so eager to get back here to London. But... many?'

'It gets worse,' Saskia said, her voice subdued. She

perched uncomfortably on the carved chest at the end of the bed.

'Tell me. Tell me everything, Saskie.'

'I'm still not sure you ought to know this, love, but Sir Piers preferred married women. Not just the hangers-on who follow jousters, but other jousters' wives and, well, he was very unpopular with them.'

'Yes, with the jousters. And so?'

'Apparently, just before he was killed, he'd started an affair with Sir Phillip Cotterell's wife.'

It took some seconds for the information to register and, when it did, Eloise's face had drained of colour. 'Sir Phillip Cotterell?' she whispered. 'Piers was having an affair with Sir Phillip's *wife*? But, for pity's sake, Saskie, they'd not been married long. So Sir Phillip found out and killed him…in a tournament…and got the king to agree to hush it up…and keep the truth from me because—'

'Hush, love! Stop!' Saskia came to sit by her mistress and hold her hand, regretting the disclosure already. 'No…wait! That's called jumping to conclusions.'

'Well, what would *you* do if someone told you that your wife was being unfaithful? It makes sense to me. It's what I've been wondering all this time.'

'It's not necessarily what happened, love, even so.'

'And where is Sir Phillip now? Disappeared, of course.'

'He's on a pilgrimage to Rome, apparently. He'd hardly be so penitent if he'd intended to kill a man in cold blood, would he?'

'Where's his wife? Did she go, too?'

'Lady Cotterell? In a nunnery somewhere.'

'So she's penitent too, is she? Which nunnery?'

Saskia heaved a sigh. 'I don't know, love, and it's no use you trying to find out when there are more nunneries in England than I've had hot dinners.'

'Hot dinners or not, Saskie, I can start with those here in London.'

'There are dozens here! Anyway, what would Lady Cotterell know about what happened? Less than you, I should think.'

Eloise sprang to her feet. 'Good grief, woman, whose side are you on? She was having an affair with my husband and *her* husband killed him. She's *got* to know more than I do.'

'Then why on earth can't you ask Sir Owain? He was there.'

'I know he was. But he doesn't want me to know, so he's not likely to give me the whole story, is he? And I want nothing less than the whole story, Saskie, even if it proves that he was deeply involved, too. I have to know exactly what all this means, and if Sir Owain is shielding his friend from my condemnation, then I need to know that, too.'

'It sounds to me, love, as if Sir Piers brought all this upon himself.'

'Very possibly, but none of them have the right to keep me in the dark. Not Father, not Sir Owain and not the king.'

The matter was put aside for the rest of the day so that Eloise and her sister could be escorted to the great cathedral of St Paul's and then to the Chepe where the shops sold more gold and silver than either of them could have imagined. At Jolita's insistence, Eloise spent the night at the house on the Strand, which might have seemed somewhat selfish, in the circumstances, had Eloise not been eager to do some solo investigating on the following day. It suited her purposes. They sent a message to Sir Owain; they would meet him at the Great Wardrobe at the Tower where her father would be waiting to show them round.

Jolita, though, was not as deceived by her sister's willingness to be parted from her newly betrothed as Eloise had believed her to be. 'Now, what is it?' Jolita asked, adopting her usual pillow-hugging position with one of Eloise's pillows. She crossed her legs like a pixie, rippling the green brocade beneath her. 'You've not quarrelled again so soon, have you, Ellie?'

Eloise smiled indulgently. 'Your faith in me is comforting, dear sister. No, we have not quarrelled. Quite the contrary.'

'What, then?'

'What?'

'Oh, don't be obscure, Ellie! You're up to something. Is it those enquiries you were so set on? It is, isn't it? Doesn't Sir Owain know?'

'Dearest, don't ask me any more. I know you don't approve and I don't want to enter into an argument about it. I shall have enough explaining to do when he finds out. That's the problem,' she added, flopping backwards onto the bed, 'with being owned again. I've been free of having to explain myself and I was just getting to enjoy it. Damn him!'

'But you can't let it rest, I know. Do you *have* to investigate, love?'

'Yes, Jollie, I do.'

'Then I'll come with you.'

Slowly, Eloise turned her head into a mass of red silken waves to look at her sister. 'You mean it?'

'Of course. That's what sisters do. Besides, it'll be much easier to explain if we're together. Now, tell me what you've discovered so far.'

Eloise would not have told another living soul how shamed she was to have found that her marriage, founded on such promise, had stood no chance of being a success. So she turned on to her face to hide the pain in her expression, and told Jolita what Saskia had told her. Except that, this time, there was not so much anger as humiliation.

The two sisters dressed with some consideration, bearing in mind their mission to seek out a penitent in a nunnery. Sober tones would be best, they said, soft reds and browns, greys, and flowing ells of white wimple to cover their heads. They also agreed that a liberal presence of gold ornament would be appropriate. Nuns did not live by bread alone, nor were they immune to inducements.

Mounted on their new palfreys, impressively elegant beasts of rich chestnut and dappled grey, and accompanied only by Saskia and three of Sir Henry's liveried grooms, they set out towards St Helen's Priory, since that was more in the direction of the Tower than some of the others.

'There's Clerkenwelle,' one of the grooms told them, 'but that's some way out of town. And there's St Mary's Spital up on the Moor Fields, and St Clare's over by the Aldgate.'

'But St Mary's of Bedlam is for sick folks,' one of the others reminded him.

'Bethlehem,' the first one corrected him. 'Aye, best stick to St Helen's, mistress. We can go on to St Clare's if that doesn't work out.'

His prediction was correct. Though they had set out early, it took them some time to wend their way through the busy narrow streets, past carts, sledges and horses, crowds of people, market-traders, drunks and piles of rubbish. They held their noses at the stench of decaying waste, no better since the terrible pestilence of two years ago, heaving sighs of relief as they gained entry to St Helen's Priory only to discover that Sir Phillip Cotterell's wife was not known to them. No, they were sorry, they could make no suggestions.

'St Clare's, then,' Jolita said.

'We'll go outside the wall, mistress, there's a track that takes us down to the nunnery,' the helpful groom told them.

The sun was well up by the time they passed out of Bishopsgate, but the track was green and thick with meadowsweet as they trotted through. But the reply at St Clare's was the same as before, though the nuns suggested that St Katherine's-by-the-Tower might be able to help.

'But that's another place for sick folks,' the groom said as they headed south towards the great white walls of the Tower. 'Was your friend sickly, m'lady?'

'I don't suppose so,' Eloise said. 'But we have to meet Sir Crispin at the Tower, so we may as well try it. It's within a stone's throw.'

This time, although the sister in charge at St Katherine's was quite sure that none of their patients bore the name of Cotterell, nor had anyone of that name given birth there within the last year, there was no reason why the ladies should not come inside to take some refreshment and be shown around the wards. The glint of obvious wealth had caught her eye, along with the tinkle of harness-bells and the titled names. Donations were never refused. It was almost noon: refreshment would be most acceptable; they would be delighted to see the wards.

It was soon apparent to Sister Anna that the elder of the two noble sisters and her maid was no novice when it came to the healing of the sick and, as they strolled through clean and airy wards, the visit that had started as a duty developed into a congenial exchange of opinions.

The nuns recruited outside helpers, men and women who lived on the hospital precincts apart from the nuns' quarters, to help with the heavy work and general duties. Before long, Jolita sauntered off to talk to one of them, a youngish woman who had been hovering in the background as if waiting to catch their attention.

'Mistress de Molyns?' the woman said. 'Forgive me. I caught the name.' Dressed in the plain unbleached linen gown of a helper, her head enclosed in an old-fashioned wimple, the woman emanated a softness that was both tender and sensual. Her wide dark eyes were steady beneath beautiful brows, her cheekbones delicate and high, though her pale lips were too tightly compressed with weariness to smile readily.

'Jolita de Molyns of Handes, in Derbyshire,' Jolita said. 'Do we know each other, mistress?'

'My name is O'Farrell,' the woman whispered. 'No, we have not met, but I know of you and Lady Eloise from your brother, Sir Rolph.'

'You know our brother?' Jolita frowned. 'How so?'

Mistress O'Farrell was not inclined to go into details while her employer was in sight. 'I would like to be allowed to speak with you both. Do you think that would be possible? Beyond the porter's lodge? I shall be on my way home in a few moments. Please,' she insisted. 'It *is* important.'

Jolita was not convinced. 'It's also rather mysterious,' she said. 'I hope you don't—'

'Thank you.' The woman turned and left as Sister Anna and her guests approached, leaving Jolita as much perplexed as curious.

* * *

Leaving Sister Anna overcome by their generosity, the three women dismounted as the figure of Mistress O'Farrell came into view where the wooden gates of St Katherine's-by-the-Tower were just hidden by the white-blossomed elders.

Intrigued, Eloise wondered how this woman could have come into contact with their brother when the hospital took in only women patients, but whatever she half-expected, the truth was more surprising.

The woman lost none of her dignity as she told them. 'I am Sir Rolph's mistress,' she said, 'for lack of a better description.'

The affairs of the last few days had helped to prepare Eloise for startling news, last night's being the most recent. Even so, while she displayed no outward sign of shock, the possibility of her brother's liaison with any woman other than the domineering Grissle was not something she had ever seriously contemplated. Her expression, to her credit, remained implacable. 'Ah! Rolph's mistress. Then you must be Marie,' she said, watching the large eyes widen in astonishment.

'You *knew*? He's already told you about me, my lady?'

Eloise's fingers found their way to her purse-chain hanging from her girdle, toying with it. Now she understood more clearly Rolph's strange request for Marie, the eldest daughter who, although dear to him, was not as close as she had suggested to Father Janos. But to have named Lady Griselle's eldest daughter after his mistress was taking a risk that

verged on madness, for if his wife should ever find
out, the repercussions would be more than Rolph
could bear. Eloise recalled his face, his words—'it's
hell...sheer hell...'—and knew that while it was not
uncommon for a man to have his own private life,
Griselle was not the kind to accept another woman
without sustained and violent protest. Harridan wives
were not uncommon either. Nor weak husbands like
Rolph.

'Our brother rarely shares his confidences with us,
Mistress O'Farrell. Well, not consciously, anyway.
But come, shall we sit over here on the bank? My
sister and I would like to hear your story. How is it
that you are working here at the convent hospital? Is
it voluntary work that you do?'

The young lady's hands, although reddened and
rough, remained demurely in her lap, twisting a stalk
of grass. 'Sister Anna would no doubt be pleased to
have it so,' she said, composedly, 'but I need every
penny I can earn. I have a child, you see. A boy.
Christopher.'

Eloise took a deep breath.

It was Jolita who asked her, 'How old?'

'He's eight,' Mistress O'Farrell said. 'But he's
been sickly now for going on two years. Sister Anna
believes me to be a widow, but I've never been married. I don't live on the convent site like most of the
others, so a neighbour cares for Christopher while
I'm at work. She's getting old, though.'

'I see,' Jolita said. 'Mistress O'Farrell, my sister

and I are sorry to hear about your child, but if you wanted to talk to us about financial problems—'

Abruptly, the grave-eyed young lady gathered her skirts and stood, not looking directly at either of them. 'Forgive me for wasting your time. I bid you good day, ladies.' She turned to walk away.

Saskia and Eloise caught at her hands just in time. 'Mistress O'Farrell...please...don't go! Please come back. My sister had no intention of insulting you. Come, sit with us again and tell us. Your son, Christopher, is he...?'

With a sigh and a slight show of reluctance, Marie O'Farrell sat again, finding it impossible to resist talking of her child. 'Yes, he is your brother's son. And it's not money I am asking you for, my lady, it's news. I've had no messages from Sir Rolph for some time, and your appearance came like a ray of hope, a chance to find out how he is. I hoped you might be able to tell me something of him, that's all.'

As gently as they could, they gave her news of the injuries which had prevented Rolph from making contact with her, and though they understood that his well-being was her main concern, it was impossible for them not to be aware that she had relied on him for some support. It was also clear that she was anxious for Lady Griselle de Molyns to remain unaware of her existence.

'He called his eldest daughter after me,' she told them, without boasting. 'We met well before his marriage to Lady Griselle, but I was not suitable, you see, being of common stock. I would never have been accepted. His friends discovered, and that was a nightmare for him, poor Rolph, but no one could have been more loyal. Never once has he blamed me.'

'Blamed you for what, mistress?' Eloise probed, gently.

'Well, for being the cause of his worries,' Mistress O'Farrell said.

There was a pause in the narrative during which Eloise hoped she might explain further, but this woman was no chatterbox. 'You are talking about blackmail, are you not, mistress? His friends blackmailed him to keep them quiet? To keep this information from Lady Griselle?'

'Only one. Not the others. They were more understanding, as it turned out.'

'My late husband? Sir Piers Gerrard? He was the one?'

'Look...Lady Eloise...please understand. I was not aware that you knew anything of this, but I was willing to risk it because I need to have news of your brother. Even to know that he lies injured is better than not knowing anything. But the last thing I want you to think is that I wish to speak ill of your late husband. I'm sure he had his reasons.'

'Believe me, Mistress O'Farrell, I need information as much as you do. I am about to make another marriage, God willing. My affairs must all be in order before I do; all ends tied up. And that means my late husband's affairs. I know about my brother's loans to him, but...'

'Loans? No, my lady, as you say, it was blackmail. Sir Rolph has been drained over the years to buy Sir Piers's silence, yet he would not give me up as I said he should. He adores Christopher, and our son adores his father.'

'When did Sir Rolph begin these payments to Sir Piers?'

'Oh, some years ago, my lady. Before you and Sir Piers were married. I think Christopher was still a toddler when Sir Piers found out. He'd probably heard it from the others. He was not a well-known jouster at that time, and I think Sir Rolph believed he'd be glad to take a one-off payment and go away. But Sir Piers did well at Crécy in forty-six, and the king gave him the Staffordshire property next to your brother's estate, as you know. It must have been the cost of rebuilding, equipping himself for tournaments, and having so many…' She hesitated, biting at her lip.

'Mistresses. Yes, I found that out, too.' Having been told only recently of the expensiveness of mistresses, Eloise understood her dilemma. All the same, the added information painted an ugly picture of how Sir Piers had systematically drained her brother of money which Sir Rolph then tried to pass off, to Eloise and to his wife, as unrecorded loans, attempting to claim them back from Eloise at his wife's insistence. In a way, it was understandable that Rolph would have desperately tried any device to hold on to this lovely woman and his son while at the same time trying to keep their existence a secret from his family.

'I'm sorry, my lady, perhaps I should not have… It was selfish of me. I was desperate for news. I must go home to my child. But…' she turned to Eloise, searching her eyes as if for some scrap of kindness '…could you get a message to Sir Rolph for me? Please?'

'Of course I can. But could you do something for me in exchange? Allow us to see Christopher, then I shall be able to tell Rolph I've seen him and, apart from that, we may be able to help him.'

Tears flooded uncontrollably into Marie O'Farrell's eyes as she stood, and she would have stumbled but for Saskia and Jolita's hands. 'Thank you,' she croaked. 'Yes, thank you.'

To both Eloise and Jolita, it was becoming increasingly difficult to untangle the information into its relevant compartments, for while neither of them were naïve, nor were they particularly artful. It was true that men had occasional mistresses and, while not being exactly condoned, this was never something a man flaunted before his wife, nor could she expect to be particularly flattered by it. Eloise, believing her husband to be as much a man as any other as far as women were concerned, would have accepted that he had one mistress, even two. But to learn that he was a shameless libertine who habitually took other men's wives and blackmailed those he called friends was news that no woman, particularly a newly married one, would accept without feeling shame, humiliation and betrayal. A man's honour was as important as his lineage, and Sir Piers's behaviour was dishonourable in the extreme.

Marie O'Farrell apparently knew nothing of the fact that her lover had been using the proceeds from his wife's dowry, raised with her permission from her estates, to pay for Sir Piers's silence. Which was probably why, both Eloise and Jolita agreed, Marie and her son were now living in such appalling conditions when they should have been comfortable. It must have been some time since he had been to visit her there or, presumably, he would have done more to help. At the same time, neither of the sisters could help pitying and liking the woman. She was modest, sweet, and unpretentious, and was concerned more for her son than for herself, and they were more relieved than shocked to find that Rolph loved a woman who was as far from his wife's ungracious nagging as it was possible to be. What a pity he had not been able to marry her. His behaviour was weak and underhand, but Sir Piers's behaviour was blatantly amoral in every respect.

Chapter Nine

The royal armoury at the Tower was every bit as diverse in its fabrications as the other departments of the King's Great Wardrobe, though neither Eloise nor Jolita had realised that the embroiderers worked here on banners, trappings and pennants for the royal ceremonials. If they had arrived at the Tower from the town, however, instead of through the postern gate in the wall, they might have been able to keep their visit to Mistress O'Farrell's home a secret from Sir Owain longer than they did. He was waiting for them with some impatience.

'Where've ye been?' he said, lifting Eloise out of the saddle.

'St Katherine's-by-the-Tower,' she replied, 'talking to Sister Anna. They have a reputation for healing second to none, you know.'

'All *this* time?'

With a promise of the full story after their visit to the Tower, Sir Owain had to be content for the time being. So while Jolita and Saskia went to visit the broderers, Eloise and Sir Owain found a corner away from the hammering of metal and the shouting of orders where they could sit on a window-ledge overlooking the wide brown river.

'What is it?' he said. 'Scandal? Gossip?'

'More than that.' She told him of Marie O'Farrell, of her relationship with Sir Rolph and of the sad conditions in which she lived in a small cottage where her precious son was growing more sickly every day from lack of proper nourishment and sanitation. The air was often polluted by butchers' offal thrown into the street, the water fouled in the well, the earth-closet leaked sewage, the nearby river alive with mosquitoes. Even in daylight, rats scampered boldly across the thatch while the lad with Rolph's sandy hair played listlessly with a mongrel bitch and her mewling pups.

Eloise and Jolita had been angry and sickened that Rolph had not done better for his mistress than that. They had given Mistress O'Farrell money, which she had not wanted but could hardly refuse, and they had promised to send some healing potions to ease Christopher's sores, as his mother would take nothing from St Katherine's pharmacy.

Well before she had concluded her tale, Eloise realised from Sir Owain's lack of surprise that he must have known of Rolph's unfaithfulness.

His eyes had hardly left her face, but now they softened with tenderness as he picked up her hand and kissed it. 'My caring one,' he said, 'yes, I did know about Rolph's London woman, but a man's mistresses are his own affair unless it affects oneself or one's friends, and then we stick together for protection. As long as Lady Griselle doesn't get to hear of it, he'll be all right.'

'Is that what you truly believe?' she said, withdrawing her hand.

'Yes, that's what I believe. And I've told you, my outraged green-eyed beauty, that I do not keep mistresses, nor do I intend to. Too expensive by half, as you've just seen.'

Eloise stood up. 'Is that the only reason, sir?'

He caught her hand before she could move beyond his reach and pulled her on to his knee, holding her helpless within his arms as he kissed her throat, moving down over the wide open neckline of her surcoat. 'It's the only reason you're going to get,' he said, between kisses, 'until tonight. I shall return to Sheen with you and your father this afternoon. I don't intend to spend another night on my own while you go off in another direction. There now, woman, let there be no more doubting, eh?' He let her up, laughing at her flushed cheeks.

Straightening her surcoat, she pretended indignation. 'So your wounds are healing, it seems.'

'Yes, my sweet. They are. You'll be able to make a full examination of them later. Now, where has your sister got to? Your father's eager to be away, and we have to eat and then call at Cold Harbour and the Strand for your belongings.'

Eloise had no intention of telling Sir Owain anything she had discovered about Sir Piers's blackmailing of her brother, knowing that he would forbid her to make further enquiries. Nor did she believe for one moment that her brother was the only man Sir Piers had tried to blackmail. But her sister's ostensibly innocent quest to see how gold thread was made had yielded far more than that, for she and Saskia returned subdued and unsmiling, unable to explain much of the process.

'Tell you later,' Jolita whispered in answer to Eloise's enquiry. She would say no more.

It was only in the privacy of Jolita's chamber at the house on the Strand that she and Saskia were able to speak. She exchanged an enigmatic glance with the maid.

'For pity's sake,' Eloise said, impatiently, 'tell me what you've found out.'

'Well,' Jolita said, 'if the two young gossips I spoke to had known I was Sir Crispin de Molyns's daughter, we'd not have found out anything.'

'So who did they think you were?'

'You're not going to believe this.'

'Try me.'

'Father's mistress.'

'Father's *what*?'

'It's going to be one of those memorable days, love,' Jolita said, 'when shocks follow each other so fast you might miss one if you blink. Apparently, Father has a mistress. And when *we* strolled along, that's who they thought I was, his mistress and her maid, come to see.'

'Jollie! I can hardly believe it! Why?'

'Why does he need a mistress? Well, it appears to be a sad fact of life, dearest, that any man who spends time away from home cannot exist for long without a woman in his bed. Not even Father.'

Eloise sat without speaking, trying to imagine what her mother would say if she knew. Perhaps she already did, like the queen knew about the king.

'And that's not all,' Jolita said, coming to sit by her side. 'These two young men, while they were busy cutting sheets of beaten gold into strips, told us what they knew about Sir Piers, too.'

Until this moment, investigating her late husband's activities in London had been uppermost in Eloise's mind. That, and the assertion of her independence. Now, the thought of hearing more disturbing revelations about what men got up to when they were on the loose began to lose its appeal. Her brother. Her father. The king. Sir Piers. 'What?' she said, softly.

'Mistress,' Saskia interrupted, 'd'ye not think it might be better if—?'

'Just *tell* me!' said Eloise. 'I know about his many women and Sir Phillip's wife, I know about the brothels at Smithfield on Cock Lane. I know about the blackmailing. What else is there to know? That he cheated at jousting, too?'

'Yes,' Jolita said, ignoring Saskia's warning looks. 'He had a reputation for it.'

Something that Sir Owain had once said about him not being able to tell the difference between jousting and warfare passed through her mind and then was lost. 'Cheating? What do two gossipy broderers know about it?'

Saskia came to sit on the rushes before them, cross-legged. 'Not gossip, love,' she said, gently. 'They knew Sir Piers just as everyone else did at the armoury. They made some of his armour there, but he was not generally well liked.'

'No, but that's hardly a surprise any more, is it? He was a rotter, but how did his breaking of jousting rules—?'

'No,' Jolita said, 'it was not so much rule-breaking as dirty tricks. You know how strict they are about rules, but Sir Piers's reputation was for winning at any price, partly because he could not afford to lose. As you know, every time a man loses he forfeits his armour and horse to the winner, and Sir Piers's debts had become more than he could handle. Because of his extravagances, mostly. And before he gained a reputation as a spendthrift, he seems to have borrowed from just about everybody. Later on, he even—' Jolita stopped abruptly as Saskia's warning frown caught her eye, but it was too late.

'Even what? Come on, tell me the rest. It can't be any worse.' Premonition told Eloise that it could.

Less enthusiastically, Jolita continued. 'He even offered one man a night with his wife if he would release him from his obligations.'

'What d'ye mean, a night with his…a night with his *wife*? Me? Is it *me* you mean? In return for a debt? Oh, no, Jollie…no, you must have misunder-

stood.' Eloise held her face between her hands, un-
believing, shattered by this newest revelation. Yet
while she denied it, she knew from his coarseness
that it could be true, for how often in that brief time
after their marriage had he boasted to her that he now
possessed what every one of his acquaintances would
kill for. He had not spared her the details of their so-
called envy, either.

'I feel sick,' she whispered.

'I'm sorry, love. Saskia was right. I shouldn't have
told you.'

'Yes, you should. Who was this man?'

'We didn't ask. We didn't want to stay any
longer.'

'But why did they think that my father's mistress
would be interested to know of his late son-in-law's
disgusting tactics? Were they hoping to put you off?'

'I don't know, love, but it was we who asked if
they knew Sir Piers, and I don't suppose it occurred
to them that it might be tactless to gossip when they
had chance to boast how well they knew what went
on behind the scenes, just as men do.'

'He offered *me*? For *money*? His own *wife*?'

Saskia got up, far from pleased by Jolita's can-
dour. Her mistress had suffered enough without
knowing every last sordid detail. 'I think we should
be away, m'lady,' she said, formally. 'Come, shall
you let me put this cloak around you? You're shivering.'

'I'm cold.'

Already feeling some remorse, Jolita enclosed her

in an affectionate hug. 'Don't dwell on it, love. Whoever it was didn't accept the offer, did he? So no real
harm done.'

Her words ran in Eloise's ears as she rode at Sir
Owain's side across the countryside to Sheen and,
although the air was heavily oppressive with a rum-
ble of thunder, she shivered beneath her cloak of soft
mulberry-dyed wool. Pale and silent, she mused upon
the disclosures of the day, wishing at times she had
not opened such an unsavoury can of worms, and
wondering how much more there was to be revealed
before she could discover the manner of his death.

Keeping his thoughts to himself, Sir Owain was
by no means sure that her morning's expedition with
Jolita had been as innocent as Eloise had suggested,
for surely the discovery that her brother had a mistress would not have affected her as much as this.
Was it, after all, Sir Piers's trail she was following?
If so, she had better be stopped.

After the noise, smells and oppressive heat of London, the fresh greenness of Sheen rippled under a
breeze that brought the gathering thunderclouds even
nearer, dousing the travellers with the first heavy
raindrops as they reached Sir Crispin's rambling wa-
terside dwelling. Now the surface of the darkening
river was pelted with a pattern of overlapping circles.
Thunder cracked open the sky, and Eloise was hauled
out of the saddle and carried inside with the rain
stinging her face.

The ride to Sheen had done nothing to clarify the
thoughts that jumbled ceaselessly through Eloise's

mind, thoughts that led her in countless directions and left her, rudderless and adrift. The state of her unease was more apparent to Sir Owain and Saskia than to Sir Crispin, who had matters of his own to occupy him, yet Sir Owain's attempts to understand the cause of Eloise's coolness were not appreciated.

He followed her along the open balcony outside the upper rooms that overlooked the busy hall where servants were lighting candles set in iron brackets. White billows of linen were settled upon long tables, and the orders of the hall-steward were muffled by the heavy thud of rain upon the roof. 'Eloise, wait!' he said. 'Where's your chamber?'

She shook her head, pretending not to hear him above the din, but he was prepared for her attempt at dismissal and, taking her by the waist, herded her along the balcony into an alcove where a large chest filled the space between two walls. 'Sit here,' he said, 'if you please.'

'Sir Owain, there are things—'

'You have to attend to. Yes, I know, but there are things I have to attend to also which will not withstand another of my lady's cold shoulders. Now, lass,' he said, sitting close to her side, 'you know what I'm talking about. What is it that's put you into this chilling mood again? And don't tell me it's nothing.'

'Then I have little to tell you. My brother, the woman and child. They concern me. That's all there is to it.'

'And you've discovered something else since we met at the Tower? You were concerned then, but not shocked as you are now. What is it?'

Her sigh was ragged and the tears that welled into her eyes were to do with the real reason for her anguish rather than for the one she used to sidetrack him. 'My father,' she said. 'He has a mistress, too.'

'And that has angered you?'

'Well, of course it has,' she replied, truthfully, 'though I suppose you're going to tell me that it's of no consequence as long as my mother doesn't find out. Well, I don't agree. It does matter. He's deceiving her. Did you know about it?'

'Yes, I knew.'

'And I expect you know whereabouts in London he keeps her.'

'Not in London; here, at Sheen.'

Suddenly immersed in a new angle to the affair, Eloise stood up as if to go in search of her. 'Where? Who is she? The woman who comes—?'

'Peace, lass!' Sir Owain pulled her back to him, fiercely. 'Not here in the house; your father's not stupid enough for that. She lives and works at the palace here in the Royal Wardrobe department. Why d'ye think he wanted to get back here so fast, eh?' He kissed her, lightly. 'Don't be angry with him, sweetheart. He's done well for you. His best. As much as any father could. You'd not deny that, would you?'

She could not trust herself to answer, her father's unfaithfulness being yet another side to his inconsistencies that seemed also to emphasise the notorious double standards that men carried. But at the same time, she had managed to evade Sir Owain's curiosity enough to give her next question an air of less consequence.

'Did you know that Rolph had lent money to Sir Piers?'

'I suspected as much, sometimes.'

'And did the king lend him money, too?'

'The *king*? I very much doubt it. Why do you ask that?'

'And what about Sir Walter de Mauny and Sir Phillip Cotterell? Did they lend my husband money? Did you?'

'Eloise, what's all this about? All Sir Piers's debts would have been recorded, wouldn't they? And paid off out of the estate? That's always the first thing to be done. In which case you must already know the answers to your questions, surely. Or is there something you've just discovered?'

He had not answered her directly. Perhaps she should not have asked. It was too direct. It would not do for him to know the extent of her enquiries. 'No...no, not at all. I was not an executor of Sir Piers's will so I have no way of knowing. It was a thought, no more than that.'

'But presumably Rolph told you of *his* loans?'

'Yes.'

'And does Mistress O'Farrell know of them?'

She knew what he was asking. The fact that he

had already suspected such 'loans' suggested that he understood the true nature of the transaction. 'If she did, she made no mention of it. I believe she's honest. I liked her. I only wish I could help her more. That child will not survive if he's not taken out of that filthy place. He's my nephew, isn't he?'

She stayed within his arms, longing for his protection yet more confused than ever by inexplicable fears and emotions. The only facts of which she could be sure were that Sir Piers had been disliked enough to make him a target, that he had misused her brother's friendship by blackmail, that he took other men's wives including Sir Phillip's, and that his debts had reached such proportions that he had offered to barter his own wife for his release. Another more personal consequence of this shameful offer was that the man, whoever he was, had not accepted it, either because he had felt the bargain to be a poor one, or because he believed he could obtain her by a cheaper method, or because the repayment of money meant more to him, or because he was too sorry for her to accept. Whatever the reasons, the discovery had severely dented Eloise's self-esteem, threatening to obliterate the events of the past few days which had helped her to begin trusting again. And still the spectre of Sir Owain's involvement in the affair loomed over it all. She longed to ask him and be given a whitewashed version of the truth, but that was not the way to a clear conscience for either of them.

'I'd like to visit Sheen Palace tomorrow,' she said into the darkness.

'Yes, my avenging angel,' he smiled, 'I'm sure you would.'

'I'm sorry, Janos. I cannot accept your advice, though I know it's sound. She's getting too close.' Sir Owain slipped his arms into the fur-lined dressing-gown that his squire held open, tyeing the leather girdle with more energy than was necessary. 'We have to go.'

'Then I fear you do the lady a disservice, sir. She's intelligent. Do you think taking her back to Derbyshire will stop her enquiries? Do you think she'll agree to go back with you?'

The reply was grim and uncompromising. 'Do I think she'll do as she's told? Not if she can help it, certainly, but my methods are quite effective, as a rule.'

'Be careful. You don't know your own strength.'

'Yes, I do, Janos, and you know my weaknesses, so no one will come to more harm than they have already. You're not concerned for my bruises, then?'

Father Janos closed the lid of his physic-chest and smiled. 'No, I'm far more concerned for the lady's. She left her chaplain behind at Handes, you know.'

'Best place for him,' Sir Owain muttered. 'And, Michael…' he turned to his eldest squire '…don't unpack everything. We shall be off again tomorrow.'

'Yes, sir. Shall I tell Mistress Saskia?'

'No, I'll tell her myself. And say your prayers before you sleep, lad. Father Janos needs someone to approve of.' He went out and closed the door silently behind him, his leather sandals making no sound upon the wooden floor that led to Eloise's chamber.

His discreet knock was answered immediately by Saskia, whose arms were full of clothes. 'My lady's not here,' she said.

'Where is she?'

'I'm really not sure, sir. She went out a while ago. Said she needed some fresh air before bed. Probably in the garden.'

'Are you unpacking, Saskia, or packing?'

'Unpacking, sir.'

'Then put them back. We're going up to Derbyshire tomorrow.'

Saskia's arms lowered. 'Oh, sir. My lady will not be best pleased.'

'All the same, mistress, we shall be going, pleased or not.'

The thunderstorm had passed over during supper when few had noticed how the pounding on the roof had softened and then ceased. The air smelt fragrant and fresh, and the grass squeaked beneath Sir Owain's sandals while heavy droplets bombarded his hair that caught at the low boughs of apple and walnut trees.

He wiped the water off his face and waited, listening, straining his eyes into the last lingering light, watching for any sign. Then, like a hound on a scent, he moved carefully towards the gate that led to the field beyond where a donkey had just snorted in greeting.

Quickly, Eloise dodged to one side, hoping to

merge into the shadows, to become invisible, transparent. The donkey's head followed her, jaws crunching noisily, nose nudging her for the next mouthful. Recklessly, and with mounting annoyance, she slid the wooden bolt out of its socket and, pushing the creature aside, bolted through the semidarkness into the long wet grass, leaving the donkey as a temporary obstruction. She ran, but stood no chance against her pursuer's speed. His hand scooped around her waist, throwing her sideways to land on top of him, then over and over in a sea of cool wetness that soaked instantly through her kirtle and chemise.

'Leave me be!' she yelped, struggling. 'Let go!'

But his arms and body held her, and she was no match for the man who had beaten all-comers to hold her. 'That I shall not do, my beauty,' he said. 'I have you and I shall not let you go. Ever. Do you hear?'

His words found one of her worst bruises. 'Lies,' she cried, weeping into the grass. 'Men are liars, cheats…deceivers…weaklings…let me go…I want no man…let me *be*!' The storm of tears raged while, hardly noticed by her, Sir Owain hauled her into his arms and began to undo her hair, letting it fall like a dark shadow into the long stalks of meadowsweet.

'Stop,' she sobbed. 'Just go home and leave me alone.' Held against his chest, her protests were absorbed against his warmth, her back-lacings nimbly undone, her kirtle peeled away with expert hands. 'You've done this before!' she snarled, between sobs.

'Never with such purpose, my beauty, and never

in a field of soaking wet grass.' Undeterred by her lack of co-operation, he pulled her arms out of her long sleeves and held her immobile as the kirtle and chemise were tucked in a damp pile beneath her buttocks, by which time both of them were slippery with rain and tears, her squeals long since overtaken by sobs of helpless anger.

She sat against him, her wrists held behind her in one of his while, with his other hand, he gathered together the stalks of lady's-mantle in which rain had gathered in the cup-shaped leaves, tipping the rainwater on to her and washing her down with slow sweeping strokes as if he was grooming her. Over her neck and breasts his hands bathed and caressed, lingering provocatively when she arched her back in a wave of ecstasy that transformed her sobs into gasps.

'That's better, sweetheart,' he whispered. 'It's been a long hot day and then a thunderstorm, and this is what you need more than tears and arguments.' He released her hands and let them push the fur-lined gown off his shoulders, and she clung to him as he bent her backwards, presenting her beautiful full breasts to the exploration of his lips.

Her mind blurred as something inside her stirred and ached, triggered by the warm tugging of his mouth. This was still new to her, this tenderness. It was all so new, even what she did next, instinctively. 'Let me...' she murmured, straddling him as he sat, guiding him into her but then, wet and slippery, fell off again, laughing, because she was unused to it.

They toppled sideways into a new patch of cool wet grass, still joined and pulsing, laughing as another shower of water shocked them into urgent and forceful action that took them by surprise with its incredible power.

Bathed, cleansed, and oblivious to the donkey grazing nearby, they lost themselves in each other, in the earth and in the night, drowning in pleasure and release. Later, Eloise could not tell whether the muffled roar she heard was herself or her lover, nor could she answer him when, wrapped inside his embrace, he lifted the wet hair from her face and whispered. 'Was that too rough for you, sweetheart? You're not hurt?'

The gentle wandering of her hands assured him that nothing less would have done, that his lovemaking was unique, his kisses sheer bliss, his aftercare remarkable. He washed her down again over the lower reaches which had escaped his attention before, rolling her on to her face, turning a deaf ear to her half-protests and washing her back and thighs with long watery fingers. He parted her legs to reach the tenderest places that, despite their fierce encounter, still ached for his touch. His ablutions lingered there as they had done before, and now Eloise held his wrist, silently pleading with him to continue.

Boldly, he swept his hand over her. 'To make up for all those times when you should have been by my side, as my woman? You'll never find me wanting, my beauty, not in any department, I swear it. We'll have sons and daughters, beautiful thoroughbred creatures, dark chestnuts, wild and wilful like their mother. Shall we?'

'Not pliant and obedient?'

'Nay, not that. That was said only to rile you, lass.'

'Then love me again, Owain. Once more, before they lock the doors on us.'

Hours later, relaxed in body and in spirit, they lay at peace in the candlelit warmth of Eloise's bed as if their wild and earthy coupling had worn the edges off all fears as a torrent does with boulders. The fears still lurked, but now she could live with them.

Stroking his chest and tenderly following the pattern of hair with her fingertips, she noted how his bruises were changing colour from purple to green. 'Why has Saskia not unpacked, I wonder?' she said. 'What was she doing when you saw her?'

'Unpacking,' he said, drowsily. 'I told her to repack.'

Her hand stopped. 'To repack? Why?'

'Because I'm taking you up to Whitecliffe later tomorrow.'

'No! No, Owain! I cannot do that, not so soon.' She squirmed away, trying to sit up. 'I cannot go tomorrow, not even this week. I haven't finished—' She stopped, just in time.

He pulled her down, pinning her to the pillow. 'Finished what?'

'My…er…visiting. I've not finished seeing London, the palaces. I wanted to visit Sheen Palace, and Windsor, too.' Her eyes clouded with anger again.

'And the merchants. I've bought no new clothes or any physics from the apothecaries. No, Owain... please...not tomorrow.'

'Leave it,' he whispered, holding her fierceness with one quelling look. 'I understand how brief the stay has been, but enough is enough, Eloise, at least for the time being. What we need now is some time to get to know each other and for you to see what you'll be marrying into. Anything else can wait. I was made to give the king my assurance that we'd be wed before September is out, and he won't tolerate any more delays.'

'September? Three months?'

'Three months. Now, I've done something to make the idea of our departure easier for you to digest.'

She frowned. He was wrong. Enough was not enough when she had not done all that she had meant to do, particularly at Windsor, and now there would be no more opportunities left to her.

'About Mistress O'Farrell,' Sir Owain said, watching the frown clear.

'Rolph's mistress? What about her?'

'I've sent a wagon and escorts for her and her child, her goods and chattels, and I've sent money and a note to Sister Anna at St Katherine's telling her that, from now on, Mistress O'Farrell will be living in Derbyshire in the household of Sir Owain of Whitecliffe and his wife-to-be. Does that help?'

A slow blink and a smile changed Eloise's expression to the softness he had hoped to see. Her hands reached up to caress the soft skin of his ears and the short hair in front of them. His eyes were almost closed with tiredness.

'Thank you…thank you,' she said. 'You think of everything.'

'I think of you, mostly,' he said before he kissed her. 'Now, lady. Shall we go home tomorrow?'

'Yes, sir. If you wish it.'

In the weeks that followed, Eloise took every opportunity to put aside the bittersweet sense of foreboding that had stubbornly pervaded all her thoughts since Sir Owain's claim on her had begun to materialise. After what he had been through to win her, she could no longer doubt his determination, nor could she continually repeat her objections to him when he had assured her they were unfounded. She must now look forward, as he had prescribed, though it was not easy to release the control and to set off in a different direction after all her well-laid plans had failed.

The new location made things easier, in one sense, for the castle at Whitecliffe was far more beautiful than she had imagined it to be, and there was much concerning Sir Owain's life that she had so far made no effort to discover. That he was the eldest of four, for instance, a brother and a sister married, the youngest brother living at Whitecliffe and, according to Sir Owain, never likely to leave.

At seventeen, Nathaniel was already a brilliant scholar who was happiest with pen, paper and books, tutor and music-master. He was shy, delightful, and physically not unlike his eldest brother except for a deformed foot that turned badly inwards. And while he hero-worshipped Sir Owain, he also admired Father Janos and fell in love with Eloise at first sight, which he could do nothing to conceal.

Other relationships had begun to form that indicated how the pattern of life was, at last, falling into place. Father Janos, after discovering that he had known Saskia's father, had found more in common with the down-to-earth Flemish maid than either of them had thought possible, and though they had no physical relationship in mind, the pleasure they derived from each other's company was obvious to everyone, especially when they spoke Flemish together. It would be a pity indeed if any calamity should bring that to an end.

Then there was Mistress Marie O'Farrell who, contrary to Eloise's expectations, showed more interest in expressing her gratitude for her deliverance from hard times than in re-establishing contact with the father of her child. 'No, I thank you,' she said to Eloise who prepared to ride over to Handes Castle with Sir Owain, 'I'd be obliged if you would tell Sir Rolph that we're here, safe and well, and that's all. It would be far better if we left things like that, especially when Lady Griselle will need his attention more than I do. I'm more content to watch the bloom return to my Christopher's cheeks and to see him wolf a meal down as he did this morning. I feel I'm doing less than I ought to earn our keep, my lady. This seems too much like heaven to last.'

Eloise had made her an infusion of calendula and chamomile petals for her hands and another of juniper berries and verjuice for Christopher's head-lice. 'Marie,' she said, 'Saskia is glad to have your help, and so am I. I never thought to have two ladies to wait on me and, in a place this size, there's far more to be done than there is at Haughton Manor.'

Too much like heaven to last. So, she was not the only one to feel it. At Handes Castle, Eloise imparted no such fears to her mother, only her happiness to have come this close to heaven, which was more than many women did. Feeling like a conspirator, she passed on loving messages from her father and, to her brother, she related how Marie was content to be liberated and well-tended without making any further demands upon him. Which appeared to do little for his sore conscience.

Sir Rolph had recovered well from his injuries and would be returning home to Staffordshire within the next few days. Did Eloise intend to return to Haughton Manor soon?

'I must, you know,' she said to Sir Owain as they rode back to Whitecliffe that evening. 'It'll be August next week, and nearly Lammas, and so far I've sent only messages to Master atte Welle. It's time I went home.'

'Home?' He regarded her from beneath lowered brows.

'Well, yes. For a few days, at least.' She smiled, keeping her eyes fixed between the palfrey's grey ears. She had purposely used her steward's title rather than his Christian name. 'Shall you come with me?'

'I'll come, my lady, if only to check out this steward of yours who had such high and mighty designs upon my woman. The place will soon belong to me, so I'd better take a look at it, I suppose. Will next week do?'

'Well enough, sir. But I must insist that you don't gloat all over the place. I shall have a hard enough job to explain to him what happens next without you looking like the cat that's swallowed the songthrush.'

His mouth twitched at the corners. 'I *shall* gloat,' he said, perversely. 'What else would he expect of me after this performance?'

With Sir Owain to take command, the forthcoming visit to Haughton Manor in Staffordshire would hold none of the problems she had implied, Stephen atte Welle having been well aware of the possible failure of her London mission. He had received her messages with equanimity, having been assured that his position as steward was safe, with or without a wife, and his former master's relatives who had once tried every device to interfere in Lady Eloise's affairs had now gone quiet at the news of Sir Owain of Whitecliffe's involvement. In that respect, Eloise's future had a more settled outlook than ever before.

Meanwhile, Sir Owain took her hawking up beyond the limestone crags where Whitecliffe sprawled against a forested hillside. At times, they went off alone into secluded dells to make love, unable to wait for the night, and Eloise made daisy-chains for his head, and for other parts too, with more joy than either of them had known for years. Watching him practice at the quintain and school his squires in the tiltyard, she discovered that the condemnation she had once voiced so loudly had turned instead to shouts of approval and even unwanted advice which he deliberately took amiss and made her forfeit a kiss when it failed. Never had she been so happy, so proud, so much in love.

Their nights were never long enough, their days too short; any thoughts of losing even the smallest part of this new happiness bringing a steeliness to her heart, a resolve that had been lacking before. Stronger and more confident, less defensive, she began to prepare a place for optimism to grow like a delicate and rare healing herb.

They saw it as little more than an ill-timed interruption to their idyll when, two days before they were due to set out for Staffordshire, a message came from Westminster commanding Sir Owain to attend a special tournament at Smithfield in London.

'Do you *have* to go?' Eloise whispered into his soapy ear as he sat in the wooden bathtub. His hair was damp and smelt of hay.

'Yes, I do, sweetheart. It's a contest against his Grace's prestigious prisoners-of-war. He wants me to lead a team and I cannot refuse. Only a few days, then I'll be back.'

'We could go as far as Staffordshire together. It's on the way.'

He kissed her arms that linked around his shoulders. 'M-m-m. I'll come with you as far as your manor and go on to London the next day. How will that do?'

'Perhaps I should come with you to protect you from all those audacious women.'

'I only know one audacious woman, and she's here.' Inch by inch he hauled her round until she lost her balance and fell sideways on to his lap, still half-dressed, laughing and protesting at the wet.

'Pliant,' he chuckled, 'but not yet obedient. Hold your noise and kiss me, woman!'

The fight that ensued was messy, and weighted heavily against Eloise.

Chapter Ten

Eloise's marital home at Haughton Manor was small compared to Whitecliffe, a problem which Sir Piers Gerrard had tried to solve by adding extensions, most of which he could not afford. Building work had been suspended, leaving piles of stone, scaffolding, rubble and timber at every corner, much of which had since been stolen by villagers for their own more modest dwellings. The stables where Sir Piers had kept his expensive destriers were now being used as grain stores, and Eloise had made a convenient distillery for her medications in the mews where he had once bred the rarest falcons.

Her three Irish wolfhounds were overjoyed to see their mistress once more; her reception from Master Stephen atte Welle, whilst more restrained, was just as warm. There was no resentment of Sir Owain's success either, only genuine congratulations, the two men spending much of the day in amicable discussion about the affairs of the manor.

The night before Sir Owain's departure for London was both passionate and tearful, though even at this stage Eloise could not bring herself to tempt Fate further by telling him of her overpowering love for him. Still fearfully hearing the last whispered warnings of cynicism, she had to agree that that would be foolish indeed.

'Don't weep, sweetheart,' he whispered. 'It's not for long. Do you not recall how you wept, only a few weeks ago, when I got too close to you? Eh?'

'I've changed my mind,' she croaked. 'Hurry back to me.'

'As soon as it's over. Nothing will keep me there, I promise. And I'll leave Father Janos with you, if you like. Since you let Father Eamonn go to Lady Griselle, I'd feel happier if you kept Janos here for support.'

'Thank you, dearest. But won't you need him?'

'Not before my return. I shall have nought to confess.'

'Owain, will you take something with you? To bring good fortune?'

'If you wish. What is it?'

'The diamond. Keep it by you and bring it back to me.'

Next morning at dawn, Sir Owain had placed the blue velvet pouch in his luggage, promising to keep it safe and kissing Eloise with a fierceness that lingered on her lips as she watched his departure, waving to the retinue of men, horses and pack-mules until they disappeared into the haze.

With Sir Owain's departure and the return of Sir Rolph to his nearby home at Coven Hall in Staffordshire, the possibility of Eloise furthering her enquiries about Sir Piers's death seemed once more to be within her grasp, for now she could visit her brother alone to question him without opposition. But days passed in which there were more attractive tasks needing her attention at Haughton Manor, for the rich summer pickings from the garden and fields would not wait. Soon, all three women were involved from morn till night in the herb-plots and still-room, hanging bundles to dry on the racks above them, decanting rosewater from the glass alembics, filling bottles, jars and boxes with lotions and ointments. The shelves began to fill and, as word got round, a queue of villagers began to wait at her door for her ministrations, as they had done before.

Each night, Eloise half-decided to use the next day for her visit, and each night she fell asleep with the memory of his arms and the opposing half-decision to leave things as they were, in case something should be revealed that would wreck her happiness unnecessarily early. Leave it, he had told her. Enough is enough. He was right.

Others had found fulfilment in the daily tasks at Haughton. Both Marie O'Farrell and Saskia had noticed how young Christopher and Stephen atte Welle had taken to each other like long-lost father and son, both being gentle mannerly souls. Stephen had found a pony of three times the lad's age, given him some lessons in how to stay in the saddle, and taken him several times to market in the nearby town.

'Aye,' Saskia said, pushing down a white sticky mess into a jar with a stick. 'Master atte Welle's been eyeing you since you arrived, Marie lass. Did you not know that?'

'Me? Rubbish! He'd not be—'

'Yes, he would. He's a man and he knows how to reach a woman's heart as well as a woman does a man's. Different route, same strategy.'

'Christopher thinks he's wonderful,' Marie said, thoughtfully.

'He's a good man,' said Eloise, 'and you two could run this place between you. Take the chance if it's offered, Marie. Don't be too proud.'

'Christopher needs a father,' Marie said, 'otherwise he'll be a bastard all his life.'

'And Marie needs a husband,' said Saskia. 'Your life has moved on, love. Keep up with it.' She tied a waxed linen lid over a pot. 'And pass me those bits of parchment, if you will. This'll need a label on it.'

Whether it was the talk of the future or whether because she was concerned that her courses had not appeared on time, Eloise could not sleep that night. Dark fears bore down on her, unnamed, irrational, her mind delving into every depressing crevice of her negativity which she thought had been replaced over the last few joyous weeks. She wept, unable to say why, unable to hold herself together. 'God in heaven,' she whispered to Saskia, 'keep him safe. For pity's sake, keep him safe, for I cannot do without him now.'

'Oh come, love, that's foolish talk. There's no reason to believe that he's not safe. He'll be back here by the end of the week, most likely.'

But three days later, that prediction was proved wrong when Father Janos strode across to the still-room in the old mews accompanied by a very breathless and red-faced messenger, one of her father's men, who looked ready to drop. The priest's expression was grave. 'My lady, there's news from London,' he said. 'From Sir Crispin.'

Eloise was able to remember those words for the rest of her life. And her own that followed. 'Bad news,' she whispered. 'I know it. Don't tell me.'

'A stool for my lady,' Father Janos said to Saskia. 'Here. Sit down here.'

The messenger leaned against the bench, gulping down the ale that Marie offered him. His clothes and face were streaked with dust from the road.

'Just tell me, Father,' Eloise said. 'It's Sir Owain, isn't it? Is he…?'

'No, he's not. Sir Owain was still alive when this man left London.'

'Where? At Cold Harbour?'

'No, he's at St Bartholemew's Hospital. You know, the one at Smithfield on the way to—'

'Yes, I know the one. But what of his injuries? They're serious, then?' She knew that they were, if they had not taken him further than Smithfield itself.

The messenger was clearly upset. 'Yes, m'lady. At the jousts. A chance blow by one of the Frenchies. He was winning, was Sir Owain, but a blow to his helm, a chance blow…' he repeated, 'an accident…and he fell…lost a lot of blood. They carried him off, but…'

'But what?'

'But he didn't wake. They say he'll not…' For all his size and strength, the young man held his head in his hands and sobbed. 'He'll not…not…'

Cold fear flooded over Eloise. 'When was this?' she snapped.

'Three days,' the messenger gasped. 'I came straight from Smithfield. Sir Crispin sent me with two others. Michael his squire is with him. The brothers are tending him. They say he cannot be moved. Gave him the last rites—'

'That's enough!' Father Janos said, firmly. 'Mistress O'Farrell, would you take the messengers into the hall and tend them? Thank you.' He turned back to Eloise. 'We must decide what's to be done. I can go immediately.'

'I shall go,' Eloise said. 'You, me and Saskia. We shall get him out of there and take him home.'

'But if the brothers say he should not be moved, my lady, we cannot…'

Trembling with shock, Eloise found a sudden and vigorous anger swamping every emotion except love, taking poor Father Janos aback with its velocity. 'Yes, we can!' she snapped at him. 'He's mine, Father, and I am his. We belong together, and I'm not

leaving him at St Bart's when we can tend him our-
selves. We have as much knowledge between us as
they do. Probably more. And if *we* can't get him
safely home, then we're not trying hard enough.' She
saw the concern in the priest's eyes. 'I'm sorry, Father, I mean no disrespect, but I'm not going to lose
him. Not now. It's not going to happen again. I
cannot let it happen.' Tears flooded her eyes, making
them sparkle like diamonds.

With a nod, the priest placed a gentle hand on her
arm and held it. 'Courage,' he said. 'It won't happen
again. We'll go together and we'll take him to Whitecliffe. Now, shall we go in and see how best to plan
this? There's no time to be lost, by the sound of
things.'

Saskia held her in comforting arms, confirming Father Janos's opinion. 'It won't happen again,' she
said, smoothing her back. 'This is not like those other
times. This is different.'

'Is it?'

'Yes. Then, you were not able to do anything
about it. This time, you are. This time, you must; and
you've got us.'

They set out for London that same afternoon with
at least six hours of daylight left to them. Marie had
pleaded to be allowed to go, but Eloise insisted it
would be best for her to stay at Haughton with her
son, though Marie had some interesting advice to offer.

'St Bartholemew's is where I worked before I

moved to St Katherine's,' she told Eloise as they packed an assortment of newly made salves and sedatives. 'It's where I met Sir Rolph when he was injured after a tournament, and I know the physician, Master John of Gaddesdon.'

'Yes? Then he must be one of the best, I suppose.'

'He has a reputation, my lady, and a conceit to go with it. He'll not take kindly to having an important patient like Sir Owain removed from his care. Be careful.'

'Thank you for the warning, Marie. Forewarned is fore-armed. But I shall have Father Janos with me, remember.'

'Ye-s.' The sound was not enthusiastic, but Eloise had had no time to ask why, or to care that it was not for a woman to enter a man's domain.

She sent a message to Whitecliffe, preparing Nathaniel and the household for their eventual arrival with Sir Owain, also one to her mother and brother. Stopping only to eat and sleep, the small party of riders used up every daylight hour to push forward, silent and intent and far removed in spirit from their last journey only a few weeks earlier. With each mile, Eloise's determination hardened, willing him to hang on to life. She could not let him go.

Exhausted, they arrived at Smithfield in the fading light to the sound of the muted Compline bell that echoed softly from the great priory church of St Bartholemew. Opposite, near the northern wall of the city, stood the hospital buildings which Eloise had never thought she would enter for any reason. At this moment, tired or not, she would have fought her way inside.

Their request for admittance was at first politely refused. 'The hours of visiting are past,' they were told, 'and Sir Owain has had a stream of visitors all day. Well-wishers have crowded our doors, and ladies are never permitted within the hospice, I fear. Only the nursing sisters and—'

'Yes, brother, we are aware of that,' said Father Janos, dismounting. 'Kindly tell the master, Richard Sutton, that we are here as a matter of great urgency. We have travelled far. The lady is Sir Owain's betrothed, and I am his chaplain.'

The door-keeper returned with the master, a dark and sensuous man who bowed gravely, welcoming them in. 'But of course, my lady,' he said, in sympathetic tones, eyeing Eloise beneath lazily hooded lids. 'Your father, Sir Crispin, has visited our illustrious patient each morning. The king himself has insisted that our physician, Master John, should tend personally to his needs. He can have no better attention than that. And who knows how much time Sir Owain has left? Of course you must see him. And you, Brother…?'

Eloise put him on the right track. 'This is Sir Owain's personal physician and chaplain, Father Janos Leuvenhoek. And my maid, Mistress Borremans. Please, can you tell me how Sir Owain is?'

Master Sutton sighed and shook his head, shifting his eyes away from Eloise's figure for the first time. 'Tch! We've tried most things to wake him, but to no effect, so far. It was a nasty blow to the head, my lady. Knocked his helm off. He fell badly, and we think there may be leg injuries.'

'You *think*?' Eloise frowned. 'Where is he? May we see him now?'

'Of course, since you are family. Almost. We've put him in a private cell, an expensive comfort, but it's only a matter of time, I fear. We pray for him constantly, my lady, I assure you.'

They followed the black-clad Master Sutton along whitewashed corridors to where a low arched doorway led into a dimly lit room, starkly furnished except for the white-covered bed, a small table and stools, and a crucifix on the wall. The monk who kept vigil at the bedside rose as they entered and, with downcast eyes, bowed and went out.

Eloise took his place, horrified by the still pale face, almost unrecognisable in a swathe of head bandages, eyes sunk deep into brown sockets, lips blue-tinged, the nose pinched. 'Oh, my God!' she whispered. 'Owain…beloved.' Her lips on his forehead tasted his cold sweat. Appalled, she stared at Father Janos.

The priest had seen. 'What treatment is he receiving?' he asked. 'May we see his wounds?' Already he had his hand on Sir Owain's pulse.

'Er…well,' Master Sutton stuttered, uncomfortable with the request and unwilling to take responsibility, '…er, perhaps it would be best if you were to ask Master John Gaddesdon in the morning.'

'I am Sir Owain's physician, Master, and Lady

Eloise is skilled at healing. None more so. We know what we are doing, I assure you. Could you provide us with a bowl of hot water and some towels, please?' Father Janos removed the black cloak that covered his white habit, anticipating Eloise's mind.

Scowling, Master Sutton disappeared. It was too late for this game and he'd already interrupted his supper for them. People could be so unco-operative.

'He said,' Eloise muttered, folding down the sheet, 'that they *thought* he might have leg injuries, but how can they not know after all these days? And haven't they given him water? Or food?' She lifted the white linen nightshirt off his legs and stared in horror at his left leg, mottled red and purple and swollen inside tight skin. 'Look at this! They've not even poulticed it.'

'We must get him out of here,' said Father Janos, grimly. 'Let's have some more light, Mistress Saskia. Over here. Saints have mercy! This is nasty. Let's take a look at his head wound, shall we, m'lady?'

'Can you ease him forward while I undo the bandage?'

A voice snapped at them shrilly from the doorway. 'What in heaven's name d'ye think you're doing? Leave my patient at once!'

None of the three paid the slightest attention.

The door closed. 'Do you hear me? I am John of Gaddesdon, Master Physician of this hospital. No one may interfere with my patients.'

'Then if you wait long enough, Master John Gaddesdon,' Eloise countered, 'Sir Owain will not *be* your patient, will he? In fact, he won't be anyone's patient. What is there to interfere with, exactly? Life? Or death?' By this time, the bandage had been removed and Sir Owain's battered head laid back on the pillow. 'Bring the light up, Saskie. I can scarce see which is hair and which is blood.'

'I was about to begin a different treatment tomorrow morning,' said John of Gaddesdon. He was very short and rotund in his all-black garb except for a rim of white surplice showing at the bottom. His face was ruddy and heavy-jowled, his lower lip hanging loosely over a chin that had lost itself in his throat. Eyes, mean and petulant, swept continually up and down the unwanted guests, particularly lingering over Father Janos's white habit. 'We would have shaved the back of his head and administered a plaster of oil or roses, verjuice and wild celery,' he said, pompously. 'And what do *you* know about wounds, sir?' He advanced to the bottom of the bed.

Eloise glared at him. 'Master Gaddesdon,' she said, 'may we ask what you know about *this* wound? Have you taken the trouble to inspect it? Personally?'

'Well…yes, of course I have. Such wounds are often best left alone, you know, and, in my long experience, the evil humours that cause false sleep must be extracted by blood-letting at the most auspicious times, which according to my reckoning, will be—'

'Which will be when he's got no more blood to give, sir, if I may say so,' said Father Janos, angrily. 'Can you not see his colour in this light? Does he look as if he has any to spare?'

'And who *are* you, sir?' Again, the Master Physician swept his eyes over Father Janos with obvious disdain.

The priest, not given to boasting, was tempted too far. 'Father Janos Leuvenhoek, chaplain to Sir Owain, trained in theology and medicine at Leuven and Bologna. A sound curriculum by anybody's standards. And yes, Master Gaddesdon, Dominican priests have two arms, two legs and one head, just like Augustinian canons, as you see. Does that reassure you?'

The man glowered uncomfortably. 'I have nothing against Dominicans,' he said, 'but I cannot have my authority challenged; there can be only one line of treatment, Father.'

'Then that's easily settled, sir. We shall remove Sir Owain from your care.'

'And condemn him to certain death. He cannot be moved.'

While they spoke, Eloise was carefully examining the patient's head under the lamp that Saskia held, parting the thick hair matted with blood and exclaiming at the damage. 'Father,' she said, urgently, 'this must be attended to immediately. It's a fracture.'

'Tut, lady,' John of Gaddesdon contradicted, 'a poultice of pigeons' droppings with honey will often cure...excessive harmful matter...' He droned on as the hot water and towels arrived carried by two white-robed nursing sisters.

Eloise took the chance to ask them, 'Where is the

young squire who was at his master's side when he was brought in here? His name is Michael.'

'Michael was dismissed, my lady,' one of them said. 'He was sent back to Cold Harbour, Sir Owain's London home.'

'I see. Thank you. Now, with St Bart's reputation for hospitality, do you think you could provide the men and horses in our retinue with food and shelter for the night? We three will stay here, but they are exhausted and they cannot reach Cold Harbour now that the city gates have been locked and the curfew sounded.'

'Certainly, my lady. We'll attend to it.'

'And tell Master Sutton, if you please, that my father will make a generous donation to the hospice.' She smiled at them. 'He'll not be out of pocket. Now, Master Gaddesdon, do you wish to assist us, or do you prefer to be a spectator? We're going to open this wound up. Saskia, bring up the physic-chest, will you?'

Unwilling, but far too curious to be left out, John of Gaddesdon followed his guests' example and rolled up his sleeves, washing his hands and watching with some scepticism as Saskia unrolled a waxed linen bag holding a mass of feathery plant-life.

'Water-moss,' she said.

'Hold his head quite still,' said Eloise, 'while I snip this hair away.' Carefully, she cut the hair close to the scalp, dismissing from her mind that this was the man she adored. She cleansed the bare patch with an infusion of St John's wort and rosemary, then she

cut the skin around the area where splinters of bone
had been crushed into small particles like spears
waiting to pierce and wound. Delicately, each tiny
splinter was lifted away without piercing the
membrane beneath, while Father Janos cleaned the
area again with a distillation made only a few days
ago of plantain, honeysuckle and white rose petals.

'I think,' Eloise told him, 'that you should have
the honour of packing your employer's head with the
water-moss. That's it. In a tidy layer. No pressure.
Now, we bind it gently and wait. Oh, my poor sweet
thing.'

It was well into the early hours of the morning
before they had finished discovering and treating his
wounds, including the cleaning and poulticing of a
badly inflamed leg. Master Gaddesdon had no explanation for not treating the swelling, nor had he discovered the broken collarbone, a common injury.

At intervals, Eloise moistened Sir Owain's lips
with boiled water sweetened with honey and, as
dawn lightened the high window of the cell, they
watched the faintest tint of pink to reach his lips, at
last.

John of Gaddesdon had bid them a subdued goodnight and left them to it, but Eloise and her two sup-
porters nibbled at a cold supper brought to them by
one of the women, too weary to taste it. 'Now for
the next battle,' she said. 'How to get him out of
here.'

Father Janos was full of admiration for her courage. 'Do you know,' he said, 'that when we came in here last night I could not have said with any certainty that he'd survive another hour or two. And he has. Unless something goes badly wrong, I believe he may yet pull through. You were right, you know.'

'About what?'

'We *do* know more than they do. But you know more than any of us. I've never seen that done before.'

'Nor have I. I'd only heard about a woman who did it on a man who fell off a cliff. And we found some water-moss just the day before we...' Her face crumpled. 'Oh, Janos! I can't...can't bear it. The thought of losing him...oh, please God...don't let him go. Please!'

The priest's hand closed over her arm as Saskia placed an arm around her shoulders and, together with Saskia's hand in the priest's, they made a circle of comfort over the unconscious form in the bed.

The problem of how to remove Sir Owain from the hospice without an undignified tussle was solved in a matter of an hour by the appearance of Sir Crispin de Molyns who, until his dawn arrival at St Bartholemew's, had known nothing of his daughter's prompt response to his message.

'Father!' Eloise flung herself into his arms, clinging like a lost child.

'Lass,' he murmured. 'Nay, I'd no idea you'd be flying down at this pace. You arrived last night, so they tell me. You must hardly have stopped for breath. Father Janos, how do you do, man? And you too, Saskia.'

'Did Master Sutton complain of the trouble we've caused him?' Eloise wanted to know.

Smiling at the radical change of heart, he hugged her. 'Well, let me put it this way, love. They're far more in awe of you than they are of me. Have they not done well for him?'

She wiped her eyes and released him. 'He's in a mess,' she said. 'Look. Heaven knows what they've been doing. Emptied him of blood, for one thing.'

'Apparently,' Sir Crispin told her, 'he bled profusely from the nose. They had a problem stopping it. I believe they did what they could.'

Father Janos was looking ahead. 'We need to get him away from here, sir. Could you use your influence to have him taken to Cold Harbour, for the time being?'

'Of course. Is that what you want?'

'Yes, Father. Between us, we can give him all the care he needs. Then we can take him up to Whitecliffe. He *must* have the best. He's very poorly. I never thought to see him like this.' Her voice broke again.

'You're tired out, lass. And you, both of you. We'll have him out of here in no time. Leave it to me.'

More than anyone else in the king's service, Sir Crispin had access to the most sumptuous wagons, the best horses and drivers, and teams of men to bear the recumbent knight, heavily bandaged, bolstered and supported, to the well-prepared chamber at Cold Harbour in which he and Eloise had spent the blissful night of their betrothal.

'And now,' Saskia said with a sad glance at the smooth bed with its unconscious occupant, 'the place looks even more like a battlefield than it did then.'

Until then, Eloise had not known what it was to devote every moment of every hour to the struggle between life and death. Being sure of her love for him was one thing, but the all-consuming and desperate compulsion to keep him and hold him against every threat now became her one and only aim in life, not only to deny Fate another success but because life was unthinkable without him. Her bouts of weeping were few and private; her sleeping and eating fitful and brief. Her anger at the state of her beloved was fearsome, and it was not arrogance that made her sure she and Janos could do better but disgust that John of Gaddesdon of international reputation had done so little. She had heard it from one of the nursing sisters that the Physician's next treatment was to have been to plunge Sir Owain into a bath in which a fox had previously been boiled so that he might absorb some of the fox's characteristics. Exactly which ones were not specified.

In theory, Father Janos, Michael the squire, Saskia and Eloise were to have taken turns to stay by Sir Owain's bedside but, in practice, Eloise could not tear herself away for long, watching for any sign, taking his pulse, bathing him, feeding him sips of an infusion made from nettles, parsley, watercress and honey to renew his blood. To their delight, he accepted it and kept it down. On the second day after their abscondment from St Bartholemew's, his eyelids blinked open long enough to show them that the man inside was aware of them, even in half-sleep and, later that evening, his fingers moved tentatively across Eloise's hand as she sat cutting his fingernails.

'Beloved?' She looked up and saw his dark eyes resting upon her, pensively. His lips moved, and she placed her head near him, straining to catch the sound upon his breath. Then she smiled and kissed his forehead. 'No, my love, you're not in heaven. Not yet. You're in bed at Cold Harbour, and Janos is here, and Michael, and Saskia. We shall care for you. You're in good hands. And that's as near to heaven as you'll be getting for a while.'

She thought he smiled at that before he sank back into sleep, but that delicate first contact was enough to prompt a hug of celebration for Father Janos and Saskia and, later, Sir Walter de Mauny who came to see his friend as he had done each day. The house at Cold Harbour was rarely empty of callers—Jolita and Henry, Sir Crispin, Lord and Lady Pace, and the French prisoner-of-war who had accidentally caused the injuries. His jousting horse, borrowed from an Englishman, was unused to his commands in French and had swerved at the critical moment, he explained to them. In trying to lift his lance up and out of the danger zone, he had caught its tip under the neckpiece of Sir Owain's helm, making his injuries more serious by a fall onto the sharp edge of the damaged head-piece.

'So *dangereux*,' he said to Eloise, gesticulating. 'Even with a *trois* teep...' he held up three pronged fingers '...ees so *dangereux*. Sir Owain ees *magnifique*! My 'eart eet go...' he pounded his chest '...when I fight with cem. I would *trés* rather fight weeth you, *belle dame*.' His laugh was soft and genuinely charming, and Eloise was touched by his concern. He had brought apricots and a message from the king, whose prisoner he was.

The visitors' talk invariably turned to the dangers of the sport, the risks and injuries. And had she not been so totally committed to saving Sir Owain's life, this might have stimulated her resolution to get to the bottom of the mystery surrounding the Windsor tournament of 1350. She came close to it during the long night hours as she and Father Janos talked quietly across the bed.

'I know I'm asking the wrong person,' she whispered to him, searching his compassionate face, 'but there's no one else for me to ask. You are his loyal friend. He is your employer. But there's something I need to know.'

'I am also his confessor,' Father Janos replied, 'and I know what it is that you need to know.'

'You do?'

'Yes. The answer is that he was not involved in any conspiracy to kill your late husband. There *was* no conspiracy. Nor did Sir Phillip Cotterell intend to kill him, any more than Monsieur de Grise intended to kill Sir Owain. It's a dangerous game. You know that.'

'Yes, I do know. So what happened, Father? Why the mystery?'

'He'll tell you himself—' he nodded to the sleeping patient '—in due course.'

But his assurance was not entirely the palliative it was meant to be, Eloise's cynicism being not altogether relinquished. If Sir Owain had wanted her to know, he would surely have told her by now. It did, however, help her to cross one more hurdle to know that the man she loved, the one she had promised to marry, was in no way responsible for her becoming a widow.

That same night, while she was alone with Sir Owain, she whispered her love to him, over and over, in every permutation of words she could devise. She told him how long she had yearned for him, denied him, and yearned still more in secret. She told him of her dreams and how the reality had been far sweeter, more imaginative, more profound. She begged his forgiveness for her perverse behaviour due, she said, to anger, insecurity, and an increasing lack of confidence. She would not let him go. They needed each other, now more than ever. They had always needed each other.

She did not expect any response, sleep having claimed him long before the start of her confession.

The following week brought gradual but positive improvements to Sir Owain's condition which con-

vinced his guardians that he was now out of immediate danger. He had lost a great deal too much
blood, and the blow to his head had concussed him,
causing pain which they relieved with warm poul-
tices of barley, betony and vervain. By mouth, they
gave him the same powdered willow-bark they had
used on Eloise's brother, and hung a bag of periwin-
kle flowers around his neck to prevent a repetition
of the dreaded nose-bleed. Eloise fed him sops of
bread soaked in barley soup which, being cool and
dry in the first degree, was excellent for dealing with
the fever caused by his inflamed leg.

To his whispered request for, 'Something that
tastes of something,' Eloise responded with spoon-
fuls of bone marrow from an ox, pounded together
with an egg yolk and baked. 'Anything,' she whispered, when they were alone. 'I will get anything you
ask for. I'll reach down the moon if you want me to.
It's made of green cheese, they say.'

'Too far,' he murmured. 'I cannot spare you.'

So she had followed the suggestion of Father Janos
that gold and gemstones, the more precious the better, should be cooked with the invalid's food. A capon, he told her, cooked in a sealed dish to which
had been added a little rosewater liquor and gold, in
the form of coins.

'The diamond?' Eloise said. 'Would that help,
too?'

'You have it, m'lady? Then why not? Put it to
some use.'

It was remarkable, she thought, that the priest

could even talk about food when he himself had fasted for a whole day as a penance for his burst of pride at St Bartholemew's. But the diamond and gold obviously had a beneficial effect, for Sir Owain ate more of the tender capon, delicately spiced, than anything so far. And the next morning, when they removed the dressing from his head wound again, the healing showed clean and wholesome with no sign of inflammation. From then on, the diamond was hardly ever allowed to leave the kitchen, even though Sir Owain believed it still to be in his keeping.

Although the initial recovery period seemed to Eloise like an eternity, it was in fact only a few weeks before they were able to consider making the long journey to Derbyshire for Sir Owain's recuperation. August had given way to September without her realising it, and once she did, it seemed somehow imperative that they should leave London behind and head for home without delay. Naturally, there were those who thought it folly to transport an injured man over rough roads, but there were others who agreed that to wait for the autumn rain and then try would be an even greater danger to him, with puddles and mud axle-deep. Only a handful of their friends and relatives knew the real reason for Eloise's urgency, including Sir Owain himself.

'I'm strong enough,' he said, holding her hand. 'Of course we must go. My head's mending nicely, and it's only this damn leg that's stopping me riding a horse.' It was far more than that, they both knew.

He was weak, and still in some pain from the leg and collarbone. He could not have sat a horse for long. 'Will you marry a cripple, sweetheart?' he said.

'Not *any* old cripple,' she replied, kissing his hand. 'Only this one.'

'Then we have no time to lose. Let's make a dash for it, eh?'

They were given every kind of assistance possible from the king downwards. He lent them his well-cushioned leather-covered wagon and a team of men to protect them on every stage of the journey, arranging for them to stay overnight at a succession of bishops' palaces, castles and abbeys from London to Whitecliffe, sparing no expense for their comfort. Sir Owain lay for much of the journey with his sore head on Eloise's lap, though it said much for his strong constitution and their care that he seemed no worse for the continual shaking his body was forced to endure each day. Each night, Eloise lay by his side, sleeping as lightly as a mother with a sick child, anticipating his needs and performing every task, no matter how intimate, rejoicing that he was alive to see each new day. Their arrival at Whitecliffe was ecstatic and without mishap, but that night Eloise wept quietly with relief, exhaustion and joy that Saskia's prediction appeared to be confirmed. This time, it was different. This time, she had been able to do something about it.

Away from the noise and bustle of London, the pace of their lives softened and slowed to imbue each day with tranquillity. The sound of abbey bells was replaced by the rush of wind and the cooing of doves, the constant stream of visitors reduced to a trickle of family friends. It was now, during these days of regeneration, that Eloise discovered more about the man she had once referred to as a punch-drunk hooligan, that he could converse fluently with his studious brother and his chaplain in Latin, French and Greek, for instance, and that the books in the library on mathematics and astronomy had been annotated by his hand in the margins, not by Nathaniel's.

Devoid of any lovemaking except mutual caresses, their days were passed contentedly in each other's company, walking a few yards further each time, watching the squires at their training, reading poetry to each other, playing chess and Sir Owain's musical instruments, often with Nathaniel and Father Janos joining in. Eloise and Saskia, apart from supervising the housekeeping and taking over the herb and vegetable plots, created a still-room where they introduced Father Janos to the art of making simples and distillations, unguents and electuaries. She was careful not to tell him that she had left the diamond in the kitchen at Cold Harbour, and he was equally careful to say nothing of the approaching deadline for the marriage.

Sir Owain was less restrained. 'Time's running out on us, sweetheart,' he said that evening. 'Are you not reconciled yet?'

'Yes, sir. I am. We'll decide on a day tomorrow, shall we? Sleep, now.'

'What are you waiting for?'

'For your hair to grow over your wound. I didn't agree to marry a monk, sir.'

He drew her softly into his arms. 'Of that I shall leave you in no doubt, woman, believe me.'

There was a spate of guests on the next day that put such matters as dates well out of her mind. Jolita, Sir Henry and Lord Pace had decided to follow them from London to prepare for Jolita's wedding, staying first at Whitecliffe before moving on to Handes. But there was another visitor far less sure of a welcome who waited on the other side of Whitecliffe village out of respect for Lady Eloise Gerrard's feelings, for the man who had killed her husband could hardly expect a greeting of unrestrained joy, not even after a year's exile.

Chapter Eleven

The two sisters were as near to quarrelling as they had ever been, Eloise being prevented from walking away only by a path that led nowhere except to a wall where a white rosebush was being shorn of its blooms. Shears in one hand and a basket in the other, Eloise was held at bay by a determined Jolita who was insisting, 'You have to face up to it, Ellie.'

'I don't have to. How can you expect me to meet the man? How could he have the gall to come here? What am I supposed to say to him? How kind of you to call, Sir Phillip? Created any widows lately?'

'Ellie! Stop it! Is that all you've learned in the last ten weeks? Sarcasm? For one thing, Sir Phillip is not the man you think he is. He's devout. He's been on a personal pilgrimage to Rome to ask for absolution and, for another thing, he's here to ask your forgiveness. Are you going to deny him that, after all his efforts?'

'His pilgrimage was his choice, Jollie, not mine. Including me in his penance puts the responsibility on me, doesn't it, and I'll not be held responsible. I have enough problems of my own.'

'Which Sir Phillip could probably solve for you, if you'd only ask him.'

'Huh! What's the point of asking? I'd be given another batch of half-truths to add to the others I've collected.'

'Ellie!' Jolita's tone softened, hoping to pacify. 'You've been through a lot. Are you not able to forgive? Is it embarrassment prevents you? Are you going to pretend to him that you're grief-stricken over Sir Piers's death; that he's ruined your life? You'll have a hard time convincing him of that when he sees you and Sir Owain look at each other.'

'Nonsense!'

'It's true. You know it is. Speak to him. He's not what you think.'

'So you tell me.'

'Meet him, Ellie, for Sir Owain's sake. They're good friends, you know, and it'll make it very hard for Sir Owain if you dislike his best friend. It's a wife's duty.'

'Where is he now? With Sir Owain?'

'Yes. He sent for him as soon as they came through the gatehouse. Shall I ask him to come and see you here, in private?'

Eloise sighed, glaring at a fat bumblebee. 'If you must, though I can't imagine what I shall find to say to him.'

'You'll find something.' Relieved, Jolita pecked her sister on the cheek and tripped away, her loose brown hair swinging from side to side, sheening in the sunlight.

But it was Father Janos who came down the path next without any greeting, taking the rose basket out of her hand and leading her to a sunny wall where a bench was already warmed and inviting. He sat by her side, removing the shears from her fingers. 'You'll not need weapons,' he said.

'So you approve of this, do you Father?'

'I approve of forgiveness when there's true repentance, my lady. Yes, every time.' He placed the shears in the basket. 'Do you recall asking me what I know of Sir Piers's death, and me saying that Sir Owain would tell you?'

'Yes. I remember. I doubted you then, and I still do.'

'Probably with good reason. Sir Owain finds it impossible to tell you. But now you have the chance to hear it from Sir Phillip instead. Owain's always said that he should be the one to explain.'

'Impossible, Father? Why?'

The priest regarded her at some length as if deciding what to say. 'I think you'll discover that for yourself. Your late husband doesn't come well out of the story, and Sir Owain has not found a way to explain it without appearing to slander him. He feels very passionately about the matter.'

'So he leaves it to Sir Phillip.'

'My lady, he does not *leave* it to Sir Phillip. It is part of Sir Phillip's penance, imposed on him by the Pope, no less, to acquaint you with the facts and to beg your understanding. And, yes, that does make you responsible, but is that such a bad thing? Were you not at one time craving some responsibility for your life?'

'For myself, Father.'

'But you've done that, my lady, haven't you? What else have you been doing since Sir Owain's accident? At every stage since the news reached you, you've made decisions, called the tune, treated him, brought him back, whole again. If that is not exactly what you had in mind at the beginning, then that's to do with God's plan rather than yours. And I'd say it's made a better woman of you than merely deciding what you want for yourself. Which He has granted you, in a roundabout manner, albeit a more painful one. What's more, in terms of personal effort, it takes far more to *ask* for forgiveness than it does to grant it, you know. If you think it's difficult for you, think how much more so it is for Sir Phillip.'

'I believe that, Father. I know that it would be false for me to pretend that he has robbed me of a happy marriage, for he has not. I didn't know what true happiness was until I almost lost it these last few weeks. I have you to thank for taking much of the burden from me. I couldn't have done it alone.'

'It was no hardship, my lady. But if you wish to thank me, do this one thing. Receive Sir Phillip. He has a young wife, you know, whom he thinks he may already have lost. The man still has grief to bear.'

She felt the vibration of footsteps on the grassy

path through the soles of her feet well before the guest appeared. 'He's coming, Father.'

'Well then, this is your chance to kill two birds with one stone. A clumsy phrase, I fear, in the circumstances.'

They stood together to meet the tall knight who came striding up, hesitated some yards away, then approached more cautiously. Whatever image Eloise had conjured up during the past year or more of the man who killed her husband, no one could have appeared more affable than the one who regarded her now with pain and guilt showing so clearly in his blue eyes. Having passed that way herself so recently, she could feel nothing but pity for him and reproach for herself. She stretched out both hands towards him. 'You are well come, Sir Phillip,' she said, kindly.

Gravely, Father Janos introduced them, blessed them both, and left them alone.

Sir Phillip Cotterell was, she guessed, about Sir Owain's age of thirty-three, some ten years older than herself, yet his sun-bleached brown hair, bronzed skin and pilgrim-lean frame dressed in plain browns and russets made him look older. Even so, she could imagine how, only a year ago, he and Sir Owain would have made an impressively good-looking pair. Had that same problem of hero-worship from which she herself had shrunk been one of the reasons why his wife had hoped to provoke him with an *affaire*? Was she, like herself, one for making statements? Had she been too jealous, too hurt, to think clearly? Like her.

'Am I indeed well come, my lady?' He spoke quietly, without any of the bluster she had feared. 'It's as though our lives have been closely linked without ever coming face to face until now. Which I regret.' His voice was cultured and deeply attractive, though his inflections held a tone of hesitancy, almost shyness.

'I have to admit, Sir Phillip, that I had not thought ever to meet you. But now you are here, we cannot let the opportunity pass without making use of it, can we? I have learned that life is not quite as long or secure as I thought it was.'

'You are referring to Sir Piers, my lady, or to Sir Owain?'

'Both, I suppose, and well before that, too. You must have been surprised to hear of our betrothal.'

'Not exactly. Owain and I have been friends for a long time, and I knew of his love for you well before your marriage to Sir Piers. Oh dear, have I said something to disturb you? Please…may we sit here, perhaps?'

Believing that she might have been hearing a figure of speech rather than the truth, Eloise sat on the bench she and Father Janos had just vacated and which the castle cat had hoped was to be his place in the sun. 'Loved, Sir Phillip? Oh, no. I think that's too strong a word in this case.'

'No, lady. Not so. Owain has always loved you since that first meeting. He was never the same after

that. We teased him, of course, but then he was sent
by the king on an errand because of his good French,
as you probably know. Sir Piers Gerrard took advantage of Owain's absence, and his own so-called
friendship with your brother, to persuade him that *he*
would be a good choice of husband for you. Which,
as you probably also know, had strings attached.'

'Sir Phillip...' Eloise looked at her hands, already
floundering '...I think you may be assuming that I
know more than I do. What strings are you talking
about?'

He shifted uncomfortably on the bench. 'Well,' he
said, slowly, 'you must have guessed by now that Sir
Piers was permanently and deeply in debt. His extravagant style of living...'

'Yes, I did discover that, though not until it was
too late.'

'And I suppose you knew of your brother's extra-
marital—'

'I know of it now. Sir Piers blackmailed my
brother over it.'

'Well, that was also Sir Piers's style. Blackmail
and bribery. Anything, legal or illegal, that would
release him from his debts. Unfortunately, my lady,
you and my wife were pawns in Sir Piers's game.'

'I had already begun to suspect as much. He offered me, I believe, to someone in return for his release from a debt. Did you know about that, Sir Phillip?'

He let out a groaning sigh. 'Oh, my dear lady. I
would rather you had not known about that, but I

suppose you were bound to, sooner or later. May I ask where you heard it?'

'In a very roundabout gossipy manner, sir. I made enquiries, but they were cut short by our return here in July. I don't think Sir Owain wanted me to find out any more, for some reason best known to himself.'

'Lady Eloise, I have Owain's permission to tell you what he cannot bring himself to say, that he was the man to whom Sir Piers made the offer. Can you imagine what construction you might have put on Owain's interest in you if you'd known of that? The wooing was difficult enough, so he tells me.'

The birdsong, a moment ago so joyful, stopped. The sun faded. The colours and fluttering shapes of the afternoon vanished as she studied the two pained blue eyes, striving to hold the words back for a second look. 'Sir Owain…it was he?'

'Yes, my lady. Sir Piers knew how much Owain wanted you, knew that he had made an offer, knew that he had been sent away and would return. Sir Piers used blackmail on your brother, forcing him to promote his offer for you knowing that, once you were his wife, he could use you as currency in exchange for his debts. Oh, yes, we had all lent Sir Piers money before we discovered what kind of a man he was. Sir Owain, too. We all lent and borrowed, using our word as knights as our bond. Too generously, I suppose. He offered Owain a night with you. Owain was disgusted and refused, calling him a filthy little worm, not because he didn't want you, my lady, but because he loved you, as he does now. No decent man would use a woman for such a purpose and still claim that he loved her. Then Owain discovered that your husband...shall I go on, lady? You are clearly shocked by this.'

'Yes. I'm all right. I have to know. Please continue.'

'Owain found out that my new wife had been seduced by Sir Piers. Instead of telling me about it, Owain told Sir Piers that, unless he stopped the *affaire* immediately, he *would* tell me, with predictable consequences. I would have had every right to kill him. I know that Owain confronted him for your sake as well as for mine. The man had not a shred of decency, my lady, and by that time we all knew it, but Owain had more courage and clout than the rest of us. He told him to stop. Reminded him that he had a duty to you. But I knew nothing of that until afterwards when it came out at the enquiry.'

'Afterwards?'

'After the tournament at Windsor last summer.'

'Ah, yes. The accident.' There was a check in the narration as if to prepare each other mentally for the facts of death, at last.

Sir Phillip felt the constraint as keenly as Eloise. 'Are you sure you wish to know? I've not come here on purpose to distress you. Shall I ask Sir Owain to join us?'

'No, Sir Phillip, I thank you. Just tell me how it happened. Leave nothing out, if you please.'

'Well, we were all three drawn to fight on the

same side, the king's. But Sir Piers bribed the herald to change him to the opposing team, to fight against Sir Owain.'

'But that's against the rules, isn't it? As well as being ridiculous. He'd not beat Sir Owain. He must have known that.'

'Against the rules, yes. But he was well known for bending them, when it suited him. He went even further on this occasion by substituting the coronel on one of the lances for the sharp tip used in war which, as you know, is against every peaceful jousting practice.'

Eloise was aghast. 'He meant it to kill, then? To kill Owain? So how did *you* come to be fighting him, sir?'

'Yes, his intention was to silence Owain once and for all. Unfortunately, or not, Owain had one of his massive nose-bleeds from a previous bump. Blood everywhere. He couldn't possibly have gone into the lists. So I asked the second herald if I could take his place against Sir Piers and he saw no reason to object. It's perfectly legal. Nor did he need to tell Sir Piers about the change-over so, naturally, by the time he saw who his opponent was, it was too late to change anything. I noticed the pointed lance as he took it from his squire on the second charge, so I was forced to defend myself, my lady, or I'd have had its point through my visor. There was no time to think about fair play, only about self-preservation. Even a swerve to one side would not have helped; he could easily have caught me with the point of his lance. So I did what I would have done in war, I went for his helm. I'm sorry.' He breathed heavily, shaken by the retelling of it, linking and unlinking his hands nervously. 'Truly, lady, I'm sorry. Forgive me. I killed him before he killed me.'

Eloise placed a hand over his and held them together. 'I don't believe you could have done anything else in the circumstances, Sir Phillip. Any other man would have done the same if he'd been quick enough to see the danger. They tell me the king accepted the explanation of what happened.'

'He did, my lady. The herald confessed to bribery; he was dismissed and heavily fined. Sir Piers's squire, who held his lances, was blamed by his master before he died, and he was sent back to his father in disgrace, though he was sworn to obey his master in all things and no one believed he was responsible. Owain later took the lad into his own service, so he tells me.'

'Michael?'

Sir Phillip looked surprised. 'Yes, of course. You'll have seen him.'

'I suppose I should have recognised him sooner but they change so quickly at that age, don't they? He's the most discreet and able young man.'

'He has a lot to thank Owain for.'

'But you went into exile, Sir Phillip. And your lady wife?'

He sighed and went silent, keeping one of her hands in his own. 'I thought,' he said, eventually, 'I wondered...if she might be pregnant, you see.'

'By Sir Piers?'

'Yes. So I sent her away, in private, to allow some time to elapse for…'

'Yes, I see. I looked for her while we were in London.'

He sat back against the warm wall. 'Not in London, my lady. In Staffordshire. Farewell Priory, not far from your manor of Haughton. You know it?'

'Indeed I do, sir. It's where I was educated. Isn't it time for her return now? To come home to you?'

'More than time. We need to start anew.'

'And was there…is there a child?'

'I don't know,' he said, 'but I still want her back.'

'Then it's time for us both to forgive, isn't it, Sir Phillip? Here's mine, for a start, though heaven knows you could have done no different.'

'Thank you, dear lady. You mean it?'

'With all my heart, I forgive you. Let's both begin anew.'

When Father Janos padded down the path a little while later, he was met by the extraordinary sight of Lady Eloise being held in the gentle embrace of Sir Phillip Cotterell whose handkerchief she was using to mop her face. Needless to say, the priest-physician did not blink an eyelid at the phenomenon since that was partly what he had expected to see.

The feast at Whitecliffe that day was a memorable event at which all of the men wore white roses and made a concerted effort to decide Eloise's wedding date for her since she seemed incapable of deciding it for herself. Father Janos was as insistent as the rest.

'For a lady who prefers to make her own decisions,' he said, smiling at her blushes, 'and who can dismiss the most renowned physician in the country in one short sentence, this shows a remarkable breakdown of resolve. Come now, Sir Owain, you are mending nicely. Assert yourself, sir.'

'I would gladly assert myself, Janos, if I did not fear that her ladyship would put me back on barley-porridge and blood puddings for another week. She's found a way of keeping the upper hand, and now I believe I may never be master again in my own home.'

There was disbelieving laughter at this and a great deal of leg-pulling about two fair sisters who had discovered how to keep their men waiting for a wedding date.

'September thirty-first,' Jolita said. 'What say you, Ellie? For both of us?'

'Agreed. The last day of September.'

'Disagreed!' called out Nathan. 'There are only thirty days in September.'

More noisy laughter was followed by cries of, 'Cheat…women's wiles…deceivers!' But by bedtime, the last day of the month had been settled on when they would share a wed-ding day at Handes Castle, giving Sir Phillip time to return from Farewell Priory with the young wife he had never ceased to love.

* * *

'Is it going to be convenient for you, my sweet?' Sir Owain later said to Eloise, catching her hand as she passed the bed on which he sat. 'We rather pressed you into it, didn't we? It won't be your… er…courses' time, will it?'

'No, sir. It won't.'

There was such finality in the way she spoke that made him hold on to her wrist and pull her gently to him. She waited, placing a hand on his shoulder, as naked as he, the summer air being still warm from the day-long sun. Her hair hung loose, almost black in the fading light, falling around him as she drew his head to her breast and bent to kiss the shorn patch that had now healed over.

'You sound very sure of that, my beauty,' he whispered, smoothing his hands over her. He kissed the full curving underside of her breast. 'Do you have something to tell me, then?'

Above him, she smiled. 'Is there something you'd particularly like to know, sir?'

'Mm-m! Yes, there is.' His hand covered her belly. 'I'd like to know what's been going on in there while I've been out of action. Eh? Something I ought to know about, perhaps?' He pulled her down onto his knee and enclosed her. 'Well, lady? I have you now, and there will be no more secrets between us.'

'I was going to wait a while,' she whispered into his hair, 'before I told you. Too many shocks in your weakened state—' The words ended in a yelp as she was tipped over backwards on to the bed and held there by his warm body. She could see his eyes laughing, shining in the last light of day, as bold as they had been at their first meeting, and as acute.

'What weakened state?' he growled. 'You want to test it, then? No? Well, Janos suggested I assert myself, so I will. Now, woman, what's this shock you have which you thought would wait? How many months is it? June? Or July?'

'July,' she laughed, soundlessly. 'Two courses I've missed. It's early to be certain, but this morning while you still slept, I was sick, and Saskia says that's a sure sign.'

His hand smoothed her forehead as if she were a creature prized above any. 'Sweetheart. My dearest most wonderful woman. You rode for days to reach me, to save me from death. You braved John of Gaddesdon and his minions and used all your skills on me, brought me home like a fierce lioness to nurse and tend me night and day, putting yourself at risk while you are breeding, to make me whole again. The very time when you should have been safely in my care. You must have suspected, yet you said nothing of it.'

'I suspected, but it got pushed aside, somehow. You were far more important. I had to keep you, beloved. Nothing else mattered. I love you, you see, and life would have ended for me too, if I'd not fought so hard for you. They'd already given up on you there.'

'You love me?'

'I adore you. That's the very first time you've heard—'

'No, it's not.'

'Not?'

'No. I heard you the first time when you thought I was sleeping. I thought I was dreaming, but I wasn't.'

'You heard all that? All my outpourings?'

'All of it. The most wonderful moment of my life, the moment I've longed for, to hear you say such things. I couldn't sleep for hours thinking it over, re-hearing it. I've loved you since I first saw you, Eloise. Do you remember that day when you stole my heart? I tried to tell you in the letter you never received. I thought I must have been too blunt, sweetheart.'

'Blunt? Tell me how blunt you were.' She touched his lips with one forefinger, now alive with a new curiosity. 'Tell me what you said.'

'Word for word?'

'Yes. With interest.'

He smiled at the taunt, pleased that she remembered, waiting to see her eyes darken as he recited the brief message, word for word. 'Lady, I fear my message must be brief, but I would have you know of a terrible fate that befell me at our first meeting. The heart that I have guarded so well these past years is now in your keeping through no effort on my part, and I believe that I may have a smaller daintier one in its place. If this is yours that I hold, be assured that I shall keep it safe until I come again, as I beg you will do for mine. Sweet lady, I am like a fool until I see your loveliness again. Guard thee well, for thou art mine against all comers. Doubt not that I will have thee and no other, for thou holdest my whole being. Yours, Owain of Whitecliffe.'

Instead of darkening, her eyes had slowly filled with tears. 'Oh, no,' she whispered. 'That's too cruel. Fate is too cruel, Owain. If only I'd known. Is that really what you felt? Even then?'

'From the first moment.'

'As I did, too. I've never recovered from it.'

'When it happens like that, one doesn't recover, one learns to live with it.'

'What courage you had. To come back again.'

His smile brought a tearful one in return. 'Is that what it was? Courage? I don't know. When I saw you again, angry and confused, and determined not to let me near you, I ached to hold you like this, quiet in my arms with my babe inside you, belonging to me and no one else. Yet by that time there were things I could not bring myself to tell you, things that you needed to know but which would have taken more explaining than I could provide. It had to come from Phillip himself, from the third party, as it were, set in the context of *his* story. It was not secrecy for the sake of it, sweetheart, truly, but we didn't want you to know the full extent of Sir Piers's treachery or you'd have felt utterly disgraced and you'd never have been able to look me in the face again, would you? You certainly wouldn't have accepted my version of the events without Phillip's full story. It was best for you not to know. I had a hard enough time of it without the added complications.'

'Did you, beloved? Did I make it difficult for you?'

His kiss was as deep and as potent as wine, for he had lost none of his skills at lovemaking. 'Aye, lass. You're a worthy opponent, but I meant to have you.'

She wrapped him with her arms and legs. 'I wanted you just as much,' she whispered. 'I told you of my dreams, and I meant every word. And I'm not afraid of Fate anymore after all that's happened. I think we've sent her packing. But I am afraid of you getting hurt again, my darling. I've seen your body after these contests and I don't believe you should go on doing that to it. I know it's all in the game, but you almost lost your life and I nearly lost the man I adore.'

'I've given it all some thought, sweetheart. Heaven knows, I've had plenty of time to think in the last few weeks. Perhaps it's time for me to retire and attend to my family and estate. Anyway, Monsieur de Grise has won my best horse and armour, damn him!' He laughed. 'At least now he'll have a good horse of his own to use.'

'Will it break your heart, dearest? You've been so successful.'

'Lord no! The king has asked me to be a member of his council and that's no half-time job. We could spend some months in London, buy a grand house on the Strand, move to the other manors throughout the year, and Haughton Manor will have to be put straight, sweetheart. Which reminds me, your brother is coming over the day after tomorrow, so he'll be at Handes for our wedding.'

'Oh, good heavens!'

'Is that a problem?'

'It could be. Mistress O'Farrell and Christopher and Master atte Welle are also due to arrive on that day from Haughton. Apparently they have something to tell us.'

He grinned. 'And can we guess what that might be?'

'Probably. But they're bound to meet Rolph.'

'So they will. Is Grissle coming too?'

'No, she's just had her baby. A boy.'

'Then we are about to start catching them up, my beauty, are we not? Would you care to make love to a member of the king's council now?'

'Er…I'm not sure. Are they those enfeebled old men with long white beards and spindly legs?' She laughed, caressing his head.

'Yes, all except one. It's been too long, my darling, and I need you. We'll go carefully, shall we?'

They did at first, Eloise discovering yet again how varied his loving could be. She also experienced a new kind of piquancy that may have had something to do with his new office, or his injuries, or the hidden presence of their new family, or even the fact that they had waited for many a painful week during which they had grown together in spirit as much as in body. With all secrets dissolved, they were both whole again.

* * *

Their guess about the purpose of Marie O'Farrell's visit proved to be correct, for she and Stephen atte Welle, Eloise's loyal steward, had begun to love each other and now came to ask permission to marry. It could not have been better planned; Haughton Manor would benefit from having a married steward whose wife would help him to administer the estate between the visits of the owner. Her son would, at last, have a real father. Already, young Christopher had grown two inches and filled out like a russet apple. The anticipated problem of their meeting Sir Rolph, however, was left to its own devices: they were adults: they could sort it out between them.

Within an hour of Sir Rolph's arrival, during which he brimmed with news about his new son, his family's health and Lady Griselle's much improved temper, he was seen to be walking sedately down the garden path, deep in conversation with his former mistress. At suppertime, Rolph and Stephen atte Welle were equally engrossed in discussion about the market price of heifers and sows and negotiating the loan of two hay-wagons for the harvest.

Just in time for the double wedding at Handes Castle, Sir Phillip and Lady Cotterell arrived at Whitecliffe, reconciled, relieved and deliriously happy to be together again. There had been no birth. Lady Cotterell was, as her husband had been, unsure of Lady Eloise's reaction to her appearance, but by this time there was no room in Eloise's heart for dark thoughts of the past, only of the future. In one respect, she had been right; the lady was indeed a woman after her own heart who had been hurt and confused that her new husband appeared to be putting his love of jousting before her, during the first few unsteady months of their marriage. Like Eloise, she had tried to take matters into her own hands with a mind-bending lack of caution which had almost wrecked the very relationship she wished to preserve. In her, Eloise saw many of her own traits, and they became instant friends.

There was one thing, however, that Eloise had not confessed to her betrothed about which her conscience had fought for weeks. So she saved it until the morning of her wedding day, when she assumed he would care about little except making their final vows before time ran out on them. The king's fines, he told her, could reduce them to begging for a living.

'Dearest, I must tell you something,' she said, arranging the full gores of gold silk around her feet.

He stifled a groan. 'Can it not wait?' Then he saw her concern and relented. 'Tell me, what have you done? Forgotten—?'

'No, not forgotten. This is more serious. I've lost the diamond.'

He was still. Clearly stunned. '*Lost* it? Where?'

'I left it in the kitchen at Cold Harbour. We came away in a hurry, you see, and I forgot about it, and I suppose it must have been thrown out with the spinach water. I'm sorry. It meant such a lot to us both.'

He sighed gustily, drooping his eyelids. 'In the spinach water,' he said, flatly. 'Not in the chicken broth or the barley soup or the nettle mush? Could I have swallowed it, perhaps?'

She blinked. 'You *knew*…about me…using it…?'

'In the cooking? Yes, my dearest and most adorable woman. You tried everything, didn't you, even that? Well, it worked and here I am to prove it. As for your losing it, well, I was not going to show you until the ceremony…' he fished inside his leather pouch '…but here is something you may recognise. I hope it doesn't smell of cooking. Father Janos re membered it and brought it back with us. He thought, in the circumstances, that it might be safer with me for a while. Eh?' He tipped the contents of the blue velvet pouch on to his palm where a gold ring set with the fabulous diamond winked blue and white like solid lightning. 'Your wedding ring with the me-mento of our first night of loving. That was a tournament of hearts, my beauty, was it not?' He laughed at her incredulity. '*Now* will you have me, at last?'

Gulping back a rush of tears, she threw her arms about his neck. 'Yes,' she said. 'Yes, Owain of Whitecliffe. I will have you and keep you. For ever.'

*   *   *   *   *

ITCHIN' FOR SOME ROLLICKING ROMANCES SET ON THE AMERICAN FRONTIER? THEN TAKE A GANDER AT THESE TANTALIZING TALES FROM HARLEQUIN HISTORICALS

On sale September 2003

WINTER WOMAN by Jenna Kernan
(Colorado, 1835)

After braving the winter alone in the Rockies, a defiant woman is entrusted to the care of a gruff trapper!

THE MATCHMAKER by Lisa Plumley
(Arizona territory, 1882)

Will a confirmed bachelor be bitten by the love bug when he woos a young woman in order to flush out the mysterious Morrow Creek matchmaker?

On sale October 2003

WYOMING WILDCAT by Elizabeth Lane
(Wyoming, 1866)

A blizzard ignites hot-blooded passions between a white medicine woman and an amnesiac man, but an ominous secret looms on the horizon....

THE OTHER GROOM by Lisa Bingham
(Boston and New York, 1870)

When a penniless woman masquerades as the daughter of a powerful marquis, her intended groom risks it all to protect her from harm!

Visit us at www.eHarlequin.com

HARLEQUIN HISTORICALS®

HHWEST27

It's romantic comedy with a kick
(in a pair of strappy pink heels)!

Introducing

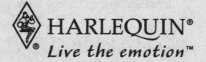
HARLEQUIN® flipside™

"It's chick-lit with the romance and happily-ever-after ending that Harlequin is known for."
—*USA TODAY* bestselling author Millie Criswell, author of *Staying Single*, October 2003

"Even though our heroine may take a few false steps while finding her way, she does it with wit and humor."
—Dorien Kelly, author of *Do-Over*, November 2003

Launching October 2003.
Make sure you pick one up!

HARLEQUIN®
Live the emotion™

Visit us at www.harlequinflipside.com

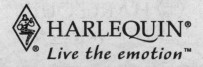